THE SEEDS OF SIN

THE SEEDS OF SIN

Anne Herries

This first world edition published in Great Britain 2006 by
SEVERN HOUSE PUBLISHERS LTD of
9–15 High Street, Sutton, Surrey SM1 1DF.
This first world edition published in the USA 2006 by
SEVERN HOUSE PUBLISHERS INC of
595 Madison Avenue, New York, N.Y. 10022.

British Library Cataloguing in Publication Data

Herries, Anne
    Seeds of sin
    1. Great Britain - History - Civil War, 1642-1649 - Fiction
    2. Historical fiction
    3. Love stories
    I. Title
    823.9'14 [F]

    ISBN-13: 978-0-7278-6389-8
    ISBN-10: 0-7278-6389-4

Except where actual historical events and characters are being
described for the storyline of this novel, all situations in this
publication are fictitious and any resemblance to living persons
is purely coincidental.

All Severn House titles are printed on acid-free paper.

Typeset by Palimpsest Book Production Ltd.,
Grangemouth, Stirlingshire, Scotland.
Printed and bound in Great Britain by
MPG Books Ltd., Bodmin, Cornwall.

One

Sir Rupert Saunders stood watching as the shores of France receded into the distance, becoming little more than a smudge on the horizon. He had fled there as a fugitive at the end of the civil wars in England, although he had been with Charles II when he was crowned at Scone in 1651, and when the King was defeated at Worcester by Cromwell later that year. After that, he had been forced to wander as his king did: bitter, angry, and sometimes close to despair, he had travelled from country to country, seeking a living until good fortune had found him at the court of the French king. The powerful Cardinal Mazarin had introduced him to the Marquis de Thouret and, as his secretary, he had risen to a position of influence and power. He had become settled and wealthy, and when the death of Cromwell had resulted in Charles Stuart being called to the throne of England, he had lingered at the French court.

The death of Mazarin in 1661 had brought changes, but even then Rupert had not considered returning to his own country. His bitterness had all but gone. Yet he had little waiting for him at home, though of late he had begun to think more of the past and to wonder about Elizabeth.

'Elizabeth . . .' He said her name softly, smiling at the memory of a sunlit wood. 'Why was it too late for us?'

His fault, not hers. Rupert's mouth twisted in a wry smile. He was the one who had thrown away his chance of happiness. It was not in the hope of rekindling the love that had once been between them that he was at last returning to his home, but because of the letter he had received from Nicolas

1

Mortimer. It seemed that both Sir John and Lady Saunders were ailing, and if he did not return now he might not see them again.

The letter had played on his conscience, even though he had fended off repeated requests from his father to return. Nicolas's letter had somehow touched his heart. He had resigned his position, said goodbye to his friends, and booked a passage for England. At first it had been merely duty that called him home, but now he had begun to think of it with pleasure, and of the daughter he had last seen as a baby.

'Angelica . . .' She must be almost a woman now, in her sixteenth year if he recalled rightly, and beautiful from all the accounts he had had of her. Old enough to be wed, he imagined. It was his duty as her father to see her married to a decent man who would care for her. He wondered what she would be like, whether she was as beautiful and as wilful as her mother . . .

Angelica stood watching the handsome man and the pretty young woman as they laughed together in the sunshine. It was April in the year 1663 and pleasantly warm that day, the kind of day that brings with it the promise of spring. Newborn lambs were playing in the far meadow, and the primroses clustered in the lanes. Angelica was happy enough, but could not help feeling vaguely envious of her companions, because they were clearly enjoying themselves, secure in the affection they felt for one another. It was always this way when they were all together.

It was not that they ignored or slighted her, but she had often felt that she was not truly important to them, that they tolerated her rather than wanted her company. She could not doubt that they made a handsome couple, for Claire was lovely and Hal . . . Hal was everything that a young man should be, of course: tall, strong, confident and handsome. As Nicolas Mortimer's adopted son, he was also the heir to the Manor of Thornberry.

He turned towards Angelica at that moment, as if sensing

her eyes on him, frowning for an instant before turning back to Claire and saying something that made her laugh.

Angelica walked away, stupid tears pricking behind her eyes. She was foolish to imagine that they were laughing at her. It was the fault of her ridiculous jealousy, something she had suffered from since they were children, perhaps because her mother was dead and her father an exile in France or one of the Low Countries. She was never quite sure where her father was, for she believed he travelled constantly, never staying long in one place as he looked for a means to earn his living, though of recent years she thought he had been in France. She knew only what she was told, for Sir Rupert did not write to her.

Her grandfather, Sir John Saunders, had written to him asking him to come home long since, for there was no need for him to remain an exile now that the King was restored to his own. Once Oliver Cromwell had died and been succeeded by his son Richard, the people of England had soon grown restless, deciding that they had lived long enough beneath the strict rule that had constrained their lives. It had been General Monk who had brought the King back, despite some resistance, and Charles had been crowned two years previously. There was no reason now for Angelica's father not to come home.

She knew that he had fought on the side of Charles I during the civil wars that had torn England apart, though she had no memory of that, only of being brought up by her grandparents – and of visiting her Aunt Caroline and Uncle Nicolas at the Manor. Angelica had never been farther from her home than the market town of St Ives, though there had been talk of taking both her and her cousin Claire to London when they were sixteen.

Uncle Nicolas, Lord Mortimer, had been for Parliament in the first war, but he had not liked the way the country was ruled during the years of Cromwell's reign, for Nicolas had fought to win fairness and justice. The Lord Protector had dismissed the parliament just as King Charles I had done before the war, imposing his will on the country. Uncle Nicolas was a fair-minded man, and he agreed that many of the laws Cromwell made were good ones, but hated it that he ruled as a dictator. After the death of Cromwell, his had been one of the voices raised for bringing back the King.

'England has struggled beneath the yoke of Puritanism for too many years,' he had been heard to say more than once in the company of his family. 'It is time to bring back the King – though he must be made to see that he rules by the will of the people and cannot be allowed the absolute rule his father imposed.'

King Charles II had come back to the joyous ringing of bells. Maypoles were brought out after years of being forbidden along with so many other simple pleasures, and now the theatres were thriving and people's lives were far less restricted than they had been. And yet still Angelica's father had not returned to his home, despite Sir John's pleas. Why was that? Surely if he cared for his daughter he would have come home as soon as he could?

Angelica was deep in thought as she walked in the direction of the woods. As a child she had been afraid of them, but she had conquered her fear to please Hal. He and Claire went to the woods often to play as children, and later to gather berries and nuts. Angelica went with them sometimes, for Claire was very good about including her in their pastimes. It was Hal who seemed to resent her, which was why she had left them to their chatter now. She was afraid that Hal did not like her, and that hurt, because she liked him very much – perhaps more than was good for her peace of mind. Was it because Claire was his true cousin and she was only a sort of second cousin, the daughter of Aunt Caroline's brother? Hal, of course, was the son of Mercy Harris, who had died giving birth to him, and Nicolas's elder brother Harry, who had been killed in the war.

Caroline and Nicolas had adopted Hal as their own, for they had no son to succeed to the title, and had made Hal their heir. Claire was Caroline's only child, of course.

Angelica had believed that Claire and Hal were brother and sister for years, and it was only since they all had grown up that she had understood the complicated relationship, for Hal had been treated as the favoured child of his aunt and uncle. Lady Saunders said privately that he was spoiled, but she had taken good care not to spoil the girl left to her charge. She was not sparing of the rod when she thought it necessary, and Angelica had gone to bed hungry and sore many a night.

Angelica and Claire had been born on the same day, within an hour or so of each other, but Angelica's mother had died a few months later. Angelica believed that there had been some sort of an accident, though she wasn't sure exactly what had happened. Her grandparents did not talk to her about her mother; she suspected that they had not liked her much. Aunt Caroline, however, had told her that she was very like her mother, who had been extremely beautiful – and that her father had loved his wife a great deal.

If that were so, why did he not love his daughter?

Angelica had puzzled over it so many times. She did not think that her father loved her, for he never wrote to her, though she did sometimes receive a gift at Christmas, and he would send his good wishes in letters to his parents. Sir Rupert had never once sent her anything for her birthday. She was not deprived in a material sense, for Sir John and Lady Saunders and her Aunt Caroline gave her everything she needed – but she longed for some sign from her father that she was loved. At her grandfather's invitation she had added a postscript to his last letter, asking Rupert to come home – but she had written a polite note, not daring to pour out her heart.

She had learned to conceal her feelings over the years, withdrawing into a cold silence when Hal mocked her, as he often did. She wished that she might tease him in return as Claire did sometimes, but once when she had tried, he had looked angry and had gone off alone.

It was cooler in the woods, but pleasant. She watched a

squirrel leaping through the branches, its coat gleaming red in the flickering sunshine. From the crown of a weeping birch tree, a thrush was trilling its song at the top of its voice. Angelica stopped to listen, and it was only as she turned around, deciding it was time to return home, that she sensed she was being watched.

She looked about her for a moment, and then, seeing a man standing in the trees a little distance away, caught her breath in sudden fear. Who was he, and what was he doing here? He began to walk towards her, and for a moment she considered running away, but as he came closer she could see his face more clearly and her heart began to beat wildly. Momentarily she thought it was Hal, for they were much alike in height, build and features. Yet when he stood just in front of her, she knew that it was not Hal. This man's hair was slightly darker than Hal's, though his eyes were equally blue – and just now they were narrowed in a look of dislike.

'Who are you?' The words sprang to Angelica's lips involuntarily, for she was shocked by his likeness to Hal. 'What are you doing here? Have you come for the fair?'

Angelica had seen some caravans drawn up in Uncle Nicolas's meadow, and she knew that the fair came to Thornberry every year in the spring or summer, and sometimes in the autumn too. The man looked as though he might be a gypsy, for his clothes were not those of a gentleman, though they were respectable, and he was not as dirty as some of the gypsies she had seen in the past.

'You may not know me – but you recognize me, don't you? You know me for who I am,' the stranger said, his face harsh with anger.

'No, I do not know you,' Angelica said. His speech confirmed her opinion that he must be with the gypsies, for it was rough and uncultured. She raised her head haughtily: he still frightened her, but she refused to show it. 'Do you have my uncle's permission to be here?'

'I need no one's permission to be here,' he said, his eyes

cold. 'I have as much right to be here as any man, for by law these woods should be mine.'

'That is nonsense,' Angelica said, surprised and shocked by his statement. 'All the land around here belongs to Lord Mortimer – and it will belong to Hal Mortimer one day.'

'No, that is a lie,' the man said, glaring at her. 'I am the true Lord Mortimer – and one day all this will belong to me. I shall take it back from those who have cheated me of my rights.'

'I don't believe you,' Angelica said, staring at him in disbelief. Her heart was pounding and she found it difficult to breathe. 'You are a gypsy. How could you be Lord Mortimer? Your claims are nonsense.'

'My father was Harry Mortimer. He married my mother during the war – but then he died, and she was too frightened to claim my inheritance.' His gaze narrowed. 'But I fear no one, and the time is coming when I shall take back what is mine.'

'You will never be Lord of the Manor,' Angelica mocked him now, for she thought his claims wild and foolish. 'Uncle Nicolas is the Lord of this Manor, and he will have you thrown off his land if I tell him what you have said.'

She moved forward, intending to walk past him, but the stranger caught her arm, his eyes glinting like splinters of ice. 'My name is Jared,' he told her, leaning towards her so that she caught a scent rather like shaven wood. She was surprised that he did not smell of sweat as many of the villagers did, but despite the poor quality of his clothing he seemed to be clean. 'Remember that, Mistress Angelica. Oh yes, I know who you are – and when I claim everything else, I shall also claim you.'

'No!' Angelica wrenched her arm from his and ran away from him as fast as she could. Her heart was racing and she was very frightened now, for there had been such a look in his eyes as he made his threats . . .

She knew that he was still standing there watching her as

she ran, but she did not dare to look back. He was wicked to tell such lies, and she knew that she must warn her uncle of what he had said, for something was very wrong here. The fact that she had mistaken him for Hal at first glance told her that there might be some truth in his claims, but she did not believe that he was the true Lord Mortimer.

As for his threats to her personally . . . Angelica shuddered at the thought of it. She admired Hal, but this other . . . this impostor . . . she hoped she might never see him again.

Hal saw Angelica running towards the house and frowned. She looked as if she were frightened of something, and that annoyed him. There was something about Angelica that aroused odd feelings in him, feelings that he preferred not to analyse too deeply. He wondered why she was not more like Claire, whom he loved with all his heart.

Once he had believed that Claire was his sister, but when Hal was old enough, Nicolas had explained the rather tangled relationship between them all. He knew that he was the love child of Mercy Harris and Harry Mortimer, and that his father would have been Lord Mortimer if he had survived the war. Because Hal had been born out of wedlock, he would not have been entitled to inherit the title and the estate if Nicolas had not adopted him, but he had been brought up as the son and heir.

'What is the matter?' he asked as he went towards Angelica now. She had seen him, and paused, clearly out of breath. 'Why have you been running like that? You are such a baby, Angelica. There is nothing to be frightened of in the woods.'

'You don't know,' she said, reacting huffily to his criticism as she always did, her cheeks pink from a mixture of exertion and hurt. 'I saw someone – a man. The things he said to me! I must tell your father. He has to know . . .'

'Slow down,' Hal commanded. He had her firmly in his grasp and would not allow her to move on if she tried. 'You are so out of breath that I cannot make head or tail of what you are saying. Tell me what is so important that my father must know it immediately?'

'He said . . .' Angelica hesitated, for she knew that Hal would react angrily to what she had to tell him, and she would have preferred to tell Uncle Nicolas. She drew a deep breath for she must tell someone and she could not ignore Hal's demands. 'He said that he was the true Lord Mortimer – that Uncle Nicolas had stolen the title and estate from him—'

'Impossible!' Hal said and his tone was as angry as she had expected. 'Nicolas inherited the title when my father died, and he adopted me to make me his heir. You are a goose to be in such a fluff about something so foolish, Angelica.'

'But you did not see him,' she said, becoming angry herself now. 'He threatened me, Hal – and said the estate would belong to him one day. And he looks just like you.'

'He looks like me?' A long forgotten memory echoed in his head, an incident that had happened when he was a small boy came back to him. 'Tell me, was he a gypsy?'

'Yes . . .' She looked at him curiously. 'His features are very like yours, Hal, though his hair is a little darker than yours, and his eyes are colder . . .'

'He is an impostor,' Hal said scornfully. 'There is no need to run to Nicolas with this foolish tale, Angelica. It is merely nonsense. He is a gypsy and has no claim on the title or the estate.'

'He said that your father was married to his mother . . .' Angelica said, and saw Hal's quick frown, for if it were true that would change things dramatically, though of course it would be difficult to prove according to the law. 'But he was only a gypsy and I dare say he was lying.'

'Of course he was lying,' Hal retorted scornfully. 'Nicolas is Lord Mortimer, and when he dies I shall take his place. I have always known it.'

He was so sure, so certain of his place, that Angelica began to feel much better. She had been foolish to allow the gypsy to frighten her. Hal was right, she was a silly goose.

'Then I shall say nothing to Uncle Nicolas,' she said and smiled at him.

'He would only think you foolish,' Hal said, frowning again. Sometimes when Angelica smiled at him he felt very odd inside, but he did not want to have these strange feelings towards her. He had decided long ago that he would marry his cousin Claire.

'You had best go home,' he told her rather brusquely. 'There is someone waiting to see you.'

'Someone waiting for me?' Angelica looked at him in surprise. Her friends did not often call without a prior arrangement.

'Sir Rupert has returned,' Hal told her. 'Grandmama sent a servant to look for you but you had vanished. That is why I came to find you.'

'My father . . .' Angelica stared at him, her heart beginning to pound. She had longed for this moment for so many years, and now, suddenly, she was nervous of meeting the man she did not know. 'What does he look like?'

'How should I know?' Hal wrinkled his brow. 'I was a child when he went away, but . . .' He saw how anxious she was and his heart softened towards her. For a brief moment he was tempted to take her in his arms and kiss away her fears, but he conquered his feelings ruthlessly. 'I seem to remember that he was quite tall and that his hair had a reddish tint – and he was always nice to me when I saw him. He bought me a saddle for my pony one Christmas.'

Angelica swallowed hard. When Hal was kind to her she felt her insides melt, and she was afraid that he could read her mind.

'That was kind of him,' she said, avoiding his eyes. She raised her head, because she was not sure why Hal was being gentle with her and she was afraid to let him close; if his mood changed, he might say something that would leave her feeling devastated. 'It was good of you to come and look for me, sir. I think I must hurry home . . . or my father will think me rude.'

Angelica's heart was beating wildly as she walked away, though she was not sure whether it was because Hal had stared at her oddly or the sudden arrival of her father. She had often wished that Hal would look at her as he did Claire, with love in his eyes, but of course it would be foolish to think that he would ever care for her. She knew that he intended to marry Claire, for he had once said as much to her – though she was not certain that her cousin felt the same way. It was difficult to know with Claire, for she was always laughing and teasing both Hal and Angelica, but there were often secrets in her dark eyes. She seemed to be a gentle, obedient girl, happy and content to do as Hal bid her most of the time, but Angelica thought that her cousin was deeper than she appeared.

As she approached the house, she noticed that servants were scurrying here and there with a new urgency. Could this change be due to the fact that her father had arrived? Angelica wondered about it. Her grandfather, Sir John, had been ill for a time now, and her grandmother hardly left her room before noon these days. She had done what she could to keep the house running as it ought, and Aunt Caroline visited at least once a week, which kept the servants on their mettle. However, she had never seen them as busy as they now were, which brought a wry twist to her lips.

She paused in the hall, her heart leaping as she heard a man's laughter. It was a long time since she had heard that sound in this house. She walked towards it, her hands clenched at her sides as she wondered what her father would be like – and, perhaps more importantly, what he would think of her. People said she was pretty – but would her father like her?

At the door of the back parlour, where her grandparents spent their afternoons, because it had a sunny aspect and looked out at the rose gardens, she paused and took a deep breath. Then, feeling as if she had run a long distance, her breathing suddenly difficult, she opened the door and went in. Sir John was sitting in the oak chair with its high, carved back by the large, open fireplace where a massive log was burning, filling the room with the fragrance of wood smoke. A fire was kept going all the year round these days because Sir John felt the cold so much. Standing with his back to her, looking down at his father's face, was Sir Rupert.

Angelica took a deep breath. 'Welcome home, sir,' she said and made a respectful curtsey. As she rose and gazed into his eyes, she was conscious that he was indeed a handsome man. No longer young, but still youthful, his eyes clear and confident, his smile as he saw her tinged with something like regret.

He was disappointed in her! Angelica felt a sharp pain in her breast, but then he was smiling, coming towards her with his hands outstretched.

'Angelica,' he said, warmly now. 'My dear daughter. I had been told that you were lovely, but you are beautiful.' She was very like her mother. For a moment Rupert had felt a stab of regret for the wife he had loved and lost, but too many years had passed, and there had been too much bitterness between them. 'I am delighted to see you and to be home again.'

'We have hoped for your return,' she said and reached up to kiss his cheek, a little shyly. 'It is good that you are home at last.'

'Yes . . .' Rupert fancied that he saw reproach in her eyes, and indeed, she had the right, for he had neglected her. It had been at the back of his mind for a few years now that his daughter needed her father, but for some reason he had delayed his return, and it was not only because he had been enjoying the life he had found in France. 'I ought to have returned with His Majesty, but it was not convenient.' A weak excuse, he did not doubt, but he could not have found the words to explain his tardiness. 'However, I am here now, and I believe it will be your sixteenth birthday this year.'

'Yes, sir. Aunt Caroline plans a large celebration for Claire, and it is to be my party too, for we were both born on the same day.'

'Yes, I remember, though unfortunately I was not here.' Rupert frowned, for that time still lingered like a bad odour in his mind. 'I shall be here for your birthday, I assure you, and we shall hold a party here to celebrate your coming birthday and my homecoming . . .' He glanced at his father, who nodded his approval. 'But in the meantime, I intend that we shall go to London. I understand that Caroline intends to visit to buy clothes for Claire, and it is time that you had clothes to befit your station, Angelica. After all, you are a young woman now, and we must begin to think about your marriage.'

'My marriage?' Angelica drew a sharp breath, for she was not sure that she wanted to think of marriage. She had met gentlemen who were friends of her aunt and uncle, but none of them had appealed to her as a husband. Perhaps if she could marry Hal . . . but she knew that he did not think of her. It was Claire he loved, Claire he wanted as his wife.

'Yes, daughter,' Rupert smiled at her. 'I do not think it a matter of urgency. You are young enough yet – but you will wish to be married one day, Angelica. All women must have a home of their own and children to make them happy, I think?'

'Yes, perhaps,' Angelica agreed. She supposed that she did want to be married one day, and she liked children. She often visited the vicar's wife, and it was a pleasure to her to nurse one of Goodwife Hernshaw's four children, all of whom were under six years of age. However, none of her friends had yet married, and she had not truly thought of it other than as something vaguely in the future. 'I had not considered it as yet.'

'And you need not,' her father replied. 'You may meet someone while we are in London. I should request a period of courtship so that you may get to know each other, for I would not have you rushed into marriage.' He knew that a hasty marriage was a big mistake, and he would not want that for his daughter. 'But I have neglected my duty towards you, my daughter, and I mean to make up for it now.'

13

His smile was tender at that moment, and Angelica felt her doubts melting away. She wanted to go to him, to put her arms about him, to hold him and be held by him, to let all the love that was damned up inside her pour out, but she felt that there was a barrier between them. He was still a stranger to her, and though he was clearly prepared to be kind, she needed time to know him.

'I shall look forward to our visit,' she said, 'and of course I shall behave as a dutiful daughter ought.'

'I want you to be happy,' Rupert told her, his eyes serious as they dwelt on her face. 'But run away now, Angelica. Your grandmother is feeling unwell and she asked for you.'

'Then I shall go to her at once,' she said and curtsied to him again.

Rupert watched as she walked from the room, her back very straight, her head high, turning to his father as the door closed behind her.

'She is a credit to you and Mother,' he said. 'I feared that she might be more like her mother, but she is all that I could have hoped.'

'Your mother has taught her to be a lady and to consider others,' Sir John told him. 'She is a modest, obedient girl – though sometimes she seems to dwell on her thoughts too much. I have thought her not quite happy at times. She needed her mother – and her father.'

'You are right to reprimand me, sir,' Rupert replied. 'I cannot excuse my behaviour, for in truth I do not know why I did not return sooner.'

'Well, you had your reasons, no doubt,' Sir John said heavily. 'I am relieved that you have come at last, and I trust that I may rely on you to do your duty by Angelica and the estate in future?'

'Yes, of course, Father,' Rupert said, a flicker of unease in his eyes. 'I am aware that I have neglected my duty to you.'

'Had it not been for Nicolas I dare not think what we would have done these past years. Times were difficult during the King's absence. God knows I did not love Charles overmuch, for in my opinion he was a bad king, and it was necessary for him to be restrained in his power, but his beheading was unlawful, and it left a shadow on this land. As a people, we have been oppressed, and but for Nicolas's influence it might have gone hard with us here, my son. Heavy fines were demanded of us because you had broken your promise after the first war. You were pardoned once, but you broke your vow not to take up arms again, at least twice over. Had I not had good friends, I might have found my estate sequestered.'

'Yes, that was foolish of me. I should have done better to stay here when war broke out again. You know my reasons for leaving, sir, but that does not excuse my tardiness in returning. I owe Lord Mortimer a debt I shall never be able to repay,' Rupert said. 'I am aware of it, sir.'

'He does not want gratitude or repayment,' Sir John said. 'But you must thank him in whatever way you can.'

'Of course,' Rupert said a little stiffly. In the last year or so he had risen to a position of importance at the French court, and was used to giving orders rather than receiving them. His father seemed to imagine he was still a reckless boy. 'I have not forgotten the time we spent together in London – when Cromwell and his rabble murdered King Charles.'

'I know how you must feel,' Sir John told him, sighing deeply. 'God knows we have lived under an iron hand these many years, Rupert, and I am heartily glad to see the new King home. However, many of our neighbours still respect Cromwell's memory, and you will not make friends by speaking of him thus.'

It was on the tip of Rupert's tongue to say that he did not give a damn what his neighbours thought, but he restrained himself. He had not come home to fall out with his father, whom he could see was ailing. Seeing how tired his father looked, he was grateful that he had been summoned before it was too late.

'What I say to you, sir, is in confidence. I shall not repeat it outside these walls, I promise you.'

Sir John shook his head, clearly too tired to sustain the conversation. 'Well, you must do as you think fit. I am an old man and these things worry me, but you are young, and the world seems a different place when you are young.'

Rupert felt a pang of remorse as he saw how weary his father was. He ought to have returned long ago. The truth was that he had left his homeland after Charles I was so cruelly beheaded, because he was a Royalist and there was no place for him in Cromwell's England – but mostly because of Elizabeth.

The memory was still painful after all these years, though there had been women enough to warm his bed. In the early days he had taken very little interest in the beautiful ladies who had offered themselves to him, sometimes blatantly. He believed he had offended some by his indifference, but eventually he had found a mistress that suited him. Louise was both beautiful and amusing, the wife of a French marquis.

'My husband prefers his little boys. He has no taste for women,' she had told Rupert before they became lovers. 'He married me because he needed an heir, and he has not once come to my bed since our son was born.'

'Then he is a fool,' Rupert replied and smiled, for her desire had been as great as his own. They had both enjoyed a relationship that satisfied their needs but made few emotional demands. It was perhaps because of Louise that he had not returned to England sooner, for he had liked her, and their friendship had outlived the passion by some years. Louise had taken other lovers since, though Rupert had not replaced her. Of late he had met no one who aroused more than a passing lust, and he wondered if that was why his life seemed empty despite the wealth and honours that had come to him these past years.

Rupert had learned to be wary of emotional tangles. Angelica's mother had ripped his heart apart with her cruel indifference and her unfaithfulness – but perhaps he had deserved it. He had become infatuated with her and married too quickly. If he had only waited, he might have seen the treasure that was his for the taking.

Elizabeth was the woman he ought to have married. She had loved him truly, but because he had hurt and neglected her, she had married someone else. Surely that should not sting after all these years? He was a fool, and should put the past behind him. He had a daughter, but he had promised his father he would do his duty, and that included a new marriage, for he must get himself an heir.

'I shall do my duty by you, Father,' he said. 'I know that I must marry and I shall choose wisely.'

'Yes, that has always been my hope,' Sir John said. 'You must not think me insensitive, Rupert – but I thought you might have married long since?'

'I believed there was time,' Rupert replied. 'Besides, I doubt you would have welcomed a Catholic wife.'

'If she was faithful to you I should have accepted her,' his father said, his tone harsh. 'Choose well this time, my son. Sarah almost destroyed you. You should look for a good woman rather than beauty.'

'Yes, Father, though she must also be intelligent and of good humour,' Rupert said. 'Beauty is but skin deep, after all.'

'Your mother is a good woman. She has been a faithful, industrious wife to me, and I pray that I may leave this life before she does, but sometimes I fear she will not wait for me. Go up to her now, Rupert. She is not well today, and I know she longs for your company.'

'Yes, Father. I shall go up to her now.' Rupert hesitated, then bent to kiss his father's cheek. 'I am glad to be home, sir.'

'I have prayed for it, and I thank God that my prayers are answered.'

Rupert walked from the room. He was thoughtful as he began to climb the stairs. Elizabeth had been much in his mind of late. He wondered where she was and whether she prospered. She had refused to leave her husband for him when he asked her, and he respected her for it – but sometimes he hated her too. Why hadn't she waited a little longer?

He smiled ruefully at his thoughts. It was all so long ago. Elizabeth would have a brood of children by now, and no doubt she had forgotten him – as he must forget her. Indeed, he had forgotten her for long periods, he admitted it to himself, but she was a part of the loneliness that had come upon him of late. Louise had kept the shadows at bay, but she was in France, and had a new and very jealous lover.

Rupert shook his head and dismissed his troublesome thoughts as he approached his mother's bedroom. He could hear laughter from inside. That must be Angelica, he thought and smiled. She was a lovely girl and he was fortunate to have her. He must try to make up for the lost years if that were possible.

He knocked and went in, watching for a moment as he saw that Angelica had been reading to her grandmother from one of Shakespeare's plays.

'What were you reading?' he asked and Angelica handed him the book. He glanced at it and nodded his understanding. 'Ah, *A Midsummer Night's Dream* . . . that was what made you laugh. Master Shakespeare's work still amuses, does it not? I have developed a taste for Molière, though perhaps he is not suitable for a girl of your age.'

'Why is that, Father?' she asked for she knew nothing of the French playwright.

'Angelica is a wonderful mimic,' Lady Saunders said, holding out her hand to him, for she did know of the Frenchman's work and thought it highly unsuitable for her granddaughter. 'She is a good and kind girl, Rupert. You have reason to be proud of your daughter.'

'I am glad to hear you say it,' Rupert said, giving Angelica a smile of approval. 'I must thank you for your care of her, Mother.'

'She has been a blessing to me,' Lady Saunders replied and laughed softly as the girl's cheeks took fire. 'No, do not blush, my love. Run along now and see if all is ready for your father. He will keep me company for a while now.'

'Yes, Grandmama,' Angelica said and glanced shyly at her father. 'We dine at four, sir – if that will suit you?'

'Of course – whatever is your usual arrangement,' Rupert said, though he had been used to a later hour. 'I have not eaten since I broke my fast this morning and I must admit that I am hungry.'

'Then I shall make sure that everything is prepared,' Angelica said and dipped a curtsey to him, but he held up his hand in protest as she left.

'There is no need for so much formality, Angelica. Please, call me Father – and do not curtsey every time we meet.'

Angelica smiled and went out, closing the door softly behind her. Rupert turned to look at his mother. She was lying back against the pillows, her face white with pain.

'You are ill . . .'

'It is nothing. The pain comes and goes. I shall be better in a moment.'

'Should I send for the doctor – or would you prefer your maid?'

'They can do little to ease me. The physician's draught makes me sleep, and I wish to talk to you, Rupert. You have been away too long and I fear I do not have much time left.'

'Forgive me . . .'

She held up her hand. 'I do not reproach you, Rupert. I knew why you went, but I am glad that you are returned in time. I want you to promise me that you will take good care of Angelica. I think she has suffered for the lack of a mother and father. We have done what we could for her – but she needs more. It is up to you to give her all that she has lacked.'

'I shall do so, Mother. Do not distress yourself for Angelica's sake.'

'She needs a mother,' Lady Saunders said, and sighed. 'She told me that you spoke of finding a husband for her – do not be in too much hurry, Rupert. I pray you will not force her into a marriage of convenience. I have a good reason for my request, though for the moment it must remain private.'

'There is perhaps someone she likes?' Rupert said, guessing what she would not say.

'Perhaps. I do not know that anything will come of it – but give her time, Rupert.'

'Yes, of course,' he said and bent closer to kiss her cheek. The skin was papery soft, and brought home to him how frail she was. 'I have thought of you often, Mother. Forgive me for staying away so long.'

'You are here now. I pray that God will grant me long enough to see both you and Angelica happy.' She reached up to touch his cheek. 'And now you may ring for my maid. I believe I shall sleep a little now.'

Two

Elizabeth Benedict was turning out her linen chests. It was her habit to do so every spring, and it was a much-needed chore, for some of it had turned yellow even though it had been packed with herbs and lavender to keep it clean and sweet. She handed a pile of sheets and cloths to her maids, bidding them wash and scrub them well, and then took a few items into her private chamber to sort them into piles. Some would be usable if they were mended, some were ready to be consigned to the fire, for they were little better than rags. She looked at a silk petticoat that had been torn and mended too many times, and placed it with the pile for burning. A pair of white stockings, sadly frayed, followed it, and then she saw the kerchief; it was for the use of a gentleman and had the initials RS embroidered into the corner.

She sighed as she recalled that she had been making it as a gift for Rupert. She had put it away after he left to return to London and she had waited to hear from him. She had waited and waited, praying that he would come back and marry her, but he had not sent a letter and she had grown weary of waiting. She had married Captain Benedict . . . Walter . . . a man she had never been able to love as she ought, though she had been a good and faithful wife to him while he lived.

It was useless to sigh for something that had happened so many years before. Elizabeth shook her head. She would not think of him, for she was sure he had forgotten her. Had he still cared, he must have come to her before this, because Caroline would have written to him to tell him when Walter died.

21

She tossed the kerchief on to the pile to be disposed of, and then retrieved it, smiling at herself for being foolish as she placed it with others to be washed. It was sentimental and ridiculous, but she would keep it yet.

'I am so excited that we are to visit London,' Claire said when she visited her cousin's home the next day. 'It is fortunate that your father has come home, Angelica. We were all to have gone together, I know, but now you will have Sir Rupert too.'

'Yes . . .' Angelica agreed happily, for Claire was always pleasant to her. It was only when Hal was with them that she felt excluded from their magic circle. 'He . . . my father has been both generous and kind to me. He brought me a beautiful gown from France, which will need only the smallest alteration – and he has given me several pretty trinkets. He says I shall have a whole new wardrobe when we go to London.'

'And why should he not be good to you?' Claire asked, for she thought it was high time that Sir Rupert returned to attend to his responsibilities, which otherwise fell on her father's shoulders. 'You are everything a daughter should be, Angelica. He should be pleased with you.' Claire knew her cousin better than most, and was aware that Angelica sometimes felt rebellious. Her own parents were less strict than Lady Saunders, and she had often felt sympathy for her cousin. Perhaps now that Sir Rupert had returned, Angelica would have more freedom – the kind of freedom that Claire had always enjoyed.

'Have you seen Hal today?' Angelica asked. She wondered whether she ought to mention her encounter with the gypsy the previous day. Hal had dismissed the man's claims as monstrous lies, and perhaps they were, but she was afraid the gypsy meant to cause trouble for her uncle.

'He went out first thing with my father,' Claire said and pulled a face. 'You know how hard Hal works, Angelica. He says he shall not come to London with us, for if his father is to go, he will be needed here to see to the estate.'

'Not come with us?' Angelica was both surprised and disappointed. She had been certain that Hal intended to accompany them. 'That is a shame – but surely if you asked him, he might change his mind?' Hal often gave way if Claire asked him nicely.

'Perhaps . . . but I am not sure that I want him to,' Claire said, and wrinkled her brow. 'I love Hal, of course I do – but he will tell me what to do all the time! I think it may be more enjoyable to visit London without him.'

Angelica stared at her in surprise. Surely she could not mean it? How could anything be better without Hal? Even when she was cross with him, Angelica always felt more alive in Hal's company. She would miss him if he did not accompany them, and would definitely have wished him to be one of their party.

'But I thought . . .' Angelica paused for nothing had been said officially about their betrothal. She had believed it was to be on Claire's sixteenth birthday, but perhaps she was mistaken.

'You thought that Hal and I were to be betrothed?' Claire flicked back her long dark curls, her soft brown eyes reflecting anxiety. 'You must promise you will say nothing to anyone?' she asked, and Angelica nodded. 'I am not certain that I wish to marry Hal. I know he thinks we shall marry one day, but I have not yet made up my mind. Perhaps I shall in time feel it is right . . . but not yet, and perhaps not ever. My mother says I must meet other young men first – and to tell the truth, I think of Hal as my brother.'

'But . . .' Angelica held back her protest. Hal would be so angry if he knew what Claire had just told her. 'Hal would not like to hear you say that . . .' She shook her head for Claire must know what Hal's reaction would be.

'You will not tell him?'

'No, of course not. I give you my word – none shall hear this from me.'

Claire touched her hand in gratitude. 'I knew that I could trust you. We have always been friends, dear Angelica – but

23

Hal tries to monopolize me, and if I speak honestly, I do not care for it. I think it better that it will be just the two of us while we are away. We shall help each other to choose our gowns, and tell each other our secrets.' She linked her arm through Angelica's. 'Now, will you show me the gown your father bought for you? I believe the French fashions are very fine, and I am eager to see it . . .'

After her cousin had returned home, Angelica visited her grandmother's room. Lady Saunders asked her to read to her from a volume of French plays that Rupert had brought for her, and the girl spent most of the afternoon there before going to her room to dress for dinner. She did not change into the gown her father had bought her, even though Claire had thought it beautiful. She stroked the soft silk lovingly with her finger-tips, but chose a plainer gown instead. She would keep the new one until she had the occasion to wear it – perhaps when Hal came to dinner.

They were to have a family dinner two nights before the promised trip to London, which was to be in ten days' time. Her father wanted to ride the estate with Lord Mortimer and set some changes in place before he left to escort his sister, brother-in-law, niece and daughter to town.

Angelica could not help regretting that Hal had refused to come with them. She knew that he was very conscientious about his duty towards the Mortimer estate, but surely it would not have hurt if he had been absent for a few weeks? Perhaps Claire had it wrong? Perhaps he would change his mind and come with them.

Angelica had at first been shocked that her cousin did not particularly wish for Hal to accompany them to London. Now, though, she had begun to wonder if it was just one of Claire's whims. In the past she had teased Hal often enough just for the devilry of it, and it might be that she was cross with him for some reason. It would be foolish of Angelica to believe that her cousin truly meant it when she said she would not marry him.

And even if Claire did mean to refuse him, it did not follow that Hal would turn to her. Angelica knew that she must not allow herself to hope that he might smile at her the way he smiled at Claire. She knew that Hal was often annoyed with her for no reason – or none that she knew of. It had always been that way. However, he loved Claire, and he would be both angry and hurt if she declined to wed him.

Angelica realized that she did not wish to see Hal hurt. He had always been so certain of his place, so sure that anything he wanted would be his – she would not like to see him humbled.

However, Claire would probably come home and marry him after all. To hope for anything else would be unkind of her, and might meet with bitter disappointment.

'Angelica.' Her father's voice reached her as she left her chamber and began to walk along the gallery. 'Pray wait for me . . .'

She did as he asked, turning to him with a slight curtsey, for she could not yet meet him on familiar terms. 'Father – is there something I may do for you?'

'Your grandmother tells me that you were reading to her from the book of plays that I brought her. She says that you have done well with your studies. Perhaps we may converse together in French this evening? I should like to hear you speak the language and see if you need improvement. As you know, French is much spoken at court.'

'Shall we go to court, Father?'

'Indeed, I am sure of it,' Rupert replied. 'I fought for the late King, and I know his son well. We spent time together during his exile – and it was through Charles's good offices in introducing me to Mazarin that I found my last post. I was a secretary to the Marquis de Thouret, who was close to both Mazarin and Louis, and I held several licences – one of which was to import French wine into England. I have a business set up in London, which has helped to repair my fortune, and it is my intention to expand to other towns.'

'I did not know that, sir. Grandfather has sometimes spoken

of the estate needing a guiding hand, for my uncle has not the time to do all that he would wish. I think it has worried him for some time . . .'

'Well, I am here now,' Rupert told her. 'Lord Mortimer has been a good steward, but the money I shall bring to the estate will make it flourish once more.'

'Then Grandfather will be content.'

'Yes, I believe so,' Rupert said and smiled at her. 'I hope that you too will be content, Angelica. I must tell you that it is my intention to marry again. I hope that the lady I choose will be a friend to you.'

'That would be pleasant, sir. I have been sad to see Grandmother confined to her bed of late so much, but you must not think that I have lacked for anything.'

'Is that so?' Rupert gave her a steady look. Could she truly be as meek and obedient as she seemed? Surely there must be something of her mother in her? 'Well, I believe you may find that your life will change for the better, daughter. I hope it may be so.'

Angelica bent her head. Could he see into her mind – see the rebellious spirit that she had learned to control as a child? She had been whipped for her tantrums as a young girl, learning to be obedient and to behave, as her strict grandparents believed was right, and she had wept into her pillow many a night. But those days were behind her. She was no longer a child, and she hid her passionate nature behind a mask of docility. To be loved, she must be good, and she needed to be loved.

'I am sure I shall be happy with your choice of a wife, Father.'

Rupert nodded, a slight frown on his brow. He wished that he might be as sure, for though he had promised his father he would marry, he had no real inclination for it. Unless he could find a lady he truly admired . . . someone like Elizabeth. But she was married to Captain Benedict, and he did not imagine that they would meet again.

'So that is the gown your father bought for you,' Hal said. He had accompanied his family to Hillgrove for the celebration dinner, because it would have been too much for Lady Saunders to travel to Thornberry, even though it was but a short distance. 'It becomes you well, Angelica.'

Since the compliment was accompanied by a frown, Angelica did not find it particularly pleasing. Hal was merely being polite, and she almost preferred it when he was brusque with her.

'You don't mean it,' she said, tossing her hair, which was the colour of spun gold and dressed in ringlets. She was a very beautiful girl, though she was unaware of it, a hint of her passionate nature showing in the fire of her eyes and the pout of her mouth. Anyone seeing at her at that moment, who had known her mother, would have seen that she was Sarah's daughter. 'Why do you not say what you truly feel?'

'I should not say it if I did not think it,' Hal said and glared at her. Something about her had got under his skin, and he struck out at her. 'If you show your true nature with other gentlemen you may never find a husband, Angelica. No man wants a shrew for a wife.'

'I am not a shrew.' Her eyes were more green than blue at that moment as she gave him a fierce look. 'Anyway, I do not care. I am not sure that I wish to be married.'

'Every woman must marry; it is her duty,' Hal told her and now there was a spark of mockery in his eyes, as if he enjoyed teasing her. 'If the right gentleman offers for you, you will have no choice. It is your father's right to dispose of you as he will.'

'My father has promised that there is no hurry for me to be wed,' Angelica said. 'I shall not marry unless I find a gentleman who is kind and gentle – and not a bit like you.'

'And then you will lead him a merry dance, I dare say,' Hal said, unsure why the thought of Angelica married to some unknown gentleman disturbed him. 'You had best not let him see your tantrums.' Hal knew that it was he who aroused her temper, for with everyone else she was mild-mannered and gentle. It was only he who had seen those cat's eyes flash with anger – and it amused him that he knew her for her true self.

'As long as he is not like you, I shall be a good wife to him,' she said and walked away to join her cousin and grandmother.

Hal found himself watching her. She looked different that evening. The dark emerald gown became her, its elegance making her look older – and more exciting. He was aware that Angelica was fast becoming a woman, and a woman who aroused feelings in him that more suitably belonged to the encounters he enjoyed with the whores he and his friends visited occasionally. But Angelica was not a whore, she was a respectable young lady – and he intended to marry Claire. Therefore it was wrong of him to have such thoughts of her.

Hal knew that his father had not been married to his mother. Harry Mortimer had been wild in his youth, and his son was determined that he would not follow in his footsteps. He owed everything to his uncle, and he would not like Nicolas to be disappointed in him. It had been long arranged, at least in his mind; he was the heir to Thornberry, and he would marry Claire – Angelica was just a foolish little girl he had always liked to tease. She had such an expressive face when she was not in control of her emotions, and the little devil in him could not resist rousing her just for the pleasure of seeing her look cross. Except that tonight she seemed different . . .

Angelica tried to put all thought of Hal from her mind as she talked to her cousin and grandmother. Lady Saunders seemed brighter that night than she had for some time, and when she asked her granddaughters if they would accompany her to her room, she surprised them by giving them each a gift.

'These trinkets were mine as a young girl,' she told them. 'I have always intended that you should have one each – and I think it appropriate that you should have them now, my dears. You are good girls, and I know you will make your parents proud of you in London.'

Claire opened her box immediately. It contained a necklet of seed pearls with a larger pearl drop. Angelica admired it and then opened her own box, discovering a similar necklet, except that hers was of gold with a small locket set with pearls and tiny turquoises.

'Oh, it is beautiful,' she said, her eyes pricking with emotion. 'It is kind of you to give us these lovely things, Grandmother.'

'I wanted to give you both something to remember me by,' Lady Saunders said and smiled at them. 'You are both dear to me – though I may have been stricter with you, Angelica, for I felt responsible for your welfare, my dear.'

'You are very good to us.' Claire kissed her cheek.

'Run along now, Claire,' Lady Saunders said. 'Angelica will send for my maid, and I want a few words with her.'

'I shall see you in two days when we leave for London,' Claire said to her cousin as she prepared to leave. 'Goodnight, Angelica. Goodnight, Grandmama, sweet dreams.'

'Goodnight, cousin.' Angelica waited until the door closed behind her. 'What may I do for you, Grandmother?'

'I just wanted to talk to you, child. Please do not be hurt by what I say – but I feel I must speak my mind. I may not have much longer left to me and there are things that must be said for your own good.'

'Have I done something to displease you?' Angelica searched her conscience, but could not think of any misdeed that might have come to her grandmother's ears.

'No, indeed you have been a good obedient girl – but sometimes I wonder if I have been too strict with you. Your mother was wilful, Angelica. She broke your father's heart . . .' Lady Saunders hesitated, and then decided it must all be said. 'She left him for another man and then died in a carriage accident. He found her body and brought it home. For a while he was like a madman in his grief. Sarah was selfish and thoughtless, though lovely to look at, and I feared you might take after her – but thankfully you have not.'

'Grandmama!' Angelica was shocked, for she had heard nothing of this. 'I did not know . . .' Though of course she had always known that some mystery shrouded her mother's death, had sensed her grandmother's silent disapproval often enough. Sometimes her silences had hurt more than the rod she beat her with, Angelica remembered.

'Well, I am sorry if it dismays or shocks you. I never intended to tell you, but you are going to London and you will meet many gentlemen. I wanted to warn you to choose wisely. Do not marry simply for advantage. If you do you may regret it at your leisure.'

'Is that what my mother did?'

'She was young and her father had died, leaving her almost penniless. I do not blame her entirely, for Rupert always had high ideals and may have expected too much of her – but I would not see you marry unwisely, Angelica. Be sure that you can like and respect your husband, my dear. Otherwise you may cause both him and yourself much pain.' She reached up to touch Angelica's cheek. 'And forgive me if I have hurt you. I have always loved you, and perhaps I have been overly harsh with you sometimes.'

'No, you have not hurt me,' Angelica said, though it was not true, and she could not deny that her grandmother had been harsh. 'I think perhaps I understand . . .' Things that had not been clear to her were explained by this revelation. 'Was it because of my mother's unfaithfulness that my father went away?'

'Yes, in part,' Lady Saunders told her. 'A part of it was because of the war, but much of it was due to your mother. As I said, she broke his heart.'

'Thank you for telling me,' Angelica said. Her chest felt tight with emotion and tears pricked her eyes, though she did not know whether she wept for her mother, her father or herself. 'Shall I ring for your maid now?'

'Just help me to my chair. I shall ring for her later. I am not tired this evening, and I wish to write some letters. I must put my affairs in order, for the time is coming . . .' She did not finish the sentence, sighing heavily.

Angelica was thoughtful as she left her grandmother. She had often wondered why her grandparents were so much stricter with her than with Claire, but now she understood. Her grandparents must have feared that she would be like her mother – and perhaps she might be if she allowed her true nature to surface.

Sometimes she felt so rebellious. It was usually Hal who made her want to strike back. Perhaps her father had made her mother feel that way . . .

Hal felt restless as he looked out the window of his bedchamber. It was a bright moonlit night and he knew that he would not sleep for some hours yet, though he was not sure what was keeping him wakeful. Unless it was Angelica in that green gown . . . there had been something about her that aroused an urgent need in him.

Perhaps if he went down to the village he might find some of his friends. It would not harm to spend a little time with them drinking at the inn, and mayhap he would find a willing wench to relieve the need Angelica's beauty had aroused in his loins.

'Damn the wench!' Hal groaned as he snatched his jerkin from the bench where he had thrown it some minutes earlier. He left his room and began to walk down the stairs that led to the Great Hall, but as he reached the bottom, he heard Nicolas's voice call to him from above. 'Yes, sir . . .' He turned reluctantly and looked up.

'Were you going out?' Nicolas asked. He was aware that Hal occasionally felt the need to go drinking with friends, accepting it because so far the lad had shown no sign of following in his father's footsteps. He was not a gambler, and it was natural for a young man to seek the company of a willing wench now and then. 'I wanted to speak with you on a matter concerning the estate, but if you have business elsewhere it can wait.'

'There is nothing that matters,' Hal said. 'Shall I come up or will you come down?'

'There are some papers in my cabinet,' Nicolas said. 'A little business you can attend to for me while I am away if you will.'

'Of course,' Hal agreed at once. He liked it that Nicolas relied on him, and his intention to spend the rest of the night drinking vanished into the mist. 'Tell me what you would like me to do, sir . . .'

In the moonlight a young man stood staring up at the windows of the house at Thornberry Manor. His eyes were angry, a stormy grey-blue that reflected the sense of resentment he harboured inside. He knew that a family gathering had been held at Hillgrove that night – and he ought by right to have been a part of that gathering. His mother had told him so; she had told him that he was the lawful Lord Mortimer, though Roald had told him that she lied and that he was merely a bastard.

Roald was the leader of the gypsies, and once Jared's mother had been his woman, but Rowena had lost much of her beauty and a younger girl had replaced her in his bed. It was her own fault, for she took no care of her appearance, letting her hair become greasy and tangled and seldom bothering to wash her clothes. As a child Jared had been neglected, dirty and often hungry, but as he grew to manhood he had learned to swim in the rivers and to enjoy the feeling of being clean. He knew that the young women of the tribe liked it that he smelled fresh, and he was popular with them – one more reason for Roald to dislike him.

Of late he had felt a growing hostility towards him from Roald. He sensed that it was because the older man feared that he would lose his position as their leader. Many of the gypsies whispered that life had been hard under his leadership and that it was Jared's time. It had been foretold that good fortune would come to them through Rowena's child.

Sometimes Jared doubted that the prophecy would come

true – for what could he do that would make their lives easier? His mother said that he should claim his inheritance. Easy enough for her to say when she sat by her fire grumbling to herself and drinking the potions she made herself from berries she took from the hedgerow. It was foul stuff, in Jared's opinion, but it eased the bitterness inside her so that she could sleep, or that was what she had said when he told her it was not good for her to drink so much ale earlier that evening.

'Go away,' she had muttered when he'd tried to take the flask from her. 'You have been nothing but a trouble to me – and trouble is all you be unless you take back what is rightfully ours.'

'Give me the proof,' Jared had asked as he had many times before. 'Without proof it is only your word against his . . . and who would believe you?'

Rowena had flown into a temper, coming at him with her fists, striking him about the face and head so that he was forced to hold her off until she calmed down. 'Call me a liar will you? I tell you I was Harry Mortimer's wife. I am your mother, but you show me no respect . . . away with you. You be a good-for-nothing and I wish you had never been born.'

Jared was smarting from the latest of her bitter tirades as he stared at the house. If his mother's tale were true, he ought to be living there as Lord of the Manor – but could he believe her? And even if it were true, he had no way of proving it. Sometimes he considered going up to the Manor and demanding to see Nicolas Mortimer, but he doubted that the great Lord Mortimer would deign to see him.

In two days the spring fair would gather in the meadows near Thornberry Manor, and there would be a wrestling competition. Jared had heard there was a purse of some ten golden sovereigns. He had won every contest he had entered in other parts of the country, and he believed he could win here. With that money he could travel to the City of Oxford, where his mother swore she had married. Perhaps there he might find proof that Harry Mortimer had married Rowena Greenslade, making him his father's rightful heir.

He was frowning as he turned away. He would go down to the village and drink a tankard of ale – and, if he were lucky, he would find the obliging wench who had smiled at him the previous evening. Perhaps he would lie with her. He might take his pick of the gypsy girls, and there was one he liked above the others: Serena was a lovely girl, dark-eyed and sweet-natured – but to take her to his bed would mean that in the eyes of his tribe he was committed to her, and he was not ready for that just yet. He cared for her, but he was not sure he wanted her to be his woman.

His thoughts returned to the girl he had met in the woods some days earlier. She was beautiful, and he had known a stirring of desire as he gazed at her, but the look in her eyes had been proud, and he had understood that she despised him. She would never look at a gypsy. He would never be good enough for her!

He had known who she was for he had seen her walking to the Manor from her home, and one of the local men had told him that she was the daughter of Sir Rupert Saunders, and therefore cousin to Mistress Claire Mortimer. She was only second cousin to Hal Mortimer . . . the bastard of Mistress Mercy Harris and Jared's father.

Jared thought it was the fact that Hal was the heir to Thornberry that irked him the most, for he was some weeks older and at least as much entitled to inherit as his favoured half-brother, even if his mother had lied about her marriage. The resentment was strong in him as he walked away that night. Why had his uncle taken the child of Mercy Harris as his heir and not his brother's eldest son? Why had Nicolas Mortimer never sought him out or given him anything to ease the hardship of his life?

The only explanation could be that Jared was the son of a gypsy woman and the Mortimers were ashamed of the connection. Anger wrenched at Jared's guts. One day he would make them sorry for their neglect – one day he would find a way to take back what was owed to him! For the moment he would seek out the tavern wench who had smiled at him so willingly. At least he could forget his anger in her arms for a time.

Angelica had hoped that Hal might come to say goodbye before they left for London that morning, but he merely sent a message with Claire.

'He had an errand for my father,' she told Angelica as they settled themselves comfortably in the coach. 'He bid me tell you to remember what he said to you the other evening, and that he wished you a pleasant visit.'

Angelica felt the familiar irritation inside, but controlled it and smiled at her cousin. Claire could have no idea that Hal was using her to mock Angelica. She glanced across the carriage at her aunt, who was settling herself with her bits and pieces about her. The three of them were to share the Mortimers' coach, while the servants and the baggage came on behind. Lord Mortimer and Angelica's father had chosen to ride.

Angelica wished that she might ride for at least a part of the way, but it was expected that she would travel with her aunt and cousin, and she had accepted the inevitable.

'Well, my dears, is this not pleasant?' Caroline asked, smiling at them. 'Are you excited, Angelica? You will find London very large and busy, I dare say. I hope you have the pomander I sent you in your purse? You may need it, for the smells are not pleasant in some parts of the town.'

'How long before we reach London?' Angelica asked. She was too nervous and excited to worry about unpleasant smells, though she had her aunt's gift somewhere in her baggage.

'Oh, some three or four days. We shall take our time, for it is more comfortable so – the roads are badly rutted in places, and we do not wish for an accident.'

The heavy coach rumbled down the drive and into the lane that led down to the village. Angelica glanced out of the window as they passed the large meadow, seeing that several caravans had begun to gather there.

'I had forgotten that the fair was due this week,' she said, a wistful note in her voice. 'The merchants are beginning to set out their stalls.'

'You will see much finer wares in London,' Caroline assured her with a smile. 'We shall visit the silk merchants and the Exchange. You may shop to your heart's content, for Rupert has told me to spare no expense in the matter of your wardrobe, Angelica.'

'He is amazingly kind to me.'

'Nonsense! It is time that he shouldered his responsibility towards you,' Caroline said. 'You are a very pretty girl, Angelica, and I dare say there will be several gentlemen in London who may wish to approach you – but you should tell them to speak to your father.'

'Father has spoken to me of this,' Angelica replied and wrinkled her brow in contemplation. 'But I am not sure that I wish to think of marriage just yet, Aunt.'

'You will be sixteen in a few weeks,' Caroline said. 'I would not care to see Claire marry before that, and I told Rupert that he should not commit you to marriage just yet – but we shall see. If you meet someone you like, you may think differently.'

'Yes, perhaps,' Angelica said and glanced out of the window once more. As she did so, she saw a man leading a handsome piebald pony on the grass verge at the side of the road, and she felt a cold trickle down her spine as she realized it was the gypsy she had met in the woods. His eyes were very blue that day, and as cold as ice. She sensed that he was watching the carriage as it swept by, and that he was angry. For a moment she wondered if she should tell her aunt, but then she remembered Hal's warning. Her uncle and aunt would both think she was foolish if she told them of the gypsy's boast. 'But Father has said that he will not force me to marry against my will.'

'Nor would I permit it,' Caroline assured her. She wondered what had caused her niece to look so oddly for a moment, but whatever it was had passed, and Angelica was smiling again as she turned to Claire. The two began talking about a book of poems they had recently been reading together, and Caroline sat back against the squabs with a little sigh. For herself, she was glad to be leaving Thornberry while the fair was here. She was always a little uneasy when the gypsies visited, though they seldom gave Nicolas any trouble. Yet of late, she had had some troubling dreams concerning Hal and a man who looked very like him.

She knew that Nicolas had forgotten Rowena's child. He had searched for the boy once, many years previously, and found no trace; he had also searched for some proof that his brother had married Rowena Greenslade, but there was no record of a marriage in Oxford, and he was certain that none had taken place.

'Harry was in love with Mercy Harris, but he needed to marry a fortune. It is unlikely that he married Rowena,' Nicolas had said when his search came to nothing. 'I do not deny that Harry may have fathered her child – we both know that he had an affair with her. But the child may have died in infancy. We can do nothing for him unless he comes to us, Caroline. You should put him out of your mind.'

Caroline had tried to do as Nicolas bid her, but she had never quite been able to forget the small boy she had once seen at St Ives with Rowena. He had been so like Hal that she was convinced he was Harry's son – and she wished with all her heart that she might have done something to help him. He had been much in her mind of late, and the disturbing dreams all concerned both Rowena's son and her darling Hal.

She was uneasy because the dreams seemed to hint at some disaster, though she could never see further than two men fighting each other in the meadow. It had come to her over and over again, but there was a veil hiding the ending of the fight from her. The vision had haunted her over the years, and she had an awful feeling that the two men were Hal and Rowena's son . . . and they were destined to fight.

The meadow was filled with people enjoying themselves when Hal rode down from the Manor that afternoon. He had spent the morning carrying out various tasks for his uncle, but now he was free to amuse himself as he chose. He knew that the wrestling matches were to begin in a few minutes, and he wanted to be sure of entering his challenge – but he would let the keener contestants go first. He had won the challenge the previous year, and he did not think that any of the local lads could beat him, but there might be a newcomer this year. He hoped that it would be so, for he enjoyed being put to the test.

'Hal!' He was accosted by one of the friends he sometimes drank with at the inn. Matthew Thomas grinned at him as he threw a careless arm about his shoulder. It was clear that he had already been drinking at the ale tent and was slightly tipsy. 'Are you going to challenge me to a bout this year?'

'I beat you last year,' Hal told him but with a look of affection on his face. 'You've been drinking, Matt. I doubt you could stand up long enough to challenge me – but we'll see what kind of competition there is this year.'

They walked together to the area that had been ringed off for the wrestling matches, passing the rows of stalls set out with various merchandise, as well as the tooth-drawer and men shooting arrows at a barrel. It was a pleasantly warm afternoon, but not hot, just right for this kind of affair.

A tall, thickset man with a swarthy complexion was already calling the challenge to any young man who stopped long enough to look interested. Hal and Matthew watched for a moment, and then went up to pay a silver crown to enter the competition. They were among the last, and it was some twenty minutes or so later before they found themselves in the ring.

Matthew did his best to give his friend a good tussle, but he was no match for Hal when sober and, having taken a drink or two, soon fell to his stronger friend. He accepted his defeat in good part, finding a place to sit on a bale of hay while he waited for the next round of the competition.

Several other bouts took place, and then he blinked as he saw a newcomer enter the ring. For a moment he thought he was seeing things, but he turned his head and discovered that Hal was still sitting beside him.

'God's body!' he ejaculated. 'Am I seeing things – or does that fellow look like you?'

'He looks like me,' Hal said grimly. He had risen to his feet to watch as the newcomer prepared to meet his first opponent. 'The damned scoundrel! I wonder he has the effrontery to be here!'

'Who is he?' Matthew asked, sensing Hal's anger. 'What do you know of him?'

'He is a gypsy, and he claims to be my half-brother,' Hal said, his lips twisting in a sneer. 'It is a damned lie, of course.'

'Yes . . .' It was on the tip of Matthew's tongue to point out that the stranger looked very like him and might be one of the late Harry Mortimer's by-blows, but something in Hal's face stopped him. His eyes narrowed as the stranger won the bout easily. 'It looks as if he knows how to wrestle.'

'Yes, I'll give him that,' Hal agreed. 'He can fight a bit.'

It was Matthew's opinion that the stranger might be this year's champion, but he held his tongue. Hal was about to fight for the second time. If he won this fight, he would meet the champion from the next fight – and that would probably mean that he would have to fight his alleged half-brother.

Matthew half wished that his friend would go down this bout, but Hal won within moments. The stranger won his next fight as easily. The ringmaster was calling for ale and water to be offered to the two remaining champions.

Matthew noticed that the stranger drank two sips of water and then tossed the rest over him. Hal drank half his ale, and tipped his water over his head. His face was set hard as he stepped into the ring and the two men eyed each other up.

'Right, gentlemen,' the ringmaster said. 'Whichever of you wins this match gets the prize of ten golden sovereigns. I want a clean fight, no gouging and no kicking or armlocks on the throat. You'll get a bucket of water over you if either of you cheats.'

Hal and Jared circled each other, eyes locked in silent challenge. Neither had forgotten their first and only meeting in the woods when they were both boys, though neither was willing to acknowledge the other. The ringmaster was taking bets on the outcome, collecting the pennies and shillings offered by eager hands and pocketing them, for he would make a good profit on the day if things went as he suspected.

Hal made the first lunge, catching Jared about the waist and lifting him off his feet for a moment, but Jared used his strength to break free, though he stumbled as he fell. In seconds he was back on his feet, and this time he reached out and grabbed Hal's arm, twisting it behind his back so that Hal groaned with the pain and sank to his knees. For a moment, it looked as if he might be forced to give in and so surrender the first fall, but with a hard, jerking movement, he brought his arm up and swung round, reversing the hold so that now he had the upper hand. His triumph lasted seconds before he found himself being tossed through the air, so that he landed on his back and lay winded as the first fall was declared for Jared.

Hal glared at his opponent, furious that he had fallen for such a trick, and battle began once more. This time they were locked into a power struggle for some time until Hal managed to throw Jared off guard and floor him, lying across his body for sufficient time to have the fall called in his favour. His victory promoted more bets, for he was a popular champion and most wished to see him win. However, he had scarcely had time to appreciate his triumph before he found himself falling over Jared's outstretched leg, and lay winded beneath his body as Jared threw himself across his chest, holding him down.

The move was so swift and treacherous that it had taken him by surprise, and he was furious as Jared offered him his hand to help him rise, brushing it aside. He refused to shake hands, stalking off as his opponent was declared the champion and awarded the prize.

'It wasn't a fair fight,' Matthew said catching up to him. 'I haven't seen a move like that before – he cheated you, Hal.'

'No, it was fair enough,' Hal muttered though it cost him to say it. 'It took me by surprise, that's all – next time I'll be ready for him.'

'Wouldn't catch me going three rounds with him,' Matthew said. 'I still say he's a trickster.'

Hal grunted, shooting a hard glance at his friend. He knew that Matthew was trying to take the sting from his defeat, but nothing would do that – it would stick like a thorn in his flesh until he had beaten the gypsy.

'It was only a stupid contest,' he said. 'Let's go to the alehouse and find ourselves some willing wenches . . .'

Three

'I never thought I should visit a theatre,' Angelica said, as she looked at her image in the small but very costly hand-mirror of burnished silver and dull grey glass. She giggled at the thought of what their former pastor would have said on the subject only a few months ago. He would no doubt have condemned her as sinful, but he had gone now, along with the strict laws that had for so long ruled their lives. 'Do you think it is a terrible sin, Claire?'

'No, of course it isn't,' her cousin replied. 'Oh, I know such things were frowned upon in the Lord Protector's time, but the King is back now and we are allowed to enjoy ourselves. Indeed, it is likely that His Majesty will be present this evening. Father says that when he and Mama came up for the coronation the whole city went mad with delight. The bells rang out from every church, people brought out the maypoles and danced in the streets and everyone was happy. It must have been the same when His Majesty married, though Father did not come up for that. Everyone is much happier now.'

Not quite everyone, Angelica thought privately. It had been said that the King would forgive his father's enemies when he was returned to the throne, but Charles had refused to forgive those who had put their names to his father's death warrant, and some ten or more traitors had met their deaths in violent ways. After that, the King had agreed the Act of Settlement, and as a magnanimous gesture spared others who might have expected to share the fate of their comrades.

However, this was not the time to be thinking of such

things. They had been in London for two days, most of which they had spent shopping at the various silk merchants in the city. Both girls were wearing new gowns that the tailors had hastily altered to fit them, and several more had been bespoken in styles they had chosen from coloured drawings of the latest fashions. They had also managed to purchase new shoes, though both were wearing their old cloaks, for there had not been time to purchase fresh ones.

Angelica had chosen to wear the necklet her grandmother had given her, but Claire had chosen some pearls of her mother's.

'We look very fine,' Angelica said, her eyes bright with excitement. 'Shall we go down now? I think the others will be waiting for we were called some minutes since.'

Even as she spoke, the door of the bedchamber opened and Caroline came in. She was wearing a silk damask gown of crimson and carrying a huge fan made of chicken skin and painted with flowers.

'Come along, my dears,' she admonished. 'The gentlemen are growing impatient. And we wish to be there before it becomes too crowded. Nicolas has taken a box for us, but there are bound to be some rowdy elements in the crowd.'

The girls gathered their own fans and followed her down the stairs to where Rupert and Nicolas were waiting. Both were wearing the latest full-skirted coats and sported matching waistcoats, their breeches cut full to the knee and their stockings silk with large bows for garters. Claire threw a sparkling glance at her cousin, for at home her father dressed very plainly, and he looked uncomfortable in his new finery. Especially his bright red stockings!

Angelica was hard put to it not to laugh, though she thought both gentlemen looked very handsome. However, she hid her smile as they were ushered outside to where three sedan chairs were waiting. Her father and Lord Mortimer would walk beside them, together with three burly servants armed with cudgels, as well as the six porters hired to carry the chairs. Even though the journey was short enough, it would have been unwise to go unescorted, for at night the streets of London were often haunted by gangs of robbers and beggars, who might attack the unwary. And then there were the Mohawks, unruly gentlemen who sometimes caused a drunken riot in the streets and behaved like foolish children, in Nicolas's opinion.

Angelica was helped into her chair, which had leather curtains pulled about it to deter the gaze of rude persons who might otherwise stare. In the small velvet purse she carried on her wrist was a kerchief soaked in lavender water and a pomander stuffed with sweet-smelling herbs and spices, which helped to mask the stench of the streets and ward off various diseases. It was said that some spices were efficacious in warding off the plague, but Caroline said that she did not believe it and the only way to escape such a terrible disease was to leave town if there should be an outbreak. However, the plague usually struck when the weather turned hotter in full summer, and as yet it was only May.

'Are you comfortable?' Rupert asked as the porters picked up the chair and began to carry his daughter. 'I shall be right here by your side.'

'I am comfortable enough,' she told him, though in truth she wished that she might be walking – but that would not be sensible, for her shoes were a pale kid leather and the streets were often strewn with filth. Many people wore wooden platforms on their shoes to avoid staining them, but this could be dangerous on the slippery cobbles.

Their journey to the theatre seemed to take an age, but as they drew closer, Angelica could hear a buzz of laughter and voices. Hearing some shouting, she peeped through the curtains and saw that a fight was going on between some young men. Since they were dressed even more finely than her father, she guessed that they were gentlemen, probably courtiers, but they appeared to have been drinking.

Lord Mortimer's servants were clearing a way for them, but some of the gentlemen seemed disinclined to move, and as Angelica was carried through their midst, the curtains were suddenly thrust back and a man put his head inside, making her give a little cry of fright.

'By God, there's a beauty in this one,' he cried, eyeing her in a fashion that made her uneasy. 'A very goddess, or Helen herself – a face to launch a thousand ships, I'll warrant. Would that I were Paris to taste the forbidden fruit.'

'Sir, you intrude,' Angelica said, for she knew the story of Helen of Troy well enough. 'Pray allow my chair to pass.'

'The goddess commands and I obey,' he said, a mocking smile on his lips as he bowed to her. 'Forgive me, Majesty . . .'

'Excuse me, sir,' Rupert said, tapping him on the shoulder as he withdrew. 'You are addressing my daughter – Good grief, Chesterford! Is it you indeed?'

'Rupert Saunders!' The sound of deep laughter made Angelica poke her head through the curtains to see what was going on. Her father was embracing the young man who had so rudely accosted her, seeming pleased to see him. 'Damn my eyes, I had no idea you were in London.'

'We arrived but two days hence,' Rupert said. 'Are you still at court, Will?'

'Where else would I be?' the other asked. 'Rochester is never far from the King, and where he goes there go I . . . We are attached at the hip, for my sins. I doubt not that we shall both end in Hell.'

'Always the same old Will,' Rupert said and grinned. 'I must not tarry, for my friends are anxious to see the play, but we shall meet soon.'

'You will come to court,' Will Chesterford said. 'And bring the beauty – but if she is truly your daughter, take care of her. It is not safe for innocents at Charles's court – especially if they look like that . . .' His eyes were quizzing her, and Angelica shut her curtains with a swish, annoyed that he had caught her looking at him. 'My apologies, Mistress Saunders. I knew you not – but I shall know you next time we meet.'

Inside the privacy of her curtains, Angelica allowed herself a smile. Master Chesterford was handsome indeed, his grey eyes merry, but with a wicked glint that warned her to be wary of him. She wondered if he would follow them to their box in the theatre, but he did not, and though she looked for him in the pit where several rowdy gentlemen had gathered to better ogle the ladies in the private boxes and the gallery, she saw nothing more of him that evening.

However, her pleasure in this first visit to the theatre was not to be diminished, and she thoroughly enjoyed watching the play, which was Shakespeare's wonderful comedy, *A Midsummer's Night's Dream.* She had read it often enough, but to see it being acted upon the stage was so much better!

Several other gentlemen came to their box during the interval, most of them friends of either her father or Lord Mortimer. They claimed to be renewing old acquaintance, but most seemed more interested in making the acquaintance of the two lovely young women in the party, and both Angelica and Claire found themselves being showered with compliments and invitations to various occasions.

It was during the second interval of the evening that Angelica noticed that her father seemed to have gone very quiet. His gaze seemed firmly fixed on a party of ladies and gentlemen in another box, and she thought he looked a little white about his mouth, as if he were labouring under some kind of distress.

'Is something wrong, Father?' she whispered to him as the curtain went up on the next act.

'No, nothing,' Rupert replied in a flat voice that covered the surging emotions inside him. He had just seen Elizabeth with three friends, and it had wrenched at his guts, shocking him. She had lowered the mask she wore for modesty's sake, as did most ladies of her class, to drink a cup of wine. Even though he had seen her but briefly, he had known her instinctively. Somehow he had not expected that she would be in London – and looking so lovely. The years had been kind to her, and she had blossomed into a beautiful woman, her face settled into a serenity that spoke of a quiet content. 'I thought I saw someone I knew from the past – but it does not matter.'

Elizabeth must be happy in her marriage. She could not look as serene if she were unhappy – and that meant she was as far beyond him as ever. Rupert felt a hard lump in his chest, for to see her, to know that she still had the power to affect him so deeply but was untouchable, was hard to bear. He brought his mind back to the play, but the actors seemed far away, their antics distant and seen through a mist as the years swept back.

He was remembering a warm afternoon when he had lain in the woods with Elizabeth, loving her, discovering the sweet passion of her nature – but he had walked away from her, caught up in his grief over Sarah's death. By leaving her so abruptly he had hurt her, making her lose faith in him. And so he had lost the woman he could not forget.

He did not think that Elizabeth had seen him. Ought he to seek her out in the next interval? He had no doubt that she would greet him kindly, but would it not be better to keep a distance? To speak with her and know that she was forbidden him would be to reopen old wounds. Perhaps it would be best if he tried to forget that he had seen her . . .

'I think that was one of the best performances I have watched in an age,' Mary Bennett said as she gathered up her fan and prepared to leave. 'Did you not think so, Elizabeth?' She frowned as she looked at her friend. 'Is there something wrong? You seem quiet. Did you not enjoy the play?'

'Yes, of course, Mary,' Elizabeth said and smiled at her. 'I was thinking of something. Forgive me if I was not attending. Yes, it was a good performance.'

Elizabeth looked about them as they followed the exodus from the crowded theatre. Some of the gentlemen were boisterous, for they had been drinking throughout the evening, and it wasn't easy for ladies to make their way through the melee. If truth were told, she thought guiltily, she had not been attending to the play for the last two acts. She had not been able to concentrate on what was going on on the stage since the moment she had glanced across at one of the other boxes and noticed Rupert sitting with Caroline, Claire and Angelica.

She had known for a few days that Rupert had come home, for Caroline had written to tell her. They still exchanged letters several times a year, though it was a while since they had visited one another. In fact, she had not seen her friend for nine years – the year Walter had died.

Elizabeth did not know why she had not accepted one of the many invitations that Caroline had sent her. Walter's estate had gone to a cousin, for though she had born a child, the boy had not seen his sixth year, which had been a source of much grief to both her and Walter. By that time, Walter's health had deteriorated and there was no chance of another child. It was but a few months after the death of their son that Walter had succumbed to a chill and died of it.

For some years Elizabeth had lived with her companion Mistress Furnley at a house on the estate, but when her friend had died, she had moved to London to live with Mistress Bennett. They had known each other for many years, and it had seemed sensible to share a home now that they were both widows. The house was large enough for both to have their own servants and apartments, but divided in such a way that they had some rooms in common. The arrangement had worked well, for neither had much family, and though both had their widow's jointure, neither was rich.

They lived comfortably enough, entertaining their friends and visiting the theatre when they chose. Elizabeth had been looking forward to that evening, but the sight of Rupert looking so handsome had thrown her into confusion, setting her heart fluttering like a moth. She had believed herself long over the tragic love affair that had almost ruined her life, but seeing Rupert that evening had brought back the painful memories.

Lost in her thoughts, Elizabeth did not notice the group of noisy young gallants until they surrounded her. She was startled more than frightened, for they were in high spirits, a little the worse for drink, but not threatening. She smiled at one of the young men who had put his arm about her waist, holding him off as he attempted to kiss her.

'Pray let me go on my way, sir,' she said. 'I wish you will let me join my friends.'

'Why the hurry, sweet lady?' the young man asked, keeping an arm firmly about her waist. 'I would spend a little time with you this night.'

Elizabeth saw that her friends had walked on without realizing that she had been delayed, and began to feel a little nervous. The young man seemed determined to hold her, and she was afraid that he might turn violent if she tried to break free.

'Please, sir. I beg you, let me go . . .'

'I will give you much pleasure if you come with me . . .'

'No!' Elizabeth tried to break free but he had hold of her wrist and she felt herself held in a vicelike grip. 'Let me go, sir . . .' Elizabeth pulled away from him, and then to her relief a man tapped the young gallant on the shoulder. 'Rupert . . . thank goodness,' she said and sighed with relief. 'This gentleman will not allow me to move on.'

'Sir, the lady wishes to be free,' Rupert said sternly. 'I ask you to take your hand from her.'

'And if I do not?' The young man squared up to him belligerently, but something in Rupert's eyes changed his mind and he let go of Elizabeth, walking off without another word.

'Thank you,' Elizabeth said, giving Rupert a grateful smile. 'I do not think that he meant me real harm, but he has kept me from my friends and they will be anxious.'

'I shall escort you to them,' Rupert said, his eyes going over her as she took his arm. 'You look very well, Elizabeth.'

'I am well,' Elizabeth said. 'And you have come home at last. Caroline wrote to me recently to tell me. I am glad of it for Angelica's sake. Lady Saunders has been an excellent guardian, but the child needs her father.'

'She is here with me this evening,' Rupert said. 'But I believe your friends are looking for you, Elizabeth. Perhaps you would care to meet Angelica another day?'

'Yes, I should like that,' she assured him. 'I have not seen her for some years – since my husband died. Caroline has invited me to stay, but for some reason I have not. However, I shall call on Caroline in the next day or so.' She looked up at him, her expression serene, giving nothing away. 'Thank you for helping me, Rupert.'

'It was my privilege,' he said, inclining his head to her. 'I did not know that I had lost your husband, Elizabeth. I am sorry to hear it.'

'Walter's health was not good for some years before he died,' Elizabeth said. 'I have accepted his death – as I accepted the loss of our son.' Her eyes lifted to his. 'Have you a son, Rupert?'

'No. My only child is Angelica,' Rupert said. 'But here is your friend – I shall leave you and hope that we shall meet again soon.'

'Tell Caroline that I shall call,' Elizabeth said and turned to Mary. 'This gentleman is an old friend who has rescued me from a young man who was a little the worse for drink.'

'Mary Bennett,' the widow said and smiled at him. 'We had not noticed that Elizabeth lagged behind. I must thank you for your help, sir.'

Rupert inclined his head and walked away, leaving the friends together. Mary looked at Elizabeth, noticing the faint flush in her cheeks.

'You have known that gentleman for some years?'

'Yes. He was once married to my cousin,' Elizabeth said. 'Sir Rupert Saunders. He went away after the war and has lived in France for most of those years. It is but two weeks or so since he returned.'

'He is very handsome,' Mary said, a speculative look in her eyes. 'Is he married?'

Elizabeth shook her head at her. 'I am not sure. I know he has only one child – the daughter of my cousin.'

'I wonder why he stayed away so long,' Mary said looking thoughtful. 'Do you suppose he means to stay now?'

'I really do not know,' Elizabeth said and laughed at her. 'Stop plotting, Mary. The others are waiting for us.'

'I have often said that you should marry again,' Mary said giving her an affectionate look. 'I think he likes you, Beth.'

'And I think that is nonsense,' Elizabeth said. 'I have promised to call on Lady Mortimer in the next few days, and you may come with me . . .'

'I shall certainly do so,' Mary said, laughter in her dark eyes. She was some years older than Elizabeth, a plump, pleasant woman who was happy with her lot. Mary had no thought of marrying again, but she believed that her friend would be happier married, for it was not yet too late for her to start another family.

Hearing some shouting and jeering to their right, they looked to see the cause of the trouble, but could not see what was going on, though Elizabeth heard some of the men shouting that the witchfinder was hunting a woman. She shuddered.

'Let us go home quickly,' she said. 'I think there is evil on the streets tonight, and I would be at home . . .'

'Did you see that lady – the one your father rescued from that drunkard?' Claire asked of Angelica when she came to her bedchamber the following morning. 'I believe it was Mistress Benedict – your mother's cousin.'

'I did not see what happened,' Angelica confessed, 'but you are right, Claire. Father told me that he happened to see Elizabeth and went to her aid. He has asked her to visit us, and she has promised to do so.'

'It is odd that she has not been to stay with us for so many years,' Claire said looking thoughtful. 'When I was little she and Captain Benedict came to our house several times, but since her husband died she has written but not visited.'

'Perhaps she was grieving,' Angelica suggested. 'Cousin

Elizabeth always sends me a gift for my birthday. I shall be happy to see her once more.'

'Yes, perhaps she was grieving,' Claire agreed. 'It will be nice to see her again . . .' She lifted her head, a sparkle in her eyes. 'My father says that we are to go to court this afternoon, and this evening there is to be a banquet.'

'It will be exciting,' Angelica said, thinking of the man who had so boldly thrust his head inside the curtains of her chair the previous evening. He had said he would remember her – and she was sure that he would be present. 'But I shall be so nervous . . . if we are presented to His Majesty.'

'Perhaps we should practise our curtsies this morning,' Claire said. 'Father said that there was nothing to be nervous about. He was kindly received when he visited last – and your father is certain to be welcomed, for he fought for the King's father.'

'It is said that His Majesty has willingly forgiven those who fought against his father – except for the men who signed their names to the death warrant.'

'Father says that he refused when he was asked to be a part of the tribunal, as did many others – but some were forced to attend and to sign their names.'

'And they have since paid for it,' Angelica said with a little shiver. 'Do not speak of it again, Claire. It is all in the past now, and they say that His Majesty is charming – though his looks are dark and not at all handsome.'

'Some call him the black boy,' Claire said with a giggle. 'But he is popular with the ladies, so I do not think that he can be so very ugly – do you?'

'What are you two giggling about?' Caroline asked as she came into the room. 'Your father has arranged for us to be received at court this afternoon. I think we should decide on the gowns you will wear – and perhaps we should practise your curtsies.'

'Yes, Mama, we were just speaking of it,' Claire told her, suppressing her mirth. 'I think I should like to wear my new green gown, if you approve?'

'I think that an excellent choice,' Caroline agreed. She turned to look at Angelica. 'I believe the blue gown we ordered yesterday has just arrived, Angelica. I have ordered that it should be made ready for you, my dear – if it will please you to wear it?'

'It will please me very much,' Angelica said. 'And I have some new slippers that will go well with it.'

'Ah, yes,' Caroline nodded. 'The embroidered ones with the leather heels that you bought yesterday. They will go well with your gown, my dear. Now, we shall play a little game if you please. You will both pretend that I am the King and make your curtsey in turn . . .'

Angelica caught the mischief in her cousin's eyes and giggled, shaking her head as her aunt raised her brows. 'I think I might imagine you better as a Queen,' she said.

'Nevertheless, you will make your curtsey to the King in a few hours, and it is a serious business,' Caroline said. 'So, my dears, let us begin . . .'

Later that day, as they went out into the streets, Angelica noticed a strong odour in the air. It was the smell of burning, but acrid and unpleasant – like fat burning on a grid.

'What is that, do you think?' she asked of Caroline, but her aunt shook her head, though a look of distaste passed across her face. Angelica saw that smoke was drifting across the city from the direction of the river, but dismissed it as she entered the carriage. Whatever it was, it did not concern her.

Claire and Angelica stood close together in the long gallery at the Palace of Whitehall, both of them a little nervous as they waited for the King to appear. He and his favoured courtiers had been to prayers, which they did several times a day, and His Majesty would pass through the gallery on his way back to his personal chambers. It was usual for those who had been summoned to wait in the gallery until the King had passed through. Sometimes he merely nodded to people at either side or lifted a hand in greeting, but at other times he would stop and speak to an individual. Not everyone invited to this gathering would also attend the banquet.

'His Majesty is coming,' Caroline whispered. 'Get ready to curtsey as he passes. If you are fortunate, he may nod his head in recognition . . .'

A small group of people was making its way down the gallery. Angelica had been told that it was best not to look directly at the King, but she could not resist turning her head to look as he approached where she and Claire were standing. She knew the King at once, for he fitted the description that had made both her and Claire giggle earlier. Indeed, no one could call him handsome, but there was a presence about him, and something more that she could not quite define. And walking beside him was the man she had met so briefly the previous evening outside the theatre!

He had seen her looking at them, and she saw a grin on his face as he returned her curious stare, and then leaned towards the King to whisper in his ear. Angelica flushed, dropping her head as she sank into a deep, reverent curtsey.

'Sir Rupert, we are glad to see you here,' a voice said, and it was a voice of such warmth and charm that Angelica knew at once why His Majesty was so popular with the ladies of his court. 'And your beautiful daughter – Mistress Saunders, you grace our court. Be sure that you visit us often while you stay in London.'

Angelica brought her head up at that, looking into the King's face and feeling the power of that dark gaze. He was smiling at her in a way that made her heart pump faster and her cheeks flush.

'Your Majesty . . . I thank you.' She sank into another graceful curtsey, but not before she had noticed the mocking gleam in Lord Chesterford's eyes. Her cheeks flushed as she bent her head once more, for she could not doubt that it was he who had brought her to the King's notice.

'Well,' Caroline said after the King's party had moved on. 'You were favoured indeed, Angelica. He did no more than nod to Claire and me – which was honour enough, I dare say.'

'It was because of Lord Chesterford,' Angelica whispered back. 'He is Father's friend – and it seems, close to His Majesty.'

'It was well that you had practised your curtsey,' Caroline said, and Angelica thought there was a note of reservation in her voice.

'Chesterford is of good family,' Rupert said and looked thoughtful. 'He does well at court, and no doubt is generously rewarded for his pains.'

Angelica's heart raced. She could not deny that she found the bold Lord Chesterford exciting – but he also frightened her. There was something a little dangerous about him, a wildness in his eyes that made her tremble inside. She knew that her father was thinking in terms of a husband for her, but she hoped that he would not make a hasty judgement. Lord Chesterford was both handsome and bold – but he was not Hal.

Angelica found herself regretting that he had not come to London with them. She knew that it was Claire he wished to marry, but she would have felt happier if he were here with them.

'We are bidden to the banquet,' Nicolas told them as the crowd began to thin in the gallery. The public audience had finished for the day, and most were preparing to leave the palace, only the favoured few remaining to partake of the feast. At certain times the public were allowed in to watch the King dine with his courtiers, but this was not one of them.

Angelica and Claire kept close together as they followed the people making their way to the great hall where the banquet was to be held. Inside the huge room with its high, vaulted roof that was hung with banners of purple, crimson and gold, tables had been set out at both sides of the room. At the head of the room was a raised dais where the King's chair and table were set. To either side of him were smaller chairs to accommodate those he wished near him during the banquet.

There was a buzz of excited voices and laughter, for the court was in merry mood. Looking round at all the rich clothes and jewels of both the ladies and gentlemen, Angelica noticed that many were dressed in the French fashion. She had thought that her father and Lord Mortimer looked fine, but some of the men were extreme in their dress, and she thought that they were wearing rouge on their cheeks.

Nicolas led the way to the places that had been allocated to them. They were seated to the right of the chamber and near to His Majesty's table, which high honour was probably due to the fact that Rupert had fought for the King's father, besides having known His Majesty while they were both in exile.

Angelica looked for and found the face she sought in the crowd, only to discover he was watching her, an expression of amusement in those bold eyes. He was sitting to the right of the King, but at the far end of the royal table, and as he saw her staring at him, he winked at her, causing her to blush bright pink. What a terrible rogue he was!

She hastily averted her gaze, looking at her cousin, who had been placed next to a gentleman dressed modestly by court standards in grey and silver. He had dark hair and steady grey eyes, and was some years older than Claire. However, his smile had a certain sweetness about it, and Angelica noticed that her cousin was responding to him readily. She herself was sitting between her father and a young gentleman who told her ingenuously that this was his first time at court. His father had brought him in the hope that he might be taken up by one of the influential courtiers.

'My father was once in the employ of Lord Rochester,' he said. 'And now my lord has found high favour in His Majesty's court, I would take service with him if he will have me.'

'And your name is, sir?'

'Forgive me, mistress,' he said, his cheeks pink. 'Perry – they call me by my surname, but my given name is Peter.'

'I am Mistress Angelica Saunders,' she said, smiling at

him. 'This is my first time at court too, Master Perry. I hope that you will have good fortune in your search for employment.'

'I know who you are,' Perry said. 'His Majesty singled you out. He stopped to speak to you, something he does rarely – unless the lady is very beautiful.' He blushed a deeper shade. 'Of course, you are beautiful . . .'

'You are kind, sir,' she replied and dared to glance at the high table once more. This time Lord Chesterford was talking with a lady to his left – a very striking lady gowned in crimson damask. Her hair was dressed high on her head with curls across the forehead, and fell in one elegant ringlet to her shoulders. Angelica thought her very proud, for she seemed to look coldly at her companion, as if she thought herself above him.

'That is Mistress Barbara Palmer,' Perry whispered in her ear. 'More properly I should call her Lady Castlemaine. She is His Majesty's mistress, and usually sits nearer to him, but it is whispered that they have quarrelled. Perhaps because the Queen is being honoured this evening. The lady has a fiery temper, it is said, and plagues His Majesty sorely. Sometimes he is forced to reprimand her. Methinks 'tis the reason she looks so sour.'

'How do you know so much?' Angelica asked. 'I thought it was your first time at court?'

'Yes, that is so,' he replied. 'But Lord Rochester and his friends sometimes drink at my uncle's tavern, and we hear his poetry, which is oft outrageous – and all the gossip from the court.'

'I see,' Angelica said and then her father addressed a remark to her concerning the food that was being served at table, and Perry turned to the lady at his other hand, leaving her with time to think.

She had heard of the King's mistress, but only in whispers from the servants, and she had not been sure whether to believe their gossip. It was said that Lady Castlemaine was not content with the honours the King had heaped upon her, and had sulked when he married the Princess of Braganza. She had married to disoblige her family, and, tiring of her husband, had become Charles's mistress. It was believed that all her children were the King's.

Angelica applied herself to the rich courses that were being brought to table, trying to do justice to the venison, pigeons in a delicate sauce and sweetbreads swimming in cream and wine. There was a remove of neats tongues, a mess of beef and onions and roasted suckling pig, and also a roasted carp and a dish of oysters. All of which was helped down with either the ever-popular sack, or a Rhenish wine, and followed by the sweet courses.

Angelica refused most of the courses, though when Perry helped her to some quince tart she accepted it, for it would have been rude to refuse. However, she took but a mouthful, and thought ruefully of so much wasted food – but when she mentioned it to her father he told her that much of it would be given away to beggars at the kitchen door the next morning.

Throughout the meal they had been entertained by minstrels who wandered about the hall accepting requests for popular ballads, especially from those who were prepared to press a coin into their hands. When the meal was over, the Queen left the hall and servants began to clear the tables away while the courtiers moved into the gallery. Musicians had gathered there, and His Majesty had graciously permitted dancing, though he himself had retired soon after his queen.

Angelica followed her father and the others in the direction of the music. As she did so, she felt a touch on her arm and turned to find that Lord Chesterford had come after her.

'I trust you are not leaving so soon, Mistress Saunders?'

'I believe we shall be leaving in half an hour or so,' she said, her cheeks pink as she saw the mocking look in his eyes.

'You must dance with me first,' he insisted. 'I shall not let you leave until you grant my request.'

Angelica glanced round, intending to ask Caroline if it

would be permitted, but her aunt had walked on ahead, and Lord Chesterford grabbed hold of her hand, pulling her irresistibly into the throng of dancers.

It was a country dance, lively and energetic. Angelica was twirled and whirled by her partner until she was almost breathless, and as the fiddler stopped his frantic playing at last, Lord Chesterford caught her about the waist, whispering in her ear, 'Come out to the courtyard with me, sweetheart. Let me show you how pleasant it is to be kissed . . .'

'You are impertinent, sir,' Angelica said, giving him a shocked stare. 'Please let me go now. I would return to my family.'

'Little prude,' Chesterford said but there was laughter in his eyes. 'Rochester bet me that you would refuse, and you have cost me five guineas, for I took his challenge.'

'Then you should not have done so, sir.' Angelica gave him a speaking look. 'It was not the act of a gentleman.'

'It was the act of a lover,' Chesterford said. 'I swear I burn for you, sweeting. Will you not take pity on me and let me taste the honey of your lips?'

'Certainly not,' Angelica said and tossed her head. 'For I know you hope to win your bet, and you shall not succeed. And now my father looks for me.' She dropped a curtsey. 'Excuse me, sir.'

Walking away from him, Angelica sensed that he was still watching her, and she could not help the smile that touched her lips as she glanced over her shoulder. He was a wicked flirt, but he was amusing, and she liked him despite his behaviour. He grinned as he saw her glance back, winking at her and kissing his fingers in an extravagant gesture. Angelica tossed her head and turned her back on him once more. He was impossible!

'We are leaving,' Rupert said as she came up to him. 'Some of the courtiers have been imbibing too freely of wine and it looks as if things may become rowdy. Your aunt and cousin have gone out to the carriage that Nicolas ordered for them.'

'Are you displeased because I danced with Lord Chesterford?'

'No, I do not censure you, daughter. Chesterford can be wild at times – he is much influenced by Rochester, but I like him well enough. Besides, you will have opportunity enough to see him. We have been invited to join a party on the river in two days if the weather is fine.'

'I shall look forward to that, Father,' Angelica said and smiled at him. She had enjoyed her first visit to court, and though she had been a little shocked by Lord Chesterford's suggestion, she was also amused by his boldness.

Hal had told her she would never catch a husband if she spoke to others as she did to him, but Lord Chesterford had not seemed put out by her plain speaking. Hal's criticism had annoyed her, and she thought it would serve him right if she made a brilliant marriage. He thought her a foolish child, but Lord Chesterford had seen her as a woman.

It was as she was undressing for bed that Claire came to her. Angelica thought that she wanted to talk about what they had done and seen that night, but her manner was grave as she perched on the edge of Angelica's bed.

'You know that awful odour we smelled as we left home earlier this afternoon,' she said. 'I wondered what it was but my mother said it was nothing – Philip told me that the Church court had condemned a woman to be hanged as a witch. She had been accused by the witchfinder – a man called Matthew Hadden – and she was found guilty.' Claire shuddered, looking sick. 'Afterwards they burned her body. Isn't that awful, Angelica? I have seen girls forced to stand in church as they are accused of being wanton, and I have pitied the scolds when they have been put in the stocks for a day to have rubbish thrown at them – but it must be terrible to hang, mustn't it?'

'Horrible,' Angelica said. 'Oh, Claire, how can people do such cruel things? I know they tried her as a witch – but hanging . . . and then to burn her body.'

'Yes, I know,' Claire said. 'I wish it had not happened, Angelica. It makes me afraid . . .'

'There is no need to be frightened,' Angelica said. 'Your

parents will not let anything happen to you – but I pity the poor woman who was treated so ill.'

'Yes . . .' Claire got to her feet. 'I hope I haven't made it impossible for you to sleep, Cousin. I think it will take me a while to forget what Philip told me.'

Angelica thought that she would never forget the awful stench of burning flesh, and prayed that she would never need to smell it again.

Four

Serena watched as Jared sawed the branches that he had taken from a fallen tree, cutting them into suitable pieces for their cooking fire. It was dangerous to build a fire with large logs, for it could set the woods around them ablaze, and they were always careful not to cause trouble. Lord Mortimer allowed them to stay here for a few weeks each spring and summer, and as long as none of their tribe became a nuisance, they were not harassed or moved on as happened in so many other places. Once, there had been plenty of wild spaces and common ground where they could graze their horses, but with the enclosure of so much land that had belonged to the people, there was little enough left. The villagers needed all that remained for their own pigs and horses, and they disliked the travelling people, regarding them with suspicion.

Serena had been to the village that morning with Rowena. Jared's mother had prepared some of her cures, and they had visited various houses and some of the outlying farms. She had been surprised when Rowena asked her to accompany her, for the older woman was often sullen, but this time she had been particular in her request. Serena had not minded being asked, for she would make a friend of Jared's mother if she could.

Her eyes turned towards him once more, dwelling on his strong back, gleaming with sweat. He was by far the most handsome of the men in her tribe, and from the time that she could walk, she had followed him about, gazing at him with adoring eyes. She thought that he liked her, but he gave no indication that he thought of her as a woman – his woman. She had tried to show him that she was willing, but he merely smiled at her and passed on. Sometimes she thought that he would never take her for his own, and at those times she felt like weeping.

'Serena . . .' She heard Rowena's voice and turned to ask what she wanted. 'I have here the mixture that we promised to the maid up at the Manor. I do not wish to go there – will you take it for me?'

They had met the maidservant on her day off and she had begged a lotion for her freckles, asking if it might be delivered to her at the big house. Serena had never been there and she felt a little nervous of going alone, but she did not like to disoblige Rowena, for she had a terrible temper when roused.

'Yes, if you wish it,' she said and took the basket from her. 'She said that we were to ask for Maria – is that not right?'

'That be right,' Rowena said. 'Mind you bring me three pennies for it, girl.'

'Yes, of course.' Serena fetched her shawl from her caravan, passing Jared as she walked through the clearing. He responded to her shy smile with a nod of his head, but did not speak. She felt a little piqued, for she had hoped that he would speak to her soon. However, he was frowning, clearly in no mood for dalliance.

Serena was at home in the woods. She loved them because they were so peaceful and so beautiful, the ancient trees having stood here for many years. Some of the oaks must be a hundred years or more old, and they had seen so much. She was singing a little ditty as she walked, her heart lifting as she saw a shy fawn bounding off to join its careful mother, and in the trees a thrush was trilling its song.

It took her some twenty minutes to make the walk to the Manor. She was not sure where to go, but a gardener directed her to the kitchen door and she asked for Maria as she had been bid. She delivered her potion and was duly paid the three pennies, which she tucked inside the pocket she wore tied under her skirt, for she would not dare to lose Rowena's money.

As she walked back the way she had just come, she saw a man striding towards her, and her heart caught with startled surprise. He looked so much like Jared that it was impossible not to know who he must be. She had heard Jared speak of the heir to the Manor who was his half-brother. She hesitated, wondering how she could avoid meeting him, but it was not possible so she bobbed a curtsey to him as he drew near.

Hal's gaze went over her. She was a pretty wench with her black hair and dark eyes, shapely and diminutive, and though he knew her for a gypsy, he found her comely.

'And what are you doing here, wench?' he demanded, towering over her, his blue eyes bright with mischief. 'Do you not know that this is private property?'

'Forgive me, sir,' Serena said, hanging her head. 'I have been to the kitchen to deliver some lotion to cure freckles to one of the maids, and I mean no harm.'

'Indeed.' Hal moved in closer, a smile flickering at the corners of his mouth. 'Now, can I believe you? Have you been up to some mischief? For if you have I must exact a penalty.'

Serena did not know whether to be frightened or not. His words seemed to threaten her, but he was smiling, and she thought he was merely teasing her. She put her head up, meeting his eyes boldly.

'Pray let me pass, sir. You know that I have done no harm.'

'Perhaps,' Hal said and grinned at her. 'Methinks I shall take my penalty either way.' Before she knew what he was about, he put an arm around her waist and drew her to him, kissing her full on the mouth. It was not a light kiss, but deep and penetrating, his tongue forcing its way inside her mouth to explore the warmth and taste of her. 'You taste like honey,' Hal said as he let her go at last, 'and you smell of flowers. I thought all gypsies were dirty, but you are not.'

'I like to be clean, sir,' Serena said and laughed up at him, for his kiss had been pleasant and not at all frightening. 'And I make my own soaps and creams – that is what you can smell, for they are perfumed with violets and other flowers from the hedges.'

'Indeed? Then you have picked my violets, and that means one kiss is not enough.' He laughed as he saw her look of fright and shook his head. 'Nay, Mistress Gypsy, I'll not harm you – though it would be sweet to lie with you, I'll warrant. But you may go on your way. I have never yet taken an unwilling woman, nor needed to, I promise you.'

Serena gave him a fleeting smile and then hurried on, her heart racing wildly. He looked so much like Jared, and he had flirted with her, kissed her in the way that she had longed for Jared to kiss her. She had not realized how exciting it would be to be kissed in such a way, and she nursed her pleasure to herself as she began to run.

The day was exceedingly warm, though on the river there had been a light breeze ruffling the sluggish brown waters. Angelica had enjoyed the boat ride, for it had been pleasant to be rowed downriver to this idyllic spot where great willows wept at the edge of the water and the grass was lush. The company had left the boat for the picnic that was to be served on shore, and everyone was walking about, talking, laughing and exchanging gossip.

Claire was with Sir Philip Rathbone, the gentleman she had met at the King's banquet. She seemed to like him very well, despite him being some few years her senior. Angelica did not think him striking. He looked a studious, serious man, of average height, dark-complexioned with straight dark brown hair that he wore short and a little beard in the Spanish style. He was plainly dressed for a courtier, but Claire had already told her that he held an important post in the King's bedchamber.

Seeing that her cousin was engrossed with her companion,

Angelica moved a little aside from the others. She stood at the water's edge watching a moorhen and its chicks for some minutes, until she sensed that someone had come to join her. Turning, she saw that it was Lord Chesterford.

'It is a warm day,' he said. He had loosened the ruffles at his throat, and had a slightly careless, even decadent air about him. His eyes held a challenge that made her lift her head proudly. 'Are you enjoying your visit to London, Mistress Saunders?'

'Yes, I have found it . . . interesting,' she said. His bold eyes raked her, and she felt that he was mentally undressing her. Since the evening he had danced with her she had heard something of his reputation from her aunt, and was determined to be careful of him.

'Interesting . . .' His eyes quizzed her, one brow arching. 'You intrigue me, mistress. Most young women wish for nothing more than to parade their finery at court, but I think you are different.'

'Am I?' Angelica raised her head, unconscious of the tantalizing effect her proud bearing had on the man. Her regal poise had been noted, admired by some and ridiculed by others. 'Perhaps I have better things to occupy me than to idle my days at court . . .'

'Ah, that is for me,' Chesterford said and smiled wryly. 'I believe you have not heard good things of me, Mistress Saunders.'

'I have heard that you and . . . others . . . enjoy pastimes that are frowned upon by some, sir.'

'You mean that we gamble, drink to excess, behave in an outrageous manner and seduce as many ladies as we can?' He mocked her with a slight bow of his head. 'I am one of Rochester's wild crowd – is that what you have heard?' Angelica was silent. She had heard that Lord Rochester was a wicked seducer and hedonist, though a clever poet, and it seemed that his friends were no better, but she turned her head away, her face flushed at his blunt speaking. 'Perhaps you are wise to listen to your friends.'

Seeing that she was disinclined to answer him, Chesterford walked off, leaving her to her contemplation of the river. A moment or two later, Claire came to join her.

'The food is about to be served,' she said. 'Is something troubling you, Cousin?'

'No . . . nothing at all,' Angelica said and smiled at her. 'It was so warm that I sought the coolness by the river, that is all. Where is your companion?'

'Sir Philip has duties to perform,' Claire said. 'He has left us to return to them.' Her cheeks were slightly pink as she said, 'I believe he only came to spend a little time with me . . .'

'Claire!' Angelica stared at her. 'You sound as if . . . as if you are much taken with him?'

Claire's colour deepened, a shy smile curving her lips. 'I know it is too soon – but I think I have fallen in love.'

'But you hardly know him,' Angelica protested. 'And . . . he is older than you, Claire.'

'But he is so gentle and so wonderfully kind,' Claire said, her eyes bright with something that her cousin had not seen in her before. 'There is such a rapport between us – an understanding that does not need to be spoken. Oh, I cannot explain, but I felt it at our first meeting, and it increases with every moment I spend in his company. Of course nothing has been said as yet, but I believe he feels the same way.'

'You would not think of marrying him?' Angelica was shocked. How could Claire think of marrying a man like that when she might have Hal?

'Why not?' Claire sounded a little hurt. 'If he asked me and my father approved – then yes, I should take him willingly.'

'But what of Hal?'

'I do not love Hal as a woman should love her husband,' Claire said. 'I care for him deeply as my brother, my cousin as he rightly is – but he is too . . . demanding. He would expect too much of me. Sir Philip would not. I think I should be very happy as Lady Rathbone.'

'Hal will be . . . upset,' Angelica said, her throat oddly tight. She knew that Hal would be furious. He had always intended that Claire should be his wife, and he would not accept her decision easily.

'I am sorry if he is hurt,' Claire said frowning a little. 'But my decision is made. I shall not marry him . . . even if Sir Philip does not ask me to be his wife.'

'Poor Hal,' Angelica said softly. She turned away to hide her feelings. Caroline was calling them to join the others for the meal, which had been set out for them on little stands. Stools and blankets on the ground had been provided for their comfort, and there were servants to wait on them and serve the delicious pies, pasties and pickles that were on offer.

Angelica took a seat on a rug near her aunt and father. Lord Mortimer had not joined them on the outing, for he had business elsewhere, but there was a merry company, and the talk was a little free as quantities of wine were drunk and tongues became loosened.

Angelica saw that Lord Chesterford had transferred his attention to a lady in a bold crimson gown. She had a full figure and her breasts were pushed high by her laced stomacher, showing off more than a more modest woman would think decent. She was flirting with her companion outrageously, deliberately flaunting her charms beneath his nose as he grew ever bolder. When she saw him dip a sly finger into the lady's décolletage, she turned away in disgust.

'Perhaps we should think of leaving?' Caroline suggested to her brother as the behaviour of some of the other guests became more and more unrestrained, the talk bawdy and even coarse.

'Oh, it would be a pity to leave too soon,' Rupert replied, for he had seen worse behaviour at court and thought nothing of it. 'I dare say some of the company may be a little free in their manner, but you cannot hide the truth from the girls. They will see more of it if they are to visit court again – and we are bidden to a ball next week. No, let them observe and be warned. I believe they are both sensible enough to know that they will be all the more admired if they refrain from such behaviour. A whore may command her price, but not respect.'

'Very well, I dare say you are right. The girls are old enough to know the way of the world, I suppose.'

'They are both too well brought up to behave in a like manner,' Rupert said. 'I am surprised at Chesterford. He was not as careless when I knew him, though he is much under Rochester's influence – yet I think it is not like him.'

Angelica listened to her father and wondered. She knew that Lord Chesterford was aware of her watching him overtly, and that his behaviour had become wilder as the day progressed – perhaps for her benefit. Was he trying to punish her for what she had said to him earlier?

She was not certain how she felt about him. He was certainly handsome, bold and exciting – and he could be charming. But she felt he might be dangerous to a girl who had little experience of men. She must take care when in his company, and never be alone with him if she wished to preserve her reputation.

And what of Hal? She had thought there was no chance for her – but if Claire had made up her mind not to marry him, it was possible that he might turn to her once his first anger and wounded feelings were over. Yet perhaps she was following a false dream that could only bring disappointment in its wake. If she wasted her chances while in London, they might never come her way again.

Elizabeth looked at herself in the mirror as she prepared to visit the Mortimers that morning. She had changed her gown three times, settling at last on a rich tawny velvet with an embroidered stomacher and a plain underskirt. She had done her hair in her usual style, but wondered if perhaps it looked a little too severe. However, there was no time to change again, for Mary was calling to her that the hire carriage they had ordered had arrived.

Elizabeth supposed that they might have afforded to set up their own carriage if they wished, for it was possible to buy a very fine one for less than sixty pounds. However, she felt that it was a shocking amount of money to take from her jointure, and the expense would not stop there, of course.

'Ah there you are, dearest,' Mary said as she went downstairs. 'You look lovely – but I thought you had settled on the green silk?'

'I thought it looked a little . . .' Elizabeth blushed as she saw the laughter in her friend's eyes. 'Well, ageing,' she admitted ruefully. 'I know that I am no longer young, but—'

'You are not old either,' Mary said, 'and you wished to look your best, as you should. Sir Rupert is a man of distinction, and he is worth changing your gown for at least twice.'

'Mary!' Elizabeth said. 'It was not for his sake. Caroline will be dressed very fine, and . . . well, not just for his sake.' She smiled at the mockery in her friend's eyes. 'I must admit that it was a shock to me to see Sir Rupert the other evening . . . but it was all so many years ago.'

'And of course he had forgotten you,' Mary teased her gently. 'That is why he came dashing to your rescue like the white knight of the fables?'

'Yes, he did, didn't he,' Elizabeth said and smiled. 'It was very gallant of him, was it not?'

'Extremely,' Mary said. 'And now, my love, we should be leaving, otherwise the horses will weary of standing.'

. Elizabeth followed her down the stairs and out into the street. It was noisy with the sounds of wagons rumbling by, the cries of an orange seller calling her wares as she walked, a basket on her arm, another balanced on her head. The oyster seller was trundling his barrow over the cobbles, and across the narrow street a woman tossed the contents of her chamber pot into the gutters without so much as a warning.

Elizabeth was relieved that she had not been standing

nearby, for if it had splashed on her clothes she might have had to go back inside and change once more.

Rupert allowed his sister to receive her guests alone, and did not enter the drawing room until they had been served refreshments. His eyes went at once to Elizabeth, his heart jerking as he saw how lovely she looked. It was not the kind of beauty that had been Sarah's, but a quiet dignity and serenity of character that was very attractive to the man he had become.

'Good morning, ladies,' he said and smiled at them. 'May I be permitted to join you?'

'Yes, of course,' Caroline said, a gleam in her eyes as she observed the expression on Elizabeth's face. It would do very well. Very well indeed! And she would do all in her power to further her brother's cause. 'I was just saying to Elizabeth that she must not be a stranger in future. It is far too long since she has visited us. I hope that she will come and stay very soon – Mistress Mary too, if she wishes?'

'Oh, I should love to visit you,' Mary said with a sly glance at her friend. 'London is very well, but in the summer it becomes too smelly – and there is a risk of plague. Yes, I think it an excellent idea. Perhaps soon after you return home? I do not know when that may be . . .'

'Mary!' Elizabeth reproved, for she knew well what her friend was fishing for. 'Would you care to dine with us one evening, Caroline – and you, Sir Rupert? I fear I did not thank you adequately the other evening for what you did to help me.'

'It was little enough,' Rupert said. 'Yes, I accept your invitation willingly, Elizabeth – but we are holding a reception here in two days. You and Mistress Mary would be more than welcome to join us.'

'Yes, of course.' Caroline added her endorsement. 'We are always pleased to see you, Elizabeth. It is to be an open-air reception if the weather is fine. We have large gardens here, and the river is close. We shall set up tables outside and roast suckling pig and capons on a spit.'

'How splendid,' Mary said. 'We would like that very much, would we not, Beth?'

'Yes, indeed,' Elizabeth said, a trifle flustered. She could not but be aware that her friends were trying to manage her life, and she wished they would not. She was not certain that Rupert was still in love with her, and even if he were, she was not sure that she wished to marry again. She had been hurt badly when she believed that he had taken her love and abandoned her, and though she had been content enough during the last years of her marriage, she had learned a hard lesson. 'It sounds most pleasant.'

She glanced at Rupert. He was frowning, as if his thoughts did not quite please him. It would be foolish of her to assume that his gallant rescue of her meant anything special. She was not a foolish young girl to break her heart over a man now, and she would not do so – but neither would she cut herself off from his company. She would merely wait and see what the future brought.

Angelica frowned when she saw Lord Chesterford mingling with the other guests that evening. It surprised her that her aunt had invited him, for she sensed that Caroline did not truly approve of him, and she suspected that it must have been in answer to her father's request.

She knew that the two were friends. Her father had met Will Chesterford when he was in France. Will must have been too young to fight in the Civil War, but she had discovered that his father had been killed at one of the last battles of the second war. For his safety, he had been taken to France by his mother, who had married again some years later to a French noble.

Angelica thought he might have been with Charles at Worcester. She had been told that he had joined the King in exile after Charles's daring adventures in the western counties where he had been hunted by his enemies, finally escaping overseas with the help of many loyal subjects who risked their lives for his. It must have been during those years of wandering on the continent, when he would have been as penniless as his King, that Will fell much under the influence of the King's friend Rochester. When the King returned to his throne Chesterford had returned to claim his father's estate, which had been sequestered during the years of the Lord Protector's reign. Like many of the others who had returned to find their fortunes much depleted, he received a pension from the King, who was himself extravagant and always in need of money. Will Chesterford, Angelica suspected, was just one of the gentlemen of the court who sought a rich marriage to help restore their fortunes.

She ignored him as best she could, though she was aware that his eyes were often on her as she wandered about the gardens, mingling with the guests gathered there that evening. From the river, where various small boats were moored, came the sound of pleasant music, and mingling with the crowd were jugglers, fire-eaters and tumblers performing for the entertainment of the guests. It was a warm night, though still early summer, and the smell of roasting pig hung tantalizingly in the air, making her feel hungry. She had sipped her wine sparingly, for she had not eaten much that day and did not wish it to go to her head. Her stomach felt empty, and she wished that the food would be served soon, for she was more than ready for it.

'You look thoughtful, Mistress Saunders,' Chesterford said coming up behind her. She had not been aware of him at that moment and jumped. 'Have you something on your mind – a lover perhaps?'

'You do me wrong, sir,' she reprimanded him with a haughty stare. 'It is merely that I am hungry.' As if to emphasize her statement, her stomach rumbled loudly, and to her embarrassment he laughed in delight.

'It seems you speak truly, mistress,' he said, much amused. 'It is a pleasure to meet a lady who thinks more of her stomach than the bedroom.'

'Indeed I do not!' Angelica said sharply and then realized

that she had fallen into a trap. 'I mean . . . it is only that I have not eaten much today.' Her eyes snapped with temper. 'And you need not look like that, for I do not think of the bedroom at all – and particularly not where you are concerned.' Which was not quite true, as she had wondered what kind of a husband he would make.

Chesterford laughed. 'Methinks the lady doth protest too much,' he murmured, a gleam in his eyes as he sensed her rebellious spirit. 'However, I shall not tease you, for I am certain that the food is ready, and like you, I am hungry. I pray you sit there on that bench, Mistress Angelica, and I shall fetch a platter to you.'

It was on the tip of her tongue to refuse, but then she reconsidered. Perhaps if Hal thought she had a wealthy, sophisticated suitor he would begin to understand that she was not a little girl. Mayhap he would realize that Claire did not wish to marry him and turn to her instead. Angelica did not wish to marry Lord Chesterford, and yet something in his manner amused her despite herself, and since he was known as a wicked seducer, it would not hurt him if she used him to help her gain her heart's desire.

Her mind made up, she sat on the bench he had bidden her to and waited for him to bring her the platter he had promised. He had brought her some of the most tender parts of the suckling pig and a piece of crisp crackling, which she held in her fingers and ate with enjoyment, the fat oiling her lips. She laughed and lifted her hand to wipe away the grease, but as she did so he caught her wrist and leaned forward, licking it away with the tip of his tongue.

Angelica felt a tingle shoot through her, for in that moment she was aware of him as a man and he cast a powerful spell over her. Looking into his eyes, she felt the pull of his masculinity and gasped, for she knew he desired her. She swallowed hard; he had aroused a need in her, and she felt herself drowning in his eyes, spinning down and down into a fiery cauldron.

'Oh, there you are, Angelica,' Caroline's voice broke the

spell. 'I was looking for you, my dear. Come and join me in handing round the sweetmeats to our guests.'

Angelica tore her gaze from Chesterford's, feeling shocked as she realized where her thoughts had been taking her. For a moment there she had been in some danger, and she was glad of her aunt's rescue, though she knew that it was merely an excuse. There were servants in plenty, and though she obediently picked up one of the platters and began to offer the sweetmeats, mince tarts and other delicacies to their guests, she understood that her aunt had removed her from Lord Chesterford's company for her own sake.

There was no doubt that he was a danger to her and her reputation. It was undoubtedly his intention to seduce her, for it was a game that he, Rochester and others played to amuse themselves. Angelica would be a fool to fall into his trap, for once he had lain with her she would be ruined.

She knew that he continued to watch her throughout the evening, like a hunter shadowing his prey, she thought. She supposed that she ought to be frightened of him, but it amused her to play him at his own game. She would not walk into his trap, for she was aware of it, but she would use him to make Hal jealous if she could.

She wished that he had come to London with them. It would have been exciting to see Hal's reaction to Lord Chesterford's pursuit of her – and yet perhaps he would not have noticed. Claire was the woman he intended to marry, and Angelica was foolish to think that he might turn to her.

She would do much better to try and find herself a husband – a man like Claire's choice, who would honour, love and protect her.

Perhaps it was some fault in her that led her to the wrong kind of men, Angelica thought. It must be that she was like her mother and a wicked wanton who did not deserve happiness.

Throughout the evening, she was aware that Claire was being courted by Philip Rathbone, and that her father was often to be seen with Elizabeth. She thought that she would be pleased if her father chose Elizabeth as his new wife. Although it was some years since she had seen her mother's cousin, she had received many letters and gifts from her and there was a bond between them.

She could see that Claire was very happy with her beau, and wished that she might be as happy, but when a gentleman in his middle years began to pay attention to her she felt trapped. He was kind and said to be generous, but she found him tedious and wished she dare disregard her aunt's advice and seek the company of Lord Chesterford.

He was not Hal, of course, but if she could not have the man she loved, he was the next best thing. Sighing, she thought of Hal and wondered what he was doing that night.

Hal watched the gypsy girl. She was dancing by the fire-light to the tune a fiddler played, and the swaying of her hips was mesmerizing him. This was the second time he had come secretly to the camp to watch her, for Serena had been in his thoughts these past few days.

Her dancing was enticing and he knew an urgent desire to lie with her, but she had run away from him when he'd seen her at his home, and again when they had met near the village. She was afraid that he might seduce her – perhaps rape her – but she wronged him. Hal would have gladly lain with her and given her some gold coins as recompense for her trouble, but he would not force her. If she came to him she must do so willingly, of her own free choice.

As her dance came to an end, he turned away, feeling foolish for having come here. She was but a passing fancy, for he knew where his future lay. As he walked away, he heard a cracking sound behind him and turned to discover that he was being watched. He saw the gypsy staring at him, his blue eyes dark with hatred, and feeling a stirring of anger, he stopped and then went back to confront him.

'Why are you staring at me like that?' he demanded.

'Why were you watching Serena? Keep away from her – she is not for you.'

'Is she your woman?'

'No. I have not chosen her,' Jared said. 'But she is of my people and I would not have her hurt.'

'What makes you think I would hurt her?' Hal was angry, on his mettle. His hands balled at his sides, for he would have taken pleasure in striking the insolence from the gypsy's face. 'I have the right to go where I please in these woods.'

'No more than I,' Jared said, eyes glittering with anger. 'I too am Harry Mortimer's son – and my mother married him. You are a bastard, taken as the heir – but I am the rightful heir.'

'Nonsense!' Hal said. 'Your mother was never married to my father – even if he was also your father, it makes no difference. He would never have married a gypsy, and he loved my mother. He would have married her if he had not been killed.'

'Liar!' Jared's eyes narrowed in anger. 'You have it all, don't you? But one day there will be a reckoning between us and then I shall take what is mine.'

'Let it be now,' Hal said, glaring at him. 'But even if you trick me and win again, that does not make you my equal. I am a gentleman. You are a gypsy and can never be more than that.'

'The time is not yet,' Jared said, refusing his challenge. He had recently returned from Oxford, where he had learned that there was no record of his mother's marriage at any of the churches, though in such desperate days during the war it did not mean that the wedding had not taken place. He meant to question his mother once more, and if she still stuck to her story he would speak to his uncle. He would demand that Lord Mortimer acknowledge him as his rightful heir. He was the eldest of Harry Mortimer's illegitimate sons, and he should inherit something even if his mother was lying about the marriage.

'The time will come,' Jared said. 'And when it does you will be sorry . . .' He stood watching as his half-brother strode away from him, and suddenly he was shivering from head to foot, for he had an awful feeling that it would be he who would most regret whatever passed between them.

Striding away from him, Hal was troubled by no such premonitions. He was angered by the gypsy's insolence, but he did not fear him or his threats. He knew that his place was secure; the law was on his side and the gypsy would never be able to prove his lies. Yet it might be better if he stayed away from their camp. There was no point in pursuing the gypsy girl, for his future was with Claire. The girl was sensual as she danced, and he had felt desire for her, but it was merely lust, the kind of lust that could be easily satisfied with the tavern whores.

Five

Angelica knew that she had drunk more wine than she ought, but the night was warm and she had danced most of the evening, several times with Lord Chesterford and once with his friend Lord Rochester. That was an experience she would not care to repeat, and she believed that the gentleman well deserved his reputation as a Godless man. It was said that the King was often displeased with his friend, both for his wild behaviour and the dangerous verse he wrote that caused anger and ridicule to spread through the court. Indeed, he had almost been banished for his ditties concerning His Majesty's mistress Lady Castlemaine, and it was only his ability to amuse that had saved him.

At the beginning of the evening the dancers had been masked, but as it grew late, the wine and the heat led to the abandonment of most masks. Even while he had been wearing a mask, Angelica had known Lord Chesterford and now that he came to her openly she saw that he too had been drinking freely.

'The hour grows late, mistress,' he said, his speech a little slurred. 'Dance with me one last time, for your father speaks of taking you home.'

Knowing that she was unwise but made careless by the wine she had taken, Angelica gave him her hand, allowing him to draw her into the thick of what was a kind of country dance that became rowdy as it progressed. Wine had heated the courtiers' blood, and she could not but be aware of the lewd behaviour going on around her. She saw men and women openly embracing, kissing and touching in a way that was surely sinful. It did not surprise her when Lord Chesterford suddenly dragged her into a small room off of the gallery, pulling her into his arms in a heated embrace. His tongue invaded her mouth as he kissed her in a way that shocked her, thrilling and yet repulsing her. When he thrust his hand into the bodice of her gown, caressing her breast, she realized how foolish she was to allow this and broke away from him, staring at him angrily.

'You go too far, sir! How dare you behave so? I have not given you leave to abuse my virtue thus.'

'You give me leave with every look from those devastating eyes,' Chesterford said and it was clear that his senses were disordered, for he looked wild and flushed. 'You are an enchantress, Mistress Angelica – you drive a man to madness, for beneath the ice there is a fire that scorches me.'

'It is the wine that talks so foolishly,' Angelica replied coldly. 'You will excuse me, sir. You take too many liberties and I wish to leave and return to my father.'

'Go then, witch,' Chesterford said, a sneer on his lips. 'One day you will push a man too far, mistress, and then you will pay for your teasing.'

Angelica's cheeks were burning as she went in search of her father. Her heart was beating very fast and she felt ashamed. Perhaps she had brought that abuse on herself, and she wished that she had not, for she did not like to be treated in such a way.

As she entered the hall, she saw that her father appeared to be anxious, and she went to him immediately, expecting him to be angry because she had allowed Chesterford too much freedom.

'Were you looking for me, Father?'

'Yes, daughter,' he said and sounded relieved. 'We must leave at once, for in the morning we go home.'

'We go home tomorrow?' Angelica was surprised, because she had expected to stay at least another week or more. 'Have I done something to displease you, Father?'

'No, of course not, Angelica,' he said and frowned. He had not intended to leave so soon, for he had hopes that Chesterford might speak for her, given enough time. 'I have been brought a letter that arrived in town this evening. Your grandmother has taken a turn for the worse, and we must hurry back. She has expressed a wish to see you, and I know that you would not wish to show her neglect.'

'No, of course not,' Angelica said. A part of her was disappointed that they must leave London, for she did not know if she would ever visit again, but in another way she was glad to be leaving. Lord Chesterford's behaviour had shocked her, making her aware of the danger she was in. 'Do you think that Grandmother is dying?'

'I fear it may be so,' Rupert said. 'The letter came from my father, and it appears that he expects the worst.'

'Then we must pray that we arrive in time,' Angelica said. She saw that Lord Chesterford had re-entered the gallery and was staring at her, but she turned her back on him. It was doubtful that she would ever meet him again, and perhaps that was for the best. 'I am perfectly ready to go home, Father.'

'I had hoped that Chesterford might speak before we left,' Rupert said with a frown. 'However, if he is serious, he may make the journey to ask for your hand.'

Angelica was silent. She did not think that Lord Chesterford had any intention of asking her to be his wife, and she did not truly wish for it.

She went to join her cousin and aunt, feeling tears prick behind her eyes as she saw their white faces. It was evident that they were distressed by the news that had arrived that evening, as indeed she was. Her grandmother had not always been kind to her, but Angelica had known no other mother, and she was sad that the woman who had raised her was so close to death.

'Oh, Angelica,' Claire said with a little sob. 'I do not want Grandmama to die.'

'Perhaps she won't,' Angelica offered, though in her heart

she knew Lady Saunders must be very ill or they would not have been sent for. 'Have you had a chance to tell Sir Philip that you are leaving?'

'Yes. He was with me when your father told us the news,' Claire said. 'He was sorry that we must go, but he is to take leave from the court next month and visit us at home. If we both feel the same then he will speak to my father.'

'Yes, I see,' Angelica said. She felt a little down as she realized that she would soon be losing her cousin. Claire would return to court with her husband, and she would rarely see her in the future. 'Then at least you have something to look forward to . . .'

'Have you said goodbye to Lord Chesterford?'

'No. I do not intend to,' Angelica said, lifting her head proudly. 'We do not have an understanding – and I do not wish for it.'

'I have thought him very taken with you,' Claire told her, looking thoughtful. 'I know that he can be a little wild, but he is too much under the influence of Lord Rochester. Perhaps if he were to break free of the life at court and retire to his estates he would be a different man.'

Angelica pursed her mouth. 'You think well of everyone, Claire. He does not deserve your concern, believe me.'

'I thought you liked him?'

'He is amusing company,' Angelica said. 'But I do not think he would make a good husband. You would not wish to wed a man like that – would you?'

'He would not do for me,' Claire agreed. 'He is too much like Hal – too arrogant and sure of himself – but I think he might make you a good husband, Angelica. And I believe the life at court would suit you.'

'Perhaps . . .' Angelica pulled a face. 'However, Lord Chesterford has no thoughts of marriage. I dare say he might have seduced me if he could, but he does not wish to wed me.'

Angelica might perhaps have thought differently, if she could have read the thoughts of the man she left staring after her, an angry, resentful glare in his eyes. She had been within his grasp, on the verge of surrender, and then somehow he had frightened her.

'Has the little innocent eluded you again?' Rochester's mocking voice was at his ear as he saw her leaving with her family. 'You owe me twenty sovereigns, Will. I told you that you wasted your time with that one.'

'Damn you, you were right,' Chesterford said ruefully. He realized that he would prefer to pay than ruin the wench's reputation. 'You shall have your money, Rochester. I would have paid thrice as much if I had succeeded in bedding her.'

'The only way to get that minx between the sheets is to wed her,' Rochester said and laughed. 'Will you give that much for the pleasure of lifting her skirts, Will? Has the little bitch got under your skin?'

Chesterford turned to look at him, and what he saw sickened him. Rochester's linen was stained with wine, his face already showing signs of the debauchery he indulged in too often. If Will continued on his path, he too would end a drunken sot, ruined and reviled.

'Perhaps,' he said more to himself than to Rochester. 'Yes, perhaps I would give that and more . . .'

Angelica was glad that her grandmother had lingered long enough for them to return from London. Lady Saunders had asked for her, so she was allowed to spend a little time alone with her.

'Come, child, kiss me. I do not have many hours left to me, and I would have your forgiveness before I die.'

Angelica took the hand she offered, perching close to her on the side of the high tester bed with its heavy covers. She thought that her grandmother looked over-hot and her instinct was to pull the covers from the bed, but the physician had ordered that she be kept warm, and there was a small fire burning in the grate even though the sun was hot outside. It seemed to her then that many of the doctor's remedies did more harm than good; he had bled her shortly before their return and she seemed very weak, but Lady Saunders believed in him implicitly, and it was not for Angelica to argue. Her views would be dismissed as foolish.

'There is nothing to forgive, dearest Grandmother,' she said now, her throat tight with the tears she must not shed. 'You did all you could for me, and if I am not good and modest, it is a fault in me, not you.'

'No, child,' Lady Saunders said. 'I would not have you think that. You have always been obedient and modest, as you ought – and I was foolish to think that you might be otherwise if I did not keep a strict rein on you. So tell me that I have not taught you to hate me.'

'No, indeed you have not. I do love you and thank you for your care of me.'

'Then kiss me one last time and send Caroline to me.'

Angelica did as she bid her, kissing her frail cheek before leaving her to go outside, where she found Caroline waiting. Her face was grey with anxiety, and Angelica knew how much it must have cost her aunt to allow her a few moments alone with Lady Saunders.

'She wishes you to go into her now,' she told Caroline. 'She seems at peace, aunt, and in no pain.'

Caroline nodded but did not answer, possibly because she was too close to tears for words. Angelica went down the stairs, avoiding the parlour where her grandfather, cousin and father sat waiting. She was confused, mixed up inside, and she needed to escape into the fresh air. In town it had not been possible for her to go walking alone, but that was exactly what she needed now.

Leaving the house through a side door, she walked through the knot garden to the orchard, and there she leaned her back against a tree as the tears flowed. She had always believed that Lady Saunders loved her cousin best, but now it seemed that she had been wrong, for there was no doubting the sincerity and the regret in her grandmother's eyes.

'You should not weep for her,' Hal's voice said close to

her, making her open her eyes with a start. 'She is old and sick, and it is better that she does not linger too long.'

'That is harsh,' Angelica said, her eyes glinting with the heavy tears. 'Do you not care that your grandmother is dying?'

'She isn't my grandmother,' Hal reminded her. 'You forget that I am no blood relation to you or the Saunders. At least, the connection was slight, through my mother, a distant cousin no more.'

Angelica had forgotten, for she was used to thinking him her cousin, but of course he was not really – except for the kinship through his father, and that only of marriage.

'She has always been as a grandmother to you.' Angelica looked at him accusingly. 'She favoured you above me – you and Claire.'

'I shall not deny that,' Hal admitted, for he had thought of Lady Saunders as *his* until now, when he had realized that he was not truly a part of her family. 'But I still see no sense in weeping for what must be.'

'One day you will truly love someone, and then perhaps you may understand that it hurts to lose them,' Angelica said, and made to turn away. Hal caught her wrist, swinging her back to face him. For a moment they stared at each other angrily, and then she was in his arms and he was kissing her, kissing her as he had in her dreams, hungrily, needing her response as she needed his. She gazed up at him, and in that moment her face was soft with love, though she was not aware of it. 'Hal . . .'

'Forgive me . . .' He drew back instantly, shocked by what he had done and by the swirling tide of desire she had aroused in him as he held her close. 'I should not have done that. It was because you were so unhappy. I wanted to comfort you, that is all.'

'Yes, of course,' Angelica said quietly. For some reason she did not feel like challenging him, and she was too shocked by her response to his kiss to be angry with him. Indeed, she had wanted it to continue, perhaps to deepen into something more. And that made her immodest! 'You are forgiven. I know that you meant nothing by it.'

'No . . .' Hal replied and yet in his heart he knew that he had meant everything by it, but it was not right. He should not have these sinful feelings for her. She was but a distant cousin, but she was a lady of good birth and reputation, and he must do nothing that would harm her. He recognized that she had become a woman in the weeks she had spent in London, and he wondered what had brought about that change. He was aware of a feeling of anger deep down, though he did not know its cause. 'Did you enjoy your visit to town?'

'Yes, it was exciting,' Angelica admitted. She was still in that state of shock, still unable to summon the righteous indignation she ought to feel. 'We visited the court on several occasions. I wish you had been there to see it, Hal – the courtiers with their painted faces and their jewels, and I promise you that I do not mean just the ladies.' A little giggle escaped her as she saw the disgust in his face. 'They were . . . well, in some cases it would not be too strong to say licentious. The behaviour of some of the women as well as the men . . . it was shameful. Many of the ladies have lovers, and their husbands are just as bad. It was not at all what I expected.'

'Little prude,' Hal said for he had recovered some of his natural superiority. 'You must have known – everyone talks of the King's mistresses, and where he leads others follow.'

'Yes, I suppose so,' Angelica agreed. 'Lady Castlemaine is very beautiful, but I thought her proud – and they say she has a fearful temper.'

'The King is very taken with her,' Hal replied, for he did not care to seem ignorant in the light of Angelica's new experiences that he now wished he had shared. 'He knew her before ever he came back to England, and they say he lay with her on the night of his return.'

'But they also say that Lucy Walter was his first love, and

that she bore him a child. Do you not think it would have been romantic if he had wed her?'

'The King had to marry a princess and he chose Portugal,' Hal said. 'Kings must marry into royal houses – though he may take as many mistresses as he pleases, and I dare say breed a whole batch of bastards by them.'

'Hal!' Angelica was shocked out of her state of unusual peace. 'You should not talk like that. I for one would not care to be married to a man who took mistresses, that is why . . .' she stopped and blushed as his eyes narrowed.

'Did a man ask you to marry him?' Hal demanded, suddenly angry again. 'What did you say to him?'

'He did not ask me to marry him,' Angelica said, a little devil prompting her. 'But he tried to seduce me several times. He would have got me into his bed if he could – but I am not so easily won.'

'I trust you did nothing to be ashamed of?' Hal's frowning look made her heart sing. Was he jealous? He looked jealous, and that made her want to shout out loud for sheer delight, though of course she did not.

Angelica laughed huskily. 'You sound just like Grandfather,' she said. 'Oh, Hal, do you really think me so foolish as to give my virginity so lightly?'

He glared at her, surprised at the feeling of relief flooding through him. He thought then that he would have killed the man who had dared to seduce her.

'I should hope you have more sense,' he said grudgingly, remembering that it was not she whom he planned to marry. 'What was Claire doing while you were being pursued?'

'I . . . do not know,' Angelica lied for she did not wish to arouse his temper. 'You must ask her that, Hal – and now I should return to the house, for they will look for me if . . .' She swallowed hard as she remembered what had driven her from the house. As she turned away, Hal caught her wrist once more, but this time he did not sweep her into his arms.

'What are you hiding from me?' he demanded.

'Why should I be hiding anything?' Angelica tried to pull

away, but his fingers tightened, bruising her soft flesh. 'Let me go, Hal. You are hurting me and I cannot tell you anything. You must speak to Claire.'

'Are you saying that she allowed someone to court her?' He glared at her, suddenly throwing her hand away from him as he felt the cold anger inside and knew that he must be careful, for if he lost his temper he could not vouch for the consequences. At this moment he was torn between strangling her and carrying her off to a secluded place where he could make love to her. 'I do not believe you. She would not do that to me.'

'I do not know, forgive me,' Angelica said and fled, leaving him to stare after her. He was going to be so very angry when he knew that Claire had plans to marry another man . . .

Claire watched Angelica flee up the stairs and wondered whether she ought to follow, but she did not believe that she could say anything to comfort her cousin, for she was hurting too much herself.

'Claire!' She was startled by Hal's voice. He must have come in soon after Angelica, and by his tone he was angry. 'You will grant me the favour of a few minutes, if you please?'

Although his words formed a request, she felt it was an order, and knew an urgent desire to deny him. Hal had too often commanded her, and as a child she had been content to let him have his way, but she was no longer bound by the need to please him. It did not matter if he was angry or sulked: her world no longer revolved around him.

'I do not think that I feel like talking to you at the moment, Hal. I am waiting to see if Grandmama sends for me.'

'We shall be nearby if you are needed,' Hal said and grabbed hold of her arm, steering her into a small chamber at the end of the entrance hall. 'I must hear the truth from you – what have you been doing in London?'

'What have you been told?' Claire asked warily. Angelica had promised she would say nothing, but had she kept her word?

'Angelica told me that a licentious rogue at court pursued her, but she would not tell me if you too had an admirer who took liberties.' His eyes were snapping with anger, his manner imperious. 'I trust you did not encourage him, whoever he was?'

'Please let go of my arm,' Claire said and raised her head. She was no longer prepared to be bullied by him, for she knew her own heart. 'I was not pursued by a rogue – but if you mean did someone pay court to me . . . the answer is yes.'

'I trust you sent him about his business!'

'And what was his business?' Claire gave him a proud look. 'It is not for you to decide who may or may not court me, Hal. Nor is it for you to dictate whom I shall allow such favours.'

Hal's fingers closed on her arm, making her wince. 'It is very much my business, for you are promised to me. We are to wed as soon as . . .'

'No!' Claire wrenched away from him, rubbing at her arm. It felt sore where he had held her and would probably bruise. He did not know his own strength! 'You are a careless brute, Hal Mortimer. We are not promised. Nothing has been spoken, though I know you have assumed that we shall marry. Had you bothered to ask instead of taking me for granted, I should have told you that I do not wish to wed you.'

Hal's gaze narrowed. 'It is this popinjay of the court who has turned your head. You know that it was always agreed that we should wed. I am the heir to Thornberry, and you were to continue here as my wife.'

'It was an idea you had fixed in your mind, but it was not in mine – at least, I was not sure. I know now that I should not be happy as your wife, and when Sir Philip comes to ask my father I shall accept him.'

'So he has not yet asked?' Hal's gaze burned into her. 'Are you doing this to punish me because I did not come to London with you?'

'No, Hal, of course not,' Claire said looking at him unhappily. Her anger had faded and she knew that what she had to say must hurt him, but it must be said for all their sakes.

'I do not love you as a woman should love her husband, Hal. I love you dearly as my brother – but you are too . . . intense, too sure of yourself for me. If we were wed I should be but a shadow in your wake, and that is not how I wish to live my life.'

'You know that is not true,' Hal declared passionately. 'I love you, Claire. You are mine by right. I shall not let this other fellow have you.'

'You cannot stop it,' Claire told him. She was trembling inside, for she found it difficult to cope with his tempers, but she knew she must be strong. 'My father would not force me to wed you, and my mother approves of my choice. You may be my father's heir, Hal, but I am not a part of the estate. You have no God-given right to marry me, and it is your own fault for taking it for granted.'

'Damn you, Claire!' Hal stared at her. He was angry and hurt by her plain speaking, his rage making him want to strike her. His fists curled at his sides, and he had to battle with his emotions, finally turning and striding away from her before he gave in to rage. She had betrayed him. She was not the loving, meek girl he had believed her, and the pain curling inside him was too much to bear.

Claire watched him go. She felt as if she were bleeding inside, for it had cost her dearly to defy him. She loved Hal, but not in the way he wanted her to love him, and she knew that if she did not break free of him he would in time crush her spirit. He needed a woman who would stand up to him, not smile and tease to gain her way, as she had so often in the past, but she did not like to see him hurt. She was on the verge of going after him to see if he would forgive her when she heard her mother call to her.

'Claire, my dearest. Your grandmother wishes to say goodbye to you.'

Claire turned obediently, pushing the painful scene with Hal to the back of her mind. He would get over it. She must go to her beloved grandmother, for she was dying.

*   *   *

Angelica sat with Claire and her aunt in the church. Sir John, Sir Rupert, Hal and Lord Mortimer stood by the coffin as the service came to a sorrowful end, accompanied by sniffles and tears from many in the congregation. Lady Saunders had been a good woman, much loved in the village for her kind works, and her funeral was well attended, the congregation overflowing outside the church.

Joining in the last hymn before the coffin was taken outside to be interred, Angelica wiped away her tears. She glanced at Hal's stony face, knowing that he was battling his emotions – emotions as much of anger as of grief. He had cared for Lady Saunders in his own way, but it was anger that was chiefly in his mind.

Claire had confessed that she had been forced to tell him that she would not marry him, her face white with grief and stained with the tears she had shed for her grandmother.

'I never meant to hurt him,' she sobbed. Her hand trembled as she clutched her kerchief, screwing it into a ball. 'I know he will hate me for it, but how could I marry him? I cannot marry him. At times . . . he almost frightens me. He is too intense . . .'

'He hath a temper,' Angelica agreed. 'And he can be cruel . . . even arrogant, but . . .' she broke off unwilling to reveal her own heart.

'I know you love him,' Claire said. 'But think carefully, Angelica – would you truly wish to wed him? You know how easily he has hurt you in the past.'

Angelica smiled, but made no answer. Hal's unkindness had cost her many tears, but she would shed a million of them willingly for the joy of being his wife. Her love was something that had come unbidden and she could not deny it, even though she knew that Claire was right. Hal was the kind of man who would always hurt those who loved him too much, for he could not help himself, and yet sometimes . . . sometimes he did or said something wonderful, something that made up for all the hurts.

'I do not know,' she confessed. 'I think perhaps I might

– but he has never thought of me in that way, and I do not believe he will.'

She had hoped that when Hal's anger faded he might begin to think of her as someone he could turn to, but thus far his anger showed no sign of abating. She had hardly spoken to him since that day, for he had not come near them until today, when he was forced to accompany his father and friends to Lady Saunders's funeral.

Angelica followed the small cortege outside to the interment in the stone vault that housed the departed of their family. She, Claire and her aunt stood outside in the warmth of the sunshine as the men followed the coffin and the vicar down the steps into the vault, for it was not thought fitting for women to be there at the last. They had paid their tributes inside the church, laying a flower each on the coffin lid, and now they would return to the house and wait for the men to follow.

The atmosphere inside the carriage was stifled with grief, for both Claire and Caroline were weeping. Angelica gave a heavy sigh. She had wept for her grandmother in privacy and her tears were done. Lady Saunders had made the peace between them before she died, and Angelica felt no need for remorse.

She glanced out of the window, looking at the countryside for it was a warm summer day and the meadows had been cut for grass, the strong sweet smell pervading the air. As they passed the woods, she saw a gypsy leading a horse, and knew him as he turned his head to look at them. His expression was one of anger, his eyes colder than midwinter ice. He seemed to look directly at her, making her heart catch. Why was he so angry? Was it something she had done?

She sat back, feeling the pounding of her heart. Something about the gypsy frightened her. She felt that he was dangerous – but to her or to Hal? She had never been able to forget that meeting in the woods, and often wished that she had spoken to her uncle about him. Hal had dismissed him as a braggart, and perhaps he was, but that smouldering anger she sensed in the gypsy had not diminished, and it worried her.

Caroline was holding the reception for family and friends at the Manor, for Sir Rupert was too weighed down by his grief to have the bother of ordering the servants. The girls followed her inside when the carriage drew up at the main entrance, standing with her in the hall to welcome the guests who had come to pay their respects. Some of them had journeyed many leagues to be here, and would stay overnight before returning home.

Angelica had never before met some of her grandmother's relatives, and she was hard put to it to remember their names, though others had visited from time to time. She knew Margaret Farringdon, a friend of her grandmother's and her aunt's, and she knew several of the distant cousins, uncles and aunts. However, the only one she truly felt comfortable with was Elizabeth Benedict, who had come with her friend Mary and was going to stay with Caroline for a while.

'It is a sad day for you all,' Elizabeth said to her when everyone had gathered in the hall. 'You will miss her, Angelica.'

'Yes. We shall all miss her,' Angelica admitted. 'She was confined to her bed much of the time these past months, but the house seems empty without her.'

'Your father and grandfather will rely on you now, my dear. But I dare say you have been helping to run the house for some time?'

'Yes, that is true,' Angelica confirmed. 'The servants are very good, but they need direction. I do not mind the task, but without Grandmother to ask for advice, I fear making mistakes.'

'It is always best to make a friend of your housekeeper,' Elizabeth told her with a little smile. 'Do not fear to ask for advice, my dear. You may take the best and discard that you think of no use. But while I am here I shall be glad to help you in any way I may.'

'You must come and visit us for a day,' Angelica said.

'Have your nuncheon with us, Cousin Elizabeth. Then you may tell me what is being neglected and what I should do.'

'I shall walk down to see you in a day or so,' Elizabeth promised, and then gave her a little nudge. 'I believe Claire is looking for you, my dear.'

Angelica saw that her cousin was giving her a look of appeal and went to join her. 'Is something wrong, Claire?'

'Stay with me for a while,' Claire begged. 'Hal is in such a mood. I am sure he is ready to quarrel with me and I do not wish to quarrel today. It would be unseemly.'

'I think he is unhappy.'

'If that is so I am sorry for it,' Claire said, 'but I cannot change things. I have had a letter from Philip. He comes next week to stay with us. He has been released from his duties earlier than he had hoped and he wants to speak to my father. I believe we shall be married quite soon, for it seems that I may be offered a place in the Queen's bedchamber.'

'I see . . .' Angelica's eyes went to Hal, her heart sinking as she saw the expression on his face. He was already bitterly angry. She did not know what he might do once Claire was promised to another. 'Perhaps the sooner it is settled the better. Until he knows that it cannot be altered he may try to change your mind.'

'That is what I am afraid of,' Claire said looking nervous. 'He thinks he can bully me into doing what he wants as he has in the past – but he will not succeed this time.'

'Has he bullied you?' Angelica frowned, for it had not seemed that way to her. She had watched from the outside, thinking how lucky Claire was to be the favoured one, but clearly her cousin saw things differently. 'I do not think he meant it so – it is just his way.'

'Perhaps,' Claire said and looked uncomfortable. 'I am sorry if Hal is hurt, Angelica, but my mind is made up. I could not marry him even if I were not in love with Philip.'

'No, I see that you could not,' Angelica said and smiled oddly. Once the news of Claire's decision might have made her happy, but now all she could feel was sympathy for Hal's pain. 'Do not worry, Claire. I shall not leave you alone with him.'

Hal was looking at them. She sensed that he was deciding whether or not to try and get Claire alone, but she gave him a defiant look, letting him know that she was not prepared to give her cousin up to him. His eyes narrowed and she sensed that he was in a black mood. He threw her a speaking glance, then turned and strode from the hall.

Angelica smothered the impulse to go after him. Nothing she could say would change what had happened. Hal would have to cope with his anger and disappointment. He had loved Claire – but she did not know if he was truly in love with his cousin as a man with the woman he would wed – or whether she was simply a part of his grand plan.

Glancing across the room, she saw that her father was deep in conversation with Elizabeth Benedict. Her gaze widened as she saw how intent her father was, and that Elizabeth seemed to be hesitant, almost as if she did not wish to be given so much attention.

Angelica had guessed that her father meant to ask Elizabeth to be his wife. She knew he admired her very much; he might be in love with her, for his eyes seemed to follow her whenever they were in the same room – but she was not sure how Elizabeth felt about him. She hoped that they would marry for her father needed a wife, and an heir.

Elizabeth was someone she could talk to, and she would be a friend when Claire was married. For years everything had been the same, but in the past few months there had been so many changes. Angelica wondered what would happen next. Claire would marry – but would Angelica?

Hal felt the anger grinding inside him as he rode towards the village. He had known that Claire was begging Angelica to stay with her so that he could not talk to her alone. He had tried to talk to her more than once since the day of her grandmother's death, but she always managed to avoid him, frustrating him at every turn.

He had not yet accepted that she meant what she'd said. Surely she was merely teasing him as she had when they were children? He was hurt that she had accused him of being too forceful where she was concerned, for surely he had given way to her many times? He had never been deliberately hurtful to her, because he loved her. Claire had always seemed content to follow his lead, laughing as they played together. It was Angelica who had turned away with tears in her eyes. It was she whom he had plagued and tormented so often . . .

He found it hard to accept that he had taken Claire's loyalty for granted as she claimed. It had never occurred to him to question the rightness of what he did. As the heir, he had imagined that she was happy to follow in his footsteps, that the idea of their marriage pleased her as much as it pleased him. He had planned it as much for her sake as his own, for he did not wish to drive her from her home. If he took another woman as his wife, Claire would not have been mistress in her own home . . . but it seemed that she did not wish to stay at Thornberry.

She had found a new lover at court. Some popinjay with an empty head and effusive manners, no doubt. He had flattered her and she had fallen for his trickery. How could she have been so foolish?

The thoughts went round and round endlessly in his head as he thundered towards the inn. It had almost driven him mad, being forced to act properly and speak politely to all those people he had never met and did not wish to know. There was so much anger in him that he had not been able to bear it a moment longer. All he wanted now was to drink himself into oblivion, so that he no longer remembered what had caused this ache inside him.

Wild thoughts of abducting Claire and forcing her to wed him had been considered and abandoned. He had discovered that his pride would not allow him to do anything so futile. If Claire preferred another man to him, be damned to her. He would forget her in the arms of one of the village wenches.

He thought of the gypsy Serena and her seductive dancing, but he had not been to the woods since the night he confronted his half-brother. The girl did not want to lie with him, and he would not force her.

Be damned to the lot of them! Women were the work of the devil and he would drink to forget them all . . .

Six

Angelica spent a little time sitting with her grandfather that morning, reading to him from his Bible. He seldom stirred from his chair by the fire in the library these days, and she thought that he seemed to grow frailer every day. It was almost as though he no longer had a purpose to his life, and was counting the days until he could lie in the grave-yard, beside his wife of so many years.

After leaving him to doze by the fire, Angelica visited the kitchens to discuss the meals that would be served that day, before making her escape into the fresh air. She needed to be alone for a while, for the atmosphere of the house was so heavy that she felt it weighing upon her.

In normal circumstances she would have walked to the Manor to spend some time with her cousin, but she knew that Claire would be preoccupied. Sir Philip had arrived the previous evening and it brought home to Angelica how lonely she would be when her cousin wed. It was true that she had other friends, but they did not live close by and she saw them only at formal affairs. Claire and Hal had been her childhood companions, and even though she had often felt excluded, she had still been happy to be with them. Now Claire would be leaving Thornberry, and Hal . . .

She caught her breath as she saw him walking towards her. As usual he looked strong, handsome, impressive, a man who would always turn heads. It was clear from his expression and his manner that he was furious, and she knew that he had finally been forced to accept that Claire's intention was to wed another.

'How could she?' The indignation burst from him as they met. 'That . . . dullard! How could she prefer him?'

The outrage in his face would have amused Angelica if she had not known how hurt he was. She wanted to comfort him, but she knew he would reject sympathy, and there was little she could say in the face of Claire's determination.

'Sir Philip is no dullard, Hal,' she protested. 'I do not dislike him even though I would not care to wed him.'

'Then you have more sense than your cousin!' Hal was carrying a whip, which he used to thrash an offending bush, swishing the handle, she thought, like an angry cat. The thought almost brought a smile to her lips but she suppressed it. 'She has betrayed me and I shall never forgive her.'

'Do not hate her,' Angelica said, her voice soft, placating, different from the tone she normally used to him. 'I know you are angry – but Claire cannot help it if she does not love you in that way.'

'What has love to do with marriage?' he demanded, beyond reason now in his temper. 'We were promised – she knew it even though she denies it. It was always meant to be.'

'In your mind,' Angelica said. 'Perhaps you should have asked Claire instead of just assuming that she—'

'Damn you! I might have known you would take her side,' Hal said and turned from her, striding away, the whip slapping at his thighs as if he enjoyed the feel of physical pain.

'Hal, I'm not on her side . . .' Angelica called after him, but he did not falter or turn to look back at her. 'But you should have known . . .' And yet how could he have known when she had not? She had believed that her cousin would be content to marry Hal. In truth, Claire had never seemed less than willing to do as he wished, and therefore she had in some part encouraged him. 'I love you . . . I'm on your side . . .' But the last words were a whisper that he could not hear, nor in truth did she wish him to. Her pride would not allow her to beg him to love her. Perhaps in time he would come to her, but she did not want him unless he loved her. She would not be a substitute for Claire.

Turning, she went inside, to seek the solitude of her own chamber, where she had many tasks awaiting her. Besides the clothes she had bought in London for her own use, she had ordered several bales of plain cloth, some of which was meant for the gowns of servants, and it was this that she had decided to sort out that day. The maids would help her cut the cloth, which would then be given to each servant, the amount and quality according to their rank. Some would wish to make their own gowns, but for others the services of a seamstress would be needed.

It was just another task that fell to the mistress of the house, a role that Angelica had assumed since her grandmother's illness, which would fall even more heavily on her shoulders now that Lady Saunders was dead. She must keep an account of each bale, and how it had been distributed, also the cost of the cloth and the services of the seamstress.

Opening her journal, she glanced at entries her grandmother had made the previous year, written in the neat hand she knew so well.

One quilted petticoat for Maria, maidservant of this house, and a length of plain stuff for her gown. Fifteen shillings and sixpence.

For Joseph, footman, one jerkin and enough cloth for a pair of breeches and coat. Also one pair of boots for Sunday wear. One pound and sixteen shillings, and twenty one shillings for the boots

For Mistress Parker, housekeeper of ten years' service, two petticoats, one quilted, and a length of best fustian. Three pounds and five shillings.

Angelica smiled. Her grandmother had left so much of herself behind in all these journals that she could almost hear her speaking to her. She dipped her quill in the ink well and began to write:

Five pairs of worsted stockings bought for five shillings the pair . . .

Her quill spluttered on the page, and she got up to sharpen it with a little knife she kept for the purpose. Her mind

100

deflected from the task she had set herself, she crossed to the window for a moment to look out.

Her father was talking to the gardeners. It was such a lovely day, and she would have preferred to be out, walking with Hal and Claire, but those days were over and it was time that she applied herself to her work. She was thinking of Hal as she returned to the trestle table where she had set out her grandmother's journals. He had been so angry earlier, but when his anger began to abate, perhaps he would begin to realize that it was better to look for a wife who would love him than spend his days in useless regret.

Hal had been drinking for most of the day. The sting of Claire's rejection was festering inside him, made worse by the realization that she truly cared for the man who had followed her from London. He had seen something in her face when she introduced them, something that made him burn with jealousy, for she had never looked at him in that way. Her love had shone from her eyes, and she looked truly happy. But why? he demanded of himself. Why should she look like that?

Sir Philip was such an ordinary fellow, nothing to mark him out in any way – so how could Claire love him? Yet he was certain that she did, and it made him angry. He had cherished his dream of wedding her for so long that it was hard to let go, but he sensed that he must. The knowledge had left him empty and hurting. He had instinctively sought out Angelica in the belief that she could somehow make sense of what had happened, perhaps hoping that she would call her cousin a fool and salve his pride – but she had taken her cousin's side, and that had made him want to strike her. He should have expected it! He had mocked and teased her so often in the past that she must be delighted with this chance to see him suffer.

Hal had fetched his horse from the stables and ridden down to the inn, where he had spent the day drinking the strong ale that had befuddled his brains enough to dull the ache inside him, and now he was ready to go home. His head was swimming as he went outside, not noticing when the innkeeper sent his servant after him.

'Should you ride, sir?' the man asked respectfully, holding the reins of Hal's horse. 'My master says you may sleep here until you are feeling better . . .'

Hal looked at him blearily, waving him away. What was the fool talking about? He was perfectly able to mount and ride his horse. However, it took him two attempts, and it was only with some help from the groom that he managed it.

'Will you not bide here, sir?'

'Away with you, man,' Hal said, angry now. Did the entire world think he was a fool just because Claire had rejected him? He wrenched the reins away from the impudent groom and kicked at his horse's flanks. 'I am perfectly capable of riding this beast . . .'

He set off at a pace, his head swimming. The angry thoughts were chasing themselves in his head: Claire's rejection, Angelica's pleasure at his pain – he was sure she had been laughing inside – and now that fool of a groom doubting his ability to ride. He would show them all! His muddled mind wasn't sure what he was going to show them, whoever they were, but he knew that he was going to throw off this mood and—

He saw the hedge ahead of him. He knew that the gate was to his right, and that he should get down and open it, for the hedge was very high and needed trimming, but something in him was not responding to what his mind was telling him. He set his horse straight at the barrier ahead. Be damned to it! He would show them all. He hardly knew what was happening as he raced the horse towards his target, and then, as it refused, veering away to the right, he found himself thrown from the saddle and fell heavily to the ground where he struck his head and then, rendered unconscious, lay still.

He was unaware that someone had seen his fall. He did not know when the girl knelt beside him, bending over him, her lovely face anxious and frightened. Nor did he see her get to her feet and run for help.

'It was good of you to come,' Angelica said as she welcomed Elizabeth to her home the next morning. 'In truth, I was hoping that you might, for I am not sure what I ought to be doing about the linen. The housekeeper says that it was my grandmother's practice to go through the linen once a year and throw away any that was beyond redemption, and send that which needed mending away to the seamstress for repairs.'

'It is a task I undertake in my house once a year,' Elizabeth told her. 'I like to oversee it myself, for if not, the maids sometimes neglect their duty. It is a tedious chore and one cannot blame them, but a small tear mended prevents the ruin of many a piece of linen.'

'Then tomorrow I shall begin the task,' Angelica said. 'I suppose I should have known, but Grandmother always told me that I was not needed at such times. I believe we should begin to make jams and preserves soon, for there is a glut of soft fruit in the gardens and we cannot use it all.'

'Yes, certainly. I think that that should take priority over the linen, for the fruit will waste if it is not picked immediately. The linen will keep for another day. I should direct the maids to begin picking at once if I were you.'

'Thank you, I shall do so,' Angelica said feeling grateful for her advice. 'We have some fine strawberries and raspberries and it would be a pity to waste them.'

'Do you have a receipt for your preserves?'

'I believe there is a book in Grandmother's room,' Angelica said, 'but if you have one we might use I would not refuse it.'

'I have a special one that uses wine as a change from the normal preserves,' Elizabeth said. 'If you wish it, I shall bring it tomorrow and show you how it is made. Let your maids make the first batch of jams, and then tomorrow we shall make something special.'

'You are very good,' Angelica said, pleased with the offer. She lifted her brows in enquiry. 'I hope my aunt will not mind us stealing you away from her?'

'I believe Caroline has other things on her mind for the moment. She is planning a wedding for Claire – and it seems that Hal went out yesterday and has not returned. I believe she is quite concerned, though Lord Mortimer says it is just a young man sowing his wild oats.'

'Oh . . .' Angelica frowned, for she knew that Hal had been in a terrible temper when he walked away from her. 'I know he was hurt because Claire had promised herself to another man – but it is not like him to stay away all night. They are haymaking in the far meadow, and he usually likes to join in with the labourers at such times.'

'Well, perhaps he needs to be alone for a while,' Elizabeth suggested with a slight frown. 'I have always thought that Hal was given more than enough freedom, and it may be that he needs to come to terms with having his will thwarted. I think it has not happened often before this?'

'No, you are right,' Angelica said, but wrinkled her forehead as she puzzled over his odd behaviour. 'I know he was hurt and angry – and yet I would not have thought he would stay out all night.'

'I believe Caroline is concerned, but Nicolas seems to think he will come home when he is ready.'

'Yes, I expect so,' Angelica said. 'My father is in the front parlour, Elizabeth. Please go in to him while I speak to the maids. We shall have some wine and cakes – and they can begin the picking . . .'

She smiled as Elizabeth went through to the parlour where her father was reading the latest news-sheet to come from London. She would delay her business for as long as possible in the hope that they would find something interesting to say to each other . . .

Hal was aware of someone bathing his forehead. His head hurt, and he thought that he must have banged it somehow, for he could not remember what had happened to him. He recalled leaving the inn and he knew that he had been drinking heavily, but his head felt tender at the back and he did not think it was merely a hangover. His eyelids blinked and he opened his eyes, staring up at the girl who was bending over him. At once he understood why he felt so strange for he was not in his chamber at the Manor . . . and it was the gypsy girl who tended him.

'Why am I here?' he asked, because he had become aware that he was in a caravan. 'Did I fall and hurt my head? It feels as if it has a hundred hammers beating at it.'

'You tried to jump the hedge in the long meadow,' Serena said, continuing to bathe his forehead with a damp cloth. Her expression did not alter, and he thought how cool and comforting her touch felt. 'Your horse refused and you fell – and the blow to your head left you without your senses. You cried out in your sleep – if sleep it was – but then after I fetched something from Rowena, you slept peacefully. She said that you would feel sore when you woke but that you should regain your wits, for it was but a slight blow after all.'

'It feels worse than a slight blow,' Hal muttered, putting a hand to the back of his head and wincing. It was very tender and sticky, as if the girl had applied some kind of ointment to the wound. 'How did I come here?'

'I saw you fall and fetched help,' Serena told him. She had left him for a moment to bring a cup filled with a dark brown liquid. She eased an arm beneath his shoulders, lifting him so that he might drink. 'Rowena said that if you drank this it would ease your headache.'

Hal tasted it and pulled a face. 'It is bitter and burns the mouth. I'll drink no more of that, wench. Give me ale or water, if you please.'

'It will not harm you, I promise you that,' Serena said. 'Not everyone is pleased that I brought you to our camp – but Rowena would not harm you. She dare not, for they would blame her, and she fears that she might be taken as a witch. Besides, I drank some of it myself earlier and I know that it is not poisoned. Take just a little, sir, and then I shall give you some honey wine to ease the bitterness.'

Hal swallowed two mouthfuls and then rejected the cup. 'No more, wench. I dare say it is not harmful, but it tastes like wormwood and I would rather have a headache.'

Serena laughed, her eyes alight with mischief. 'Why are men such babies?' she asked, teasing him. She fetched him a cup with a little ale sweetened with honey. 'I have seen women in childbed drink far worse than this and make nothing of it, but this will take away the taste.'

Hal pushed himself up cautiously, looking about him with interest. He had never been inside a gypsy caravan before, and he was surprised at how clean and neat it looked. He was lying on the bed, which was little more than a thick mattress piled with pillows and quilts. There was a bench at one side, which he thought must be used as Serena's table, and beneath the bench a chest for storing things. Above the bench hooks had been set into the wood and utensils for eating and cooking hung from them. He could see evidence of herbs, bread and cheese and he thought that she must have been preparing the ingredients for a meal.

'How do you live in such a place as this?' he asked, for it seemed so cramped to him, and he did not think he could manage to find room for a tenth of his possessions. 'Where do you put everything – your clothes and books?'

'I have no books and few clothes,' Serena said. There were two gowns in her chest, and they served her well enough. 'It is a simple life we lead, sir, and much of it lived outside. When it is warm I sleep on the grass with a rug and pillow beneath my head, and I cook outside, unless it is raining, and then I eat bread and cheese or cold meat.'

'What have you been preparing today?' Hal asked, for he could smell something appetizing, the scent of it drifting in through the open door.

'It is a stew made from rabbit, herbs and roots taken from the hedgerow,' Serena said. 'I am cooking it slowly so that it will be tender, and you may eat a little, or simply drink the broth.'

'It smells very good,' Hal said, and felt his stomach clench at the thought of food. 'How long is it since you brought me here?'

'It was only last night,' Serena told him. 'Rowena said you would recover your wits soon, and you see that she was right.'

'Yes – thanks to your nursing,' Hal said. 'I must thank you for your good offices, Mistress Gypsy. Had I lain on the ground all night unattended it might not have gone so well with me.'

'Perhaps not,' Serena agreed, for she knew that Rowena's potions and cures had helped him, though she would not tell him too much, for he might not be pleased with all that had been done for him. 'But anyone would have acted thus, sir.'

'Would they?' Hal felt the bitterness of Claire's rejection twist inside him. 'Has anyone sent word to the Manor?'

Serena hesitated. The gypsies had been afraid to draw attention to themselves, and Rowena had advised caution.

'Wait and see what happens to him,' she had said when Serena had had his unconscious body carried to her caravan. 'If he dies we might be blamed. You would have done better to leave him there, girl.'

'I feared that he might die,' Serena had answered, and yet she knew in her heart that she might have acted differently. She could have gone to the Manor for help, but she had chosen her own people, and had him carried to her home. 'He will not die. I shall not let him.' She had answered defiantly and sat by his bed all night, tending him, stroking his hair as he cried out in his sleep, and her tender heart had ached for him. Something told her that he was suffering from a grief that had not come to him through his accident, and when his restlessness was at its height, she had bent to kiss his lips. After that he had settled, seeming to sleep peacefully.

'We thought it best to wait,' she said awkwardly, for she did not lie easily. 'Forgive us if we did wrong, sir.'

'No, you did right,' Hal said, for he was pleased that no word of his accident had reached his home. He did not want anyone to know that he had made a fool of himself, especially Claire and her lover. 'What of my horse?'

'We brought it here. It has been tended and is not harmed.'

'Good . . . you and your people have done well, Mistress Gypsy – or may I call you Serena? That is your name, I believe?'

'Yes . . .' she smiled at him shyly. 'You may call me by it if you wish, sir.'

'Then I shall . . . but you must call me Hal.'

'Oh no, sir, it would not be fitting.'

'Then I shall call you Mistress Gypsy.' He grinned at her as she hesitated. 'Come, you need not fear me, Serena. Do you think that I would harm you after what you have done for me? I am in your debt. Tell me what you would like – shall I buy you a new gown, or would you have a gold ring for your finger?'

'I wish for nothing,' she said, not yet daring to use his name but avoiding the title he had disowned. 'You were hurt and I helped you. Now you are better, and that is reward enough.'

'You are generous but I must find some way to reward you,' Hal said. 'When I am well I shall go home, and then I shall bring you a present – not as payment, but as a gift. Shall you take it?'

'Perhaps, if it is given as a gift,' she said, a faint flush in her cheeks, 'but I ask for nothing.'

'That stew you are making smells good,' Hal said. He threw off the coverlet and attempted to push himself up, but immediately his head began to go round and round, and he fell back against the piles of cushions and pillows. 'Damn it! I am weaker than I thought.'

'You must not attempt to rise,' Serena said. 'If you wish

it we shall send to your home, and people will come to carry you there.'

'No!' Hal frowned. He did not wish to be carried home. It would do his family good to wonder where he was for once – especially Claire. He hoped that she would be worried and that she would blame herself. 'Do not send to the Manor. I have no wish to be fetched home. I shall go when I am ready – if you will permit me to stay with you a little longer, Serena?'

'Yes . . . Hal,' she said, and her cheeks flushed red with colour, for his smile was mesmerizing her. In appearance he was very like Jared, whom she had adored since she was a child, but this man looked at her differently. He saw her as a woman, and she sensed that he liked what he saw. She knew that he had come to watch her dancing by the camp-fire, and when she danced, it had been for him. She was aware that she was foolish to be attracted to him, for she was too far beneath him, and yet she felt her insides melt when he smiled at her. Tending him, as he lay unconscious, she had felt something deep inside her reaching out to him, and she thought that she had begun to love him. 'You may stay for as long as you wish . . .'

'Good . . .' Hal's eyes caressed her. She was a very pretty girl, proud but modest, and he was grateful to her. She had helped him when he lay out of his senses, and he knew that he might have died where he lay if she had not seen him and come to his aid. His injuries were not so very terrible, but had he lain all night he might have choked on his own vomit. But more than that, he was grateful to her for caring . . . for looking at him as if she liked him . . . really liked him. Her shy smile was easing the wound that Claire had dealt him. He had gone to Angelica for comfort, but she had taken Claire's side; this girl had taken him in and cared for him, and he knew that some of her people would have been against it. She had risked much for him: if he had died, she might have been taken as a witch. 'I do thank you for your kindness, Serena.'

'It was my pleasure,' she said, meeting his eyes momentarily. 'And now I shall fetch you some of the stew, for I think that it will help you to recover your strength.'

Hal studied her as she went down the steps of her home. Her feet were bare, brown and slender. He could see her moving about, see the colour of her bright red skirt, smell the broth, which had made his stomach begin to rumble. That foul mixture she had given him had eased his head, and he took pleasure in watching the girl. She was pretty and generous, and he had wanted to lie with her from the moment he first saw her.

Claire was lost to him now. He vowed that he would think of her no more. The future was uncertain, but for the present he would simply take what he could of life.

'It is very strange that there has been no word from Hal,' Angelica said as she and Elizabeth worked together in the stillroom the next morning. 'If something had happened to him, it would surely have been reported to the Manor by now?'

'Yes, indeed,' Elizabeth agreed, lifting the pan of boiling hot strawberries in wine and sugar and beginning to spoon the thick mixture into earthenware pots, ready for Angelica to tie the little muslin caps with ribbon. 'Nicolas says it proves that he is staying away of his own will, though both Caroline and Claire are distressed by it.'

'Claire is upset because she knows that Hal was angry with her,' Angelica said, and frowned. 'He could not believe that she preferred Sir Philip to him – and to be honest, I cannot either. Sir Philip is very ordinary, and I think Hal a much better match for any woman.'

'Did you tell him that?'

'No – perhaps I should have,' Angelica said and looked thoughtful. 'I begged him not to hate Claire, for she could not help it that she loved someone else more than Hal.'

'I dare say it did not please him to hear that,' Elizabeth said. 'Men are vain creatures, my dear. You might have pleased him better if you had told him what you have just told me.'

Angelica laughed and shook her head. 'Surely not? I do not think it would have made him less angry.'

'It might have eased his hurt,' Elizabeth said and looked thoughtful. 'But you will learn in time, my dear. Most marriages are give and take – and the woman in the house must do most of the giving to keep her husband happy.'

'Is that true?' Angelica looked at her seriously. 'Was it that way for you, Elizabeth?'

'Yes, for me more than most perhaps. I married a man I did not love, and he knew it. I had to make recompense, and he was ill for some years – I became more his nurse-maid than his wife in the end. It might have been better had we had more children – but as you know, our son died.'

'Yes. We were all very sad when we had your letter.'

'It was a source of much grief to us. It left our lives sadly empty.'

'Poor you,' Angelica said. 'Were you very unhappy?'

'At times, yes,' Elizabeth said. 'You see, I loved someone else, but I had given my word to be faithful when I married and I could not break it. I did my best to be a good wife to Walter – but I never loved him as I ought.'

'I see . . .' Angelica was curious. She hesitated, then, 'Was the man . . . was it my father you loved?'

'Has someone spoken to you of this?'

'No, not at all,' Angelica assured her. 'It is merely that I have seen the way he looks at you when you are not aware . . . as if he is starving and you are a juicy plum cake, and he wants to gobble you up.'

'Oh, Angelica!' Elizabeth cried, throwing up her hands as she laughed. 'My dear – what a thing to say!'

Angelica's eyes danced with merriment. 'It is true,' she said. 'He does look at you that way. I think he wants to marry you, Elizabeth – and it is not just because he needs an heir. I think he loves you – but I am not sure if you love him?'

'I have not been sure myself,' Elizabeth said truthfully. 'I would not wish to be married simply for the sake of comfort or the getting of an heir . . . but if Rupert—'

She got no further, for one of the maids came running into the room, looking very distressed. 'Oh, Mistress Angelica, come quick,' she said. 'It is Sir John. I think . . . I think he is dead . . .'

'Dead?' Angelica was shocked. She had left her grandfather sitting in his chair not an hour before. He had seemed a little tired but in good heart. 'But he said that he felt better this morning.' She looked at Elizabeth in distress. 'My father will not be back until later. He had some business at the other side of the estate . . .'

'Then it is as well that I was here,' Elizabeth said, and took off the white apron she had been using to bottle the preserves. 'Let us go and see, my dear. It may be that Sir John has fallen into a stupor, in which case we shall send for the physician . . .'

Sir John was found to be in a stupor, though still breathing when he was carried to his bed. The physician was duly sent for, but he held out very little hope when he made his examination.

'Your grandfather has had a seizure,' he told Angelica. 'I fear that he may not last the night, and perhaps it would be as well for him if he did not, for otherwise he might be paralysed.'

'Oh, poor Sir John,' Angelica said, tears stinging her eyes. 'It is so soon after my grandmother . . .'

'It often happens that way when a couple have been married for a long time,' Elizabeth said after the doctor had gone. She looked at Angelica's white face and made up her mind. 'I shall send word to Caroline, my dear. She will want to know about her father – but it is in my mind that I shall stay here if you wish it? I can help with any nursing, and you will not want to take the whole burden on your own shoulders.'

'I did not mind helping to care for Grandmother,' Angelica

said. 'But I should feel awkward in this case – Grandfather is different . . .'

'Yes, that is what I thought,' Elizabeth said. 'I am very glad that I was here with you, and you may rely on me to do all I can for Sir John. I nursed Walter through a series of apoplexies, but he lingered for many months. It was an unkind fate, and I pray that your grandfather may be spared it.'

The doctor had left some medicines should Sir John recover, and Elizabeth said that she would sit with him for an hour or two until Caroline came. Angelica returned to the stillroom to finish potting the preserves, and messages were sent to the Manor and to Sir Rupert.

Caroline came within the hour. She was naturally very upset, and sat with her father for two hours, though there was no change in him. She was grateful that Elizabeth had offered to sit with the invalid for, as she said, it would be difficult for her to do much nursing at the moment.

'Claire has asked that the wedding be soon,' she told Elizabeth. 'I have no quarrel with that, for she has made a good choice. I have sent a message to Sir Philip's parents, and we hope that they will visit us shortly.'

'I thought it would be awkward for you at the moment,' Elizabeth said, 'and I nursed my husband through a similar illness. The doctor seems to think there is little hope of a recovery, but we shall see. I never gave up hope for Walter, and I shall not do so for Sir John.'

'We are very lucky to have you here,' Caroline said. 'I should have been anxious for Angelica had you not been; she is too young to have the care of an invalid thrust entirely upon her. Besides, it is her birthday soon, and she must be free to come to the feast we shall give for Claire.'

'Yes, of course. They were born on the same day,' Elizabeth said, remembering the way Sarah had complained because Caroline's mother had left her to go to her daughter. 'It would be unfair if Angelica were tied to her grandfather's side. But you need not worry, for I shall not desert the family while I am needed.'

'It is my hope that you will stay for a long time,' Caroline said, smiling despite the heaviness of spirit her father's illness had laid on her. 'But I shall not tease you – though I hope that Rupert will put right the mistake he made so many years ago, dearest Elizabeth. I have always wished that you had been my sister-in-law, as you know.'

'Yes, I know it,' Elizabeth said and kissed her cheek. 'Go home, Caroline. Tell Mary she is welcome to visit here if she wishes . . . but I shall not leave while I am needed.'

After Caroline had gone, Angelica took a turn at her grandfather's side, watching as he lay with his eyes closed, his breathing deep and tortured. She knew that the doctor was right and his life hung in the balance; he could die within a few hours or linger on for weeks, perhaps months. She did not want him to die, but neither did she like to think of him being confined to his bed, for he had always been a strong, determined man.

She was bathing his forehead with cool water when her father came in. She could see from his expression that he was very distressed, and her heart ached for him. He had been away so many years, and already he had lost his mother. Now it looked as if they would lose Sir John too.

'Elizabeth says we should not despair,' she told him. Going to her father, she put her arms about him, laying her head against his chest. Her fear of being almost a stranger in his life had gone, and she felt closer to him than she ever had before, tears springing to her eyes as he closed his arms about her, kissing the top of her head. 'She is going to stay with us and help us to nurse him.'

'That is very good of her,' Rupert said, a catch in his voice. 'You are too young to have such a burden, Angelica. I am glad that Elizabeth will be with you.'

Angelica gazed up at him, her eyes wide and clear. 'Why do you not tell her that you wish to marry her, Father? She would be an excellent wife for you – and I like her very well.'

'Do you, daughter?' Rupert smiled oddly. 'I like her very well too. I have for a long, long time – but I am not sure she would have me.'

'You will not know unless you ask her.'

'That is very true,' Rupert said, and there was a faint hint of mischief in his eyes. Just for a moment an attentive observer might have seen the likeness between father and daughter. 'I am grateful for your advice, and perhaps I shall speak to her soon.'

Angelica heard the little snort of breath from her grandfather, and turned to see that his eyelids had flickered open. She left her father at once and went to Sir John's side.

'Grandfather – how do you feel?'

He made a horrid gurgling in his throat as he tried to speak, but was unable to get the words out, saliva trickling from the side of his mouth. She saw that the side of his face was twisted, and pulled up oddly. He was trying to move his hands, but only the left one responded. The other seemed to lie uselessly on the coverlet.

'Is there something I can get for you?' she asked, seeing that his inability to communicate was distressing him. 'Would you like a cup of water?'

His lips moved but no words came out, but she thought that he was trying to say yes and went to fetch some water from a jug on the side table, bringing it back to him. She slipped an arm beneath his shoulders, supporting him as he managed to swallow a couple of sips, but then he lay back, evidently exhausted by the effort.

'Go now, Angelica,' Rupert told her. 'I shall sit with Father for a while, and I dare say you have other things to do.

Angelica did as he bid her, for it was clear that the nursing of her grandfather was going to be time-consuming. She would need to spend some hours with him every day, and she was grateful that Elizabeth was there to share the task with her, which would be difficult enough. Alone, she would have found it daunting.

She was thoughtful as she went downstairs to speak with

the servants about supper. She had been too busy to dwell on her feelings of disappointment that Claire would soon be leaving them – and had hardly a moment to wonder what had happened to Hal . . .

Seven

'What are you doing?' Hal ventured down the steps of the caravan to where Serena sat working, twisting lengths of some light-coloured woody material into each other to form a circle. 'You have scarce come near me all day.' In truth, he was feeling neglected, and he suspected that she was avoiding him. 'Have I done something to upset you?'

Serena looked up from her work, a grave expression in her dark eyes. 'I am making reed baskets to sell at the fairs,' she told him. 'We shall be moving on soon, and I must earn my keep.'

'Must you?' Hal felt oddly reluctant to see her go. As a rule he took little notice of the gypsies, interested only in the wrestling that took place at the fairs. 'Why do you not stay here for a while?'

'When my people go, I must go. We are waiting for Roald's return. He went somewhere on business of his own, as he does from time to time, but he will return soon, and then we shall go where he tells us. He is our leader and we must do his bidding.'

'Could you not find work here in the village?' Hal asked. He was aware of a fierce desire swirling inside him.

'Perhaps,' Serena agreed. 'For a while, if I chose – but I shall go when Roald returns.'

'Even if I ask you to stay?'

Serena's eyes met his briefly, seeming to question and then fell. She appeared to be interested in her work. 'You do not truly wish me to stay,' she said at last. 'I am a gypsy, and you are son to the lord of the Manor.'

She had spoken the truth, and Hal was silenced. He might persuade her to stay, but for what? She had helped him when he was injured – she might even have saved his life. It would be wrong of him to repay her by seducing her, even though he was aware of the burning need in his loins. He ought to go, leave now before he did something he might regret.

'I think I shall go home today,' he said. 'I shall bring you a present this evening. What would you have me give you?'

Serena glanced up. 'I ask for nothing. You may give me something or nothing – the choice is yours.'

'I shall bring you a gift this evening,' he promised. 'Will you dance for me, Serena? If you are soon to move on, it may be for the last time . . .'

'We shall return another year,' Serena said, though she was not sure that was true. Roald did not like the Thornberry fair, and came this year only because Jared and others of the tribe had asked it of him. 'But I shall dance for you this evening, if you wish it.'

'I do,' Hal assured her. He wondered what she would do if he tried to take her in his arms, but he had become aware that he was being watched from the other side of the clearing. He knew that Jared had spoken against his being brought to their camp, but others had ignored his protests. It was well known that the gypsy had no love for his half-brother – if the relationship was valid, and Hal had a sneaking suspicion that Jared's claims might at least in part be true. 'Expect me after sunset this night, Serena.'

He gave her a last, lingering look and crossed the clearing to where the horses were tethered, his own amongst them. Jared had been giving them water he had fetched from the stream in a bucket, not forgetting Hal's horse. It was a tedious chore, and Hal was aware that he was indebted.

'I thank you for your care of my horse,' Hal said. 'I know that you have no liking for me or my family, but still, I thank you.' He reached into his pocket and brought out a gold piece, holding it out to the gypsy, who gave him a scathing look. 'Will you take my money and my hand?' If the man accepted, it would be an end to the quarrel between them.

'You can give your gold to those that need it,' Jared said. 'I want nothing from you but my rights.'

'You will never be lord of Thornberry Manor,' Hal said. 'But if you spoke to my uncle, he might give you something – if he believed your story.'

'He has cheated me,' Jared said, glaring at him. 'Even if my father never married my mother, I am the eldest. I should have been the heir.'

'You are a fool if you think that,' Hal said, and lifted his saddle from the tree stump where it had been deposited, sliding it across the horse's back. He untied the bridle which had been secured to a post, and then swung himself into the saddle. 'Refuse my gold and my advice then – and to the devil with you!'

He rode off without a backward glance. It was time that he returned home, for he did not wish to truly alarm either his uncle or his aunt, only to punish Claire a little for her rejection. He had woken to the discovery that the sting of her desertion had lessened. He was still angry with her for preferring another man, but it did not hurt as it had. She had chosen to marry someone else, and she was the loser, for she would have to leave Thornberry.

Hal began to whistle a tune as he rode. He must find a suitable present for Serena, and the only thing he could think of was the ruby ring that had been given him as a keepsake by Lady Saunders. He had intended it for Claire as a betrothal gift, though he would have bought her something better when they wed – but now he would give it to the gypsy girl.

He smiled as he anticipated the dance she would perform for him that evening. Perhaps if she were pleased with her gift he might steal a kiss from her later. No harm could come from a few kisses, after all.

Serena looked up from her work as Jared came to her a few moments after Hal Mortimer had gone. The look of calm that Hal had admired faded as she saw that Jared was scowling at her. She had once hoped that he might take her as his woman, but he had grown surly of late, obsessed with the wrong he claimed had been done him, and she knew that he was angry because she had brought the lord's son here.

'Did he offer you his gold?' Jared asked harshly. 'Do not expect more from him, Serena. He will never wed you. You will end as my mother did, with a child to care for, abandoned by the man she loved.'

'I do not think that Hal is as unkind as you claim,' Serena told him, for she had fallen in love with the lord's son as he lay helpless in her bed. He had been gracious and pleasant to her, and all Jared did was scowl. 'He was grateful for my help, and has promised me a gift.'

'Do not be fooled by fair words,' Jared said. 'Ask Rowena. She will tell you that the Mortimers cannot be trusted.'

Serena tossed her head, her eyes flashing with pride. 'Are you not one of them? It is what you claim. Does that mean that you also are not to be trusted?'

Jared felt the scorn of her dark eyes, and muttered beneath his breath before walking away. Serena stared after him. She had loved him once. If he had smiled at her as the lord's son did, she would never have looked at another man. Her good sense told her that there could never be a meaningful relationship between her and Hal Mortimer, but that did not stop her feeling excited because he was to bring her a gift – and she had promised to dance for him.

Angelica saw Hal from the landing window. Her heart jerked with a feeling of overwhelming relief, swiftly followed by anger. He was unharmed and seemingly perfectly well. Why had he not sent word before this?

She went down to the hall, and was in time to see him enter the house by the main door. He seemed to hesitate as he saw her, and then he smiled, making her treacherous heart leap with joy.

'Angelica,' he said as he came towards her. 'I was on my

way home when I heard from one of your servants that Sir John had had a seizure, and so came straight here—'

'Where have you been?' she demanded imperiously. She had been as anxious as Claire and Caroline for his safety, and now he was behaving as if nothing had happened! 'Why have you let everyone worry about you?'

'I fell from my horse and was unconscious for a time,' Hal said, and grinned at her. Nothing changed Angelica! He did not know why that should please him, but it did. 'I am sorry if you were worried.'

'Why should I worry about you?' she said glaring at him. 'I have had other concerns to keep me occupied. We were in the middle of making preserves when Grandfather was taken ill. Besides, I guessed that you were doing it only to punish Claire. I know that she was stupid to prefer him to you – but that does not excuse you—'

'Did you think her foolish to choose him instead of me?' Hal's eyes narrowed as he looked at her hard.

Angelica's instinct was to deny him, but then she recalled what Elizabeth had told her. 'Yes, of course,' she said with a little toss of her head. 'He is not half the man you are, Hal. I would never marry someone like that, and I think her foolish – but Claire loves him. I suppose she cannot help herself . . .'

'No, perhaps she cannot,' Hal said seeming thoughtful. 'But I am glad that you think as you do, Angelica.'

'Well . . .' Angelica smiled a little shyly. 'That does not mean I forgive you for upsetting us all, Hal. Caroline and Claire were very distressed – and with Grandfather's illness, they have enough to bear.'

'Yes, you are right. I shall make my apology to Caroline,' Hal acknowledged. 'I needed a little time to come to terms with Claire's rejection, that is all . . .'

'But where have you been?'

'Staying with the gypsies. One of them saw me come off my horse and they carried me unconscious to their camp and nursed me there. They would have sent to the Manor, but I think they feared they might be blamed – especially if I had died.'

Angelica was startled. She had thought him merely away sporting with his friends, and this altered things. 'Were you badly hurt?' she asked, her eyes intent. He might have been killed!

'Not as badly as I might have been had they not taken me in,' Hal said. 'My head was sore for a day or so and I turned dizzy when I tried to rise – but I am better now.'

'You might have sent us word . . .'

'Yes, but . . .' He pulled a wry face, for there was truth in what she said. 'Perhaps I should have. I did not think you would care what had happened to me, Angelica?'

'Perhaps I should not,' she said, but reined in her clever tongue, holding back the cutting remark that rose to her lips to punish him. 'But I did. You know I always care what happens to you, Hal.'

'Do you?' His gaze deepened. 'Truly?'

Angelica turned warm under his look. Was he mocking her again? She was not sure, and felt relieved as she heard Elizabeth calling her.

'I must go,' she said. 'I am glad you paused on your way home to inquire for Grandfather – but you must go now, for Caroline must be anxious. And I must help Elizabeth. Sir John has survived thus far, but he is poorly and needs constant nursing.'

'I am sorry for it,' Hal said. 'I shall come another day . . .'

'Yes . . .' Angelica turned from him quickly. If she were not careful she would give herself away. She did not want Hal to turn to her out of pique. He must recover from the wound Claire had dealt him, and then, in time, if he came to love her, she would confess her love for him.

'I do not know what we should have done without you these past days,' Rupert said as Elizabeth came downstairs that evening. He thought how fresh and lovely she looked despite the hours spent caring for his father. There was such serenity about her, such comforting goodness, that he knew she was the only woman he wanted for his wife. 'Angelica has been very good, but you have been a tower of strength to us all. I am sure that it is due to you that my father still lives.'

'I have done very little,' Elizabeth said, 'but he needs constant nursing care, and it would be too much for Angelica alone – and Caroline has a wedding to plan. The banns are to be called for the first time this Sunday, and she expects Sir Philip's parents to arrive next week. She will be giving several dinners to introduce him to the neighbourhood, and we must not expect her to do much nursing.'

'As you know, she was here earlier for an hour or so,' Rupert said. 'She told me that your friend Mary is to return to London next week. Shall you go with her?'

'No, I have already told Mary that I shall stay here as long as I am needed,' Elizabeth replied. 'That is . . . if you wish it?'

'You must know that I do,' Rupert said and moved towards her, his eyes tender as they dwelled on her face. 'You know that I am grateful for what you have done for my father – but there are other reasons I would wish you to stay, Elizabeth.'

'Are there?' she asked softly. 'And what might they be, Rupert?'

'The main one is that I am still in love with you. I shall not deny that there were women in my life while I lived abroad, for I would have no lies between us, but I have loved no one else since you, Elizabeth.'

'I had thought you must have forgot me. Did Caroline never tell you that Walter was dead?'

'She says that she wrote to tell me at the time, but I never received that letter from her. I was travelling a great deal, sometimes Antwerp or Bavaria, sometimes France, and letters did not always reach me. Besides . . .' He reached out to touch her cheek. 'I thought that I had learned to forget you, and I believed that you had forgotten me.'

'I thought that I had learned to be content without you,'

Elizabeth admitted. She hesitated, then said, 'When the King made his unlucky attempt to wrest his throne from Cromwell, I did wonder if you might come with him, but you did not, at least I did not know of it – nor yet when he returned to England. Why was that, Rupert?'

'In truth I do not know,' he confessed. 'I had become settled in my ways, and I had struggled to put the past behind me, and I believed you settled in your marriage, of course – but then, when I was summoned home for my father's sake, I began to see that the years had changed nothing. I knew when I saw you that I still felt the same.'

'I was not certain, though it was a shock to me to see you that night at the theatre, and it reawakened memories that I had thought buried.'

'And to me. I knew from the moment I saw your face that I still loved you.' Rupert stroked her cheek with his finger-tips, bringing his thumb across the softness of her mouth. 'I have never forgotten the sweetness of our loving, Elizabeth. Nor have I ceased to regret that I did not marry you instead of Sarah.'

'We all make mistakes,' Elizabeth said, a little shiver running through her, her mouth sensitized to his touch. She was aware of feelings she had forgotten she was capable of experiencing. 'Had I waited a little longer, we might have had all these past years together. It was a bitter regret to me – but I could not betray the vows I had made.'

'And that is why I have never forgot you,' he replied softly. 'You are a pearl amongst women, Elizabeth. Very few would have done what you did – especially when Walter was an invalid for so long.'

'I was more his nurse than his wife for most of our marriage,' she said on a sigh of regret. 'I should not have minded that so very much if our son had lived, for he was a good man in his way.'

'I have no son,' Rupert told her. 'But I hope for one – a son with you, Elizabeth. Will you give me a chance to make up for all that I have done to wrong you?'

'I am not in the first flush of youth,' Elizabeth replied with a faint smile. She gazed up at him, searching for truth. 'Supposing I cannot give you a son – will you regret your choice?'

'If I have you I shall be content,' he said and drew her close to him. 'We shall both hope for a son, Elizabeth – but we shall have Angelica, and her children shall be our heirs if we have no other.'

'Then I shall wed you,' Elizabeth said and lifted her face for his kiss. She gave a little shudder of pleasure as his lips covered hers, his kiss soft at first and then deepening to passion. All at once the years were swept back and she was a young girl again, thrilling to her lover's touch. She arched into his body, allowing herself to feel the delight that his kiss was giving her. 'As soon as it is possible . . .' she breathed, for she knew that more happiness lay in becoming his wife than she had ever experienced.

'My father will not want us to wait,' Rupert said. 'We shall have the banns called next Sunday week and be wed the week following Claire and Philip. It will please my father to know that I have wed at last, and it means that you will be here to care for him. We may not have a wedding trip, but I shall take you to France one day, I promise. I have many friends there, and also a house you might like to visit sometimes.'

'I need no such promises,' she told him, gazing up at him lovingly. 'I am content to care for your father and daughter. If Sir John recovers his health we must think of taking Angelica to London again. There is no hurry – but I would see her happily wed to a man of her choosing.'

Rupert frowned. 'I had hoped that Chesterford might come up to scratch . . .'

'I am not sure that he is the right husband for Angelica,' Elizabeth said. 'But we have time enough, dearest. At least I can be sure that she will welcome me as your new wife, for she has already told me so. She told me that you loved me.'

'Has she indeed?' Rupert chuckled. 'It seems that my daughter is wiser than I knew.'

Hal found the ring that had been given him as a keepsake from Lady Saunders in his coffer. It was fashioned of heavy gold with a large deep red ruby set into the metal, and he knew that it was valuable. Claire had admired it when he showed it to her, and he was sure that her grandmother had expected it would eventually go to her – but now he would give it to the gypsy girl who had nursed him.

Caroline had been cross with him for not letting them know he was safe, but Claire had merely stared at him with reproachful eyes and said nothing. She had known that his silence was to punish her, and she was angry with him for being so unkind to her. Hal had begun to regret his behaviour, which had been the result of pique. He knew that he must make his peace with Claire at some time, but as yet he had made no move towards it. She had betrayed him. It was her fault that there was this breach between them.

Hal was careful how he dressed that night, choosing one of his favourite linen shirts but leaving the neck undone, and wearing only a leather jerkin over his shirt and breeches. If he went dressed too fine he might make Serena nervous, and he wanted to see her smile for him, as she had once or twice while she was tending him.

She was a pretty girl, and he had enjoyed being touched by her. If she had been of decent family he thought he might have wed her, for she was kind and she looked up to him as her superior. She made him feel that he was special and important, and he was still smarting from Claire's rejection, even though he had realized that his heart was not broken. He cared for his cousin, but he had discovered that it was not a grand passion after all – just a pleasant dream that he had cherished since childhood. He was still unwilling to let go of his dream, but in his mind he had accepted it.

It was best to push Claire's coming wedding to the back of his mind and think of Serena. It would be amusing to see if he could charm her into becoming his lover that night. Hal sensed that she liked him very much. Would the gift of the ring be enough to lower her defences? A smile curved his mouth, his eyes bright with mischief. He thought only of the excitement of the chase, of his own pleasure if he should snare his prey. Of Serena's feelings afterwards, for such an affair was doomed from the start, he did not think at all.

Angelica was delighted when her father told her the good news that evening. She hugged him and kissed Elizabeth, her face alight with happiness for them.

'That is the best news I have had in an age,' she said. 'I am so pleased, Father. Elizabeth has always been kind to me, and I know that she loves you – as you love her. This time you will be happy in your marriage, and I shall pray that your happiness will be completed by the birth of a son, if God grants it.'

'You are a good girl,' Rupert told her, well pleased with her words. 'It makes me happy to know that you are content to have Elizabeth as my wife – and your mother.'

'Perhaps not as her mother,' Elizabeth said, for she had seen the shadows in the girl's eyes for a moment when her mother was mentioned. 'But she is my very best friend, and we shall love each other dearly.'

'Yes, we are and shall be friends,' Angelica said, the shadows banished by Elizabeth's good sense. 'I know that my mother was not all that she ought to have been to you, Father, for Grandmother told me – but I hope that you have some kind memories of her?'

'I did not mean to condemn your mother,' Rupert said at once, realizing his mistake. 'I loved her truly when I wed her – but I was not the right husband for her, and we drifted apart. Yet I do not hate her. I never have.'

'And we both love you,' Elizabeth told her. 'When you were born, I held you in my arms and wished that you were mine. I held you as often as I could, but when I married I was forced to part with you, because your grand-parents wished to care for you, and I believed that you were safe with them.'

'I knew that you thought of me, for you always sent a gift for my birthday. Even when you did not visit, you did not forget me.' Angelica looked lovingly at them both. 'I shall go up and spend a little time with Grandfather now. He likes me to read to him, and it may help him to sleep.'

Angelica was thoughtful as she went up to Sir John's room. She was happy that her father and Elizabeth were to marry, but she could not help wondering if she would ever find happiness in the arms of a loving husband. Would Hal ever love her as she loved him – or would he look elsewhere for his wife?

She wished that she could read his heart, and wondered where he was and what he was doing that night.

It was perhaps as well that Angelica could not see into Hal's mind that night as he watched the gypsy girl dancing by the flames of the campfire. Her dance was provocative, sensual, and it heated his blood to fever point, making him burn for her. When she came to him, pulling at his hands, he got up and went with her to the fire, trying to match his steps to hers, though he knew he was a clumsy fool compared to her.

'I am no dancer,' he said as he stumbled over the intricate steps and saw the laughter leap in her eyes. 'You have grace and beauty, I am but a fool to worship at your feet.' He reached for her hand, his fingers curling about it tightly, taking her with him, away from the light of the fire to the shadows at the far side of the clearing. 'Enough, you have tempted me enough, sweet enchantress. I shall give you the present I promised you.' He took the ring from the inside of his jerkin and slipped it on to the third finger of her hand, where it fitted neatly. It was only as she gave a gasp of surprise and delight that he realized he had pushed it on to her betrothal finger. It was not what he had intended, for he had not meant to deceive her, but he could see from the wonder in her eyes that she thought he was making her a promise.

'Hal . . . is this truly for me? Such a beautiful, costly ring must mean . . .'

Hal smothered his conscience as he took her hand, turning it up to drop a kiss in the palm. 'The ring is nothing compared to your beauty and your goodness, Serena. I am not worthy of you, but I care for you . . .' In Hal's mind he was merely being gallant, leading her gently down the path to seduction, but in Serena's it was a declaration of love.

'Then I am yours,' she said simply, for it was the gypsy way. When a man came to a woman and danced, when he gave her a gift such as this and declared his love, it was enough. She needed no words from the parson nor the grandeur of church and hall, she was his woman, his for their life long. 'Take me to my caravan, Hal. We shall seal our love this night.'

'Not in the caravan,' Hal said, for he did not wish the other gypsies to know that they had lain together. 'Let us sneak away into the woods for this our first time. I do not wish to be seen or heard . . . this is our special time, and I would not have it spoiled.'

Serena smiled and gave him her hand, for she believed herself loved. 'I know a secret place where we can be alone,' she said, her fingers twining with his. 'Come, Hal, for we shall be truly as one in love.'

Hal smothered his qualms. She must surely know that this could only be a fleeting thing? She could not expect that he would marry her? He could not know that in her innocence, Serena already considered herself his wife.

She led him to a sheltered grove, and there on the dry bracken that made their bed, the gypsy girl gave her heart and her body to the man she had fallen in love with. Smiling up at him as he took her mouth with little pecking kisses that made her giggle before he deepened the kiss to a hungry, passionate demand, she made no protest as his hands and mouth explored her. He stroked her lovely firm breasts, trailed down the flat, soft surface of her stomach, down to the warmth and moistness of her femininity. Her body arched, as she moaned and whimpered beneath him, her natural, unfettered abandon giving Hal the impression that she was skilled in the arts of love. And then, when he realized that she was a virgin, and her love was innocent, it was too late and he could not hold back.

Afterwards, he lay, his head against her breasts, breathing hard, and his conscience smote him. 'You were a virgin,' he said, looking down into her dark eyes. 'Why did you not tell me?'

'It is our way amongst those of the true blood to hold ourselves pure for our man,' she said, smiling at him, still secure in his love, for the ring was a sacred promise. 'I have given myself to no other nor shall I. This I swear on the ring you gave me. I am yours until I die.'

Hal looked into her eyes, and his stomach curled with regret for what he had done. She was so sweet, so giving in her love, and he had taken both lightly without a thought for the future. He had desired her, wanted her to ease the sting of Claire's rejection, but he did not love her – and one day he knew he would break her heart.

'What is it?' Serena asked, feeling the first flicker of doubt as she saw his expression. 'Have I displeased you?'

'No, of course not,' Hal said and kissed her. He did not love her, but she gave him pleasure and he liked her, and in his own way he was grateful to her. He would not dismiss her lightly from his life. They could continue in this relationship for a while, perhaps a few weeks or months – and then he would give her something to ease the sting of his rejection. He would give her lots of presents, pretty shawls and gowns, anything to please her for the time they were together, and he would think of a way to let her down gently. 'You could not displease me, Serena. I just did not realize that it was your first time.'

Serena was a little uneasy, for surely if he loved her he

must have known that she was chaste? But he had begun to kiss her again, and she could not resist him, nor did she wish to wonder if she had deceived herself.

'Of course you must attend Claire's birthday celebration,' Elizabeth told Angelica a day or so later when she had suggested that it would not be noticed if she were not there. 'I would be most grieved if you did not. Your father will take you, and I shall stay here to care for Sir John. You need not worry that he will miss you, for I shall read to him and sit by his side until he sleeps.'

'Thank you,' Angelica said, for she had not wanted to miss the feasting. It was her birthday too, though she had understood when her father had told her that it would not be suitable for them to hold a celebration at the house with his father still so ill. 'Claire was insistent that I must go, but I felt it my duty to stay here.'

'No, you must and shall go,' Elizabeth told her. 'I have a birthday gift for you, my love, and I know your father has something special for you – but it would be a shame if you were to miss the feasting.'

'I am fortunate that you are so kind to me,' Angelica said and kissed her.

'What will you wear?'

'I have a new dress that was commissioned in London,' Angelica told her. 'It was not finished when we left town and it has been sent on to me. I like it very much, for it is a deep emerald green and, I think, becomes me well.'

'That is good,' Elizabeth said. 'I had wondered if there was enough time to make you a new gown, but if you have one that you have never worn it will do well enough.'

On the morning of her birthday, Angelica was presented with a beautiful cloak of velvet trimmed with soft grey fur from her father, and a French lace neckerchief from Elizabeth. She thanked them both with kisses, pleased with her gifts, for she had needed a new cloak, and the lace was very fine. However, when she went to visit her grandfather, he presented her with a beautiful gilded wood casket.

'This is for you with my love,' Sir John said. He spoke awkwardly, his words slurred and hesitant, though making perfect sense. His mind remained unaffected despite his partial paralysis. 'Most of the jewels are family heirlooms, and though a few have been reserved for Elizabeth, we all wanted you to have these.'

'Grandfather!' Angelica cried as she opened the casket and discovered the pearl necklace, earrings and matching bracelet inside. The clasps on both the necklace and the bracelet were made of small roughly-cut diamonds that had a greyish tinge but caught the light from the window and shed a rainbow of colours on to the white linen coverlet. 'Thank you so much for giving me these. But are you sure you wish me to have them all? Perhaps Claire should have some part of the set . . .'

'Caroline was given some family heirlooms when she married,' Sir John said. 'I believe she may today give her daughter a necklace she had then. I have sent her a gold and sapphire chain for my part – but you are Rupert's daughter, and therefore you should have the more important gift.'

Angelica's eyes were wet with tears as she thanked him. She had not expected this: to be put above Claire on their joint birthday was something that surprised and shook her.

'I shall take great care of them, Grandfather, and pass them down to my children in time . . .' If she ever had any, that was.

'That is as it should be,' Sir John told her, a trickle of saliva ran over his chin. It was painful to watch his efforts to wipe it away, but she knew he hated anyone to fuss over him and repressed her urge to do it for him. He did not add, and Angelica did not know, that her mother had once stolen many of the jewels, and it was only by good fortune that they had been returned by Sarah's lover. 'Go to your cousin's feast with a good heart, child. I shall do well enough with Elizabeth to care for me.'

Angelica thanked him, kissed him again, and went away to prepare for the feasting at the Manor. She had no duties for the day. Now that Elizabeth was staying with them, she had taken on most of the work usually done by the mistress of the house, though Angelica helped her as much as she could. However, on her birthday she was allowed to do nothing but greet the friends who called to bring her small gifts of flowers, homemade wine, a book, sweetmeats and soap perfumed with roses.

She spent the morning entertaining her callers and thanking them for their kind wishes, a little surprised to discover that so many people had remembered her. For as long as she could recall, she and Claire had shared their birthday, and though she had always received gifts, she had thought that it was for Claire's sake that they came. Now she had learned differently, and it felt nice to have had the chance to have at least a part of her birthday to herself.

It was as she was about to go upstairs to change for the afternoon's feasting that she received her last visitor of the day. She was surprised when Hal walked in and wished her a happy birthday, and even more surprised when he handed her a parcel. Opening it, she discovered a beautiful silk kerchief with her initials embroidered in the corner, and pinned to it was a small pearl and diamond brooch in the shape of a flower.

'Oh, Hal,' she cried, genuinely surprised, for he had never given her an individual gift before, always being accredited with the joint gift presented to her by the Mortimer family. 'This is beautiful. Where did you get it?'

'I went into St Ives earlier this week,' Hal told her. He was conscious of a faint heat about his neck making him uncomfortable, for he had gone to St Ives to buy gifts for Serena and had belatedly thought of Angelica. He had bought Claire a silk kerchief, but to Angelica's he had added a brooch at the last moment, though he was not sure what had moved him to do so. Seeing her pleasure in the gift, he was glad that he had made the gesture. Angelica was beautiful when she smiled that way, and he had discovered recently that he thought of her more than he had used to. 'I am glad that you like it.'

'It will go well with the pearls Grandfather gave me,' Angelica told him and on impulse darted forward to kiss his cheek. Hal turned his face and for a moment their lips met until she drew away, feeling almost as if she had been stung. 'Oh . . . I meant to kiss your cheek . . .'

Hal's eyes danced with wickedness for he had enjoyed the kiss, especially as he knew she was shocked. 'I know well what you intended, dear cos,' he said and laughed huskily. 'But it was sweeter so. I brought your gift here for I wished to give it to you privately. I know Caroline has a gift for you later, but I shall not be there.'

'Not be at Claire's feast?' Angelica stared at him in dismay. 'But you always come to the feasting for our birthdays . . .'

'Not this year,' Hal said, and wished for some reason that he had not arranged to meet Serena. Angelica looked so disappointed that he almost changed his mind, but then he remembered that he had a gift for his gypsy lover and that she would give him something more than a kiss in return. 'Claire will have Sir Philip with her. I shall not be missed.'

'I shall miss you,' Angelica said, her face reflecting her dismay, for she had hoped that they might dance. 'When shall I see you again?'

'I am not sure. Father is sending me to Norwich on some business. Perhaps when I return . . .'

'Shall you be here for Elizabeth's wedding?'

'Yes,' Hal smiled and agreed. 'I shall return for that I promise you. I do not wish to be here when Claire is wed, and Father understands that. He had business and thought to send me on it – but I shall return for your father's wedding.'

'I shall look forward to it,' Angelica said, and the smile she gave was shy and unsure, causing Hal to feel something odd inside. He had often felt that he would like to seduce Angelica in the past, sometimes because he wanted to punish her for her wicked words. Now, suddenly, he found himself thinking how pleasant it would be to walk with her on a summer afternoon, to hold her hand and . . . court her. 'Hal . . .' She stopped and blushed, for he was frowning, the spell that had momentarily held them broken.

'I must go,' he said, for he had remembered Serena waiting for him. He was committed to her for a while at least, and he was uncertain what this new feeling towards Angelica meant. 'I shall see you when I return . . .'

Angelica stared after him as he left the room abruptly. For a brief moment she had felt something between them, something that made her heart race wildly. She had thought Hal felt it too, but in the next instant he was frowning, and he had left so abruptly that she feared she must have given herself away.

She puzzled over his odd behaviour for a moment, but then Elizabeth was calling to her, telling her that it was time to get dressed. She pushed Hal's strange look to the back of her mind. It was her sixteenth birthday, and she meant to enjoy herself.

Hal saw Serena waiting for him in their secret place, and put away the tormenting thoughts that he had carried with him since leaving Angelica. He did not understand why his feelings towards her had changed these past weeks, but there was no doubting them. She was intriguing him more and more, though he did not wish to become involved with her – not yet at least.

Serena ran to him as she saw him, throwing herself into his arms. He held her and kissed her, feeling his blood heat as he smelled her perfume. She was lovely, generous and passionate. He ought not to be thinking of another woman while he was with her.

'You are late,' she said when he had kissed her thoroughly. 'I had begun to wonder if something kept you from me.'

'I should not have left you waiting here,' Hal said. 'When I do not wish to see you I shall tell you, Serena.' He smiled and touched her chin, for he loved to tease her and see the light in her dark eyes begin to glow like coals. 'I have a gift for you . . . what shall you give me in return?'

'A kiss,' Serena said promptly, for he had played this game before.

'Oh, no, I think it is worth much more,' Hal said catching her to him to steal his kiss. 'This is what I want . . .' and he whispered in her ear, making her blush and giggle at his mischief. 'But have your present, for I think that it will pleasure you as much as me.'

Serena took the parcel he offered, opening to reveal a beautiful scarlet silk petticoat, embroidered on the hem with beads of jet. She gasped, for it was a costly gift, and not the first such he had given her.

'You spoil me,' she said looking at him with bright eyes. 'I do not need so many gifts, Hal. What I give to you is freely given of my heart.'

'Yes, I know it, sweeting,' Hal said and caught her to him. 'But it pleases me to buy you things – and it pleases me to love you.' He kissed her mouth, stopping her protests as he bore her down to the dry earth, the smell of bracken strong in his nostrils, so that he thought he would never be able to smell it again without thinking of Serena and her sweetness. 'Love me, my pretty gypsy, for tomorrow I must leave you on business for my father, and it will be two weeks before I see you again.'

Lost beneath his kisses, swept away by the seeking caresses of his hands, drawn on the crest of a crashing wave, Serena was unable to think clearly. Her love for him had become stronger with every caress and smile he gave her, and she could not think of anything but the joy of being with him, of being loved so thoroughly that every part of her tingled even after he had left her.

It was only later as she lay in her caravan that night that she began to think and wonder. Had Hal given her so many gifts for a reason? She knew that it had surprised him that she was virgin when he first took her, and she wondered if he was trying to pay for that which he had taken and could not give back.

A single tear squeezed from the corner of her eye as she thought about her life if Hal should tire of her. She would be an outcast from her tribe, for she had not been able to keep her secret from them. Nothing had been said, but she had seen knowledge in the eyes of the other women, and she knew that some of them despised her. They thought her the lord's son's whore – and perhaps she was. Hal had given her the costly ring, placing it on the finger where he would place his marriage ring and she had taken it as a promise – but had it been?

Serena had begun to doubt. She did not know why, for at the start she had been convinced of his love, but today . . . she had sensed that his thoughts were not really with her.

It might simply be that he had business for his father that made him distant as they lay together after their loving, but she had felt him withdraw – had felt him leave her when he said goodbye. It was foolish, but she had a terrible premonition that he was saying a last farewell . . .

Eight

The Mortimer family had given Angelica a set of beautiful combs and brushes for her hair. They were fashioned of silver and set with tiny turquoises, and she knew they must be very costly. Caroline had ordered them from London especially for her, and Angelica was both pleased and touched by the gift.

The feasting had been merry that day, and Angelica had danced with her uncle, her father and several young gentlemen of her neighbourhood. One or two of them were most gallant towards her, which, she supposed, was because she was now considered of an age to marry. She smiled at them all with equal warmth, showing no favour to any of them, and in her heart wished that Hal had been amongst them.

Claire was excited by the gifts she had been given, for she had received many lovely things from Sir Philip as well as her grandfather, her Uncle Rupert and her parents. The thing she treasured most was a ring that Philip had given her as their betrothal token. It was fashioned of thick gold with an emerald set into it, and she wore it on the middle finger of her left hand because it was too large for the third.

'Philip says he shall give me another for our wedding,' she told Angelica with a sparkle in her eyes. 'I shall wear this then on my right hand, for it fits better there.'

'It is very like one that Grandmother left to Hal, is it not?' Angelica said thoughtfully, for she had seen the ring once when Lady Saunders was wearing it. 'But that had a ruby instead of an emerald.'

'Yes, I know. He showed it to me,' Claire said, her cheeks

heated. 'I think he hates me now. He refused to attend my feast and he has given me nothing for my betrothal, though he did give me a kerchief for my birthday.'

Angelica thought of the gift she had received, and knew that Claire was right. 'He was very angry. I am sure that he does not hate you, cousin.'

'I should be sad to think it,' Claire said, 'but he did not say goodbye to me before he left.'

'As I said, he was angry and hurt.' Angelica smiled a little. 'He has always been used to having his way, you know, and I dare say that we have all encouraged him in it.'

'Yes, perhaps,' Claire said ruefully. 'But do not let us talk about him anymore. This is our birthday, and we may not always spend them together in the future.'

'I know.' Angelica put an arm about her, squeezing her waist. 'It will seem strange at first, no doubt, but you will be busy in your new home, and at court, of course.'

'Yes, for we shall return there in six weeks' time. Philip has told me that he wishes to remain in His Majesty's service for another year or two, and then he may retire to his estates.'

'And you will stay with him,' Angelica said. 'I think it will be a very different life, cousin.'

'Yes, I expect so,' Claire replied, a little smile on her lips. 'But I do not really care as long as I am with Philip.'

'No . . .' Angelica thought that she might feel the same if she were marrying Hal. 'I do not suppose you do . . .'

Her thoughts went to Hal, and she wished again that he had attended their party. She wondered how he was faring on his journey, and what he was thinking of now.

Norwich was a bustling market town, and one of the richest in England because of its links with the wool trade. Hal admired the half-timbered houses of the wealthy merchants, which were much finer than in many towns of England. He frowned as he looked about him, not quite sure where to seek the house of the man he had come to meet.

Nicolas had sent him to negotiate with one of the most

important cloth merchants. The export of raw wool, leather and some other goods had been recently banned, and the importation of various clothing prohibited. Therefore, Nicolas had decided that he might make more profit in becoming partners with a wealthy wool merchant. It could greatly increase their fortunes if Hal's negotiations were successful, and he felt proud that his uncle had trusted him with this important mission.

He leaned down from his horse to inquire the direction of Lower Castle Street from a young woman carrying a basket of vegetables on her hip. She had just come from the bustling marketplace, which was thronged with people and animals, the sound of laughter and cows blaring mixing in a noisy cacophony. She smiled at him, pointing out the route he must take, her firm strong arms bare to the sun, and her ample charms on show from the plunging neckline of her bodice.

'When you have done your business, sir, a welcome awaits you at my father's inn. Seek out the sign of the Red Cockerel and you will sleep well this night.' Her dark eyes flashed an invitation he could not mistake.

Hal thanked her for her good offices, frowning as he watched her walk away, her hips swaying enticingly. She would make a fine armful in any man's bed, he thought, but for some reason he was not tempted to lie with her. It was strange, but the last time he had lain with Serena it had not pleased him as much as previously. He believed that he had begun to tire of her – and he did not enjoy the feeling that gave him.

Was he such a shallow fellow that he could tire of someone as lovely and sweet as Serena so easily? It lay heavily on his conscience, for he knew that he was ready to break with her, and the prospect was not one he relished. He had an awful feeling that his rejection would hurt Serena badly no matter how many gifts he gave her to sweeten the pill.

The truth was that he ought not to have taken her virginity so lightly. He should have known that she was innocent, but he was used to the tavern whores, who plied their trade carelessly, not caring who they took to their beds. He had known Serena was different, and yet he had still imagined that she must have lain with other men. He had wronged her, both in his thoughts and the way that he had used her, and he was shamed by it – but he did not see that there was much he could do to repair the damage.

He could not marry her. It was impossible, and besides, he did not wish for it. He was not yet certain what he wanted, but he knew that he had recovered from his anger and hurt at Claire's rejection. He would look elsewhere for his bride, and there was no need to be hasty. This time he would be certain of his feelings, and of the lady's, before he made plans. However, that still left the problem of Serena and how he was to let her down gently.

He had turned into the quiet street he sought, the rattle of his horse's hooves on the cobbles sounding louder now that the bustle and stench of the market was left behind. It was time that he forgot his own plans and concentrated on the business in hand.

'Oh, Claire, you look lovely,' Angelica said as she saw her cousin in her bridal gown of pale grey trimmed lavishly with lace shot through with silver. It was split down the middle over a petticoat of white silk, and it suited Claire well. 'And those pearls – are they a present from Sir Philip?'

Claire was wearing a heavy choker of large pinkish pearls around her throat, together with a longer strand that she had been given by her father. She had pearl drops fastened to her lobes and a sapphire and silver chain worn loosely around her wrist, from which hung a tiny book of hours.

'Yes, they were one of Philip's gifts to me,' Claire said, her eyes shining with excitement. Angelica was to be her chief handmaiden, and had come to her room to help her finish dressing. She accepted the fan her cousin gave her, feeling a little nervous. 'He has been so kind . . . so generous. I so much want to be a good wife to him, Angelica.'

'And of course you will be,' Angelica said. 'You have no

need to be nervous, cousin. You love Philip and he loves
you – that is surely the best receipt for marriage?'

'Yes, of course it is,' Claire said and gave her a wobbly
smile. 'It is just that it will all be different – away from
everyone . . .'

Had she married Hal, her life would have carried on much
as it always had. Claire had rebelled against that, but now
she was having a few doubts, though she knew that it was
normal for brides to be nervous.

'Do not be anxious,' Angelica told her. 'You will be very
happy, and I dare say you will see us from time to time.
We cannot come to London while Grandfather is so ill,
but . . .' She held back her final words, for it would not
do to say that she thought Sir John could not live long on
this her cousin's special day. 'I am sure we shall see each
other now and then – and you will be so busy you will
hardly notice.'

'I know you are right,' Claire said. 'I am just being silly.'

'Caroline sent me to see if you were ready,' Angelica said
after a pause, in which Claire seemed to gather herself. 'Are
you?'

'Yes, of course I am,' Claire said. 'Go down and tell them
and I shall follow in a moment.'

She looked around her bedchamber after Angelica had
gone. It was dear and familiar, and she was leaving it for
perhaps the last time – or the last time as Claire Mortimer.
Soon she would be Lady Rathbone. It was what she wanted.
Claire lifted her head proudly and went down to meet the
family, who waited for her below.

This was her special day, and she was marrying the man
she loved. She would not allow her foolish nerves to spoil it.

Angelica was feeling a little flushed with wine from toasting
the happy couple when she saw the newcomer enter the hall.
She was shocked to see him, and for a moment her breath
caught in her throat. What had brought Lord Chesterford here?
He was standing alone, his eyes surveying the gathering,

searching until they lighted upon her, and then he smiled, making his way through the guests to her side.

'I was told that you were here today,' he said, bowing to her gallantly. 'I believe it is your cousin's wedding?'

'Yes, indeed, sir,' Angelica said recovering her poise. 'She has this day been wed to Sir Philip Rathbone . . . but what do you here, my lord? What business can bring you this far from London and the court?'

'Personal business,' he said, a rueful glint in his eyes. 'Do you think me such a vain fellow that I cannot be happy away from the court?'

'I had not thought about it,' Angelica said. 'But I am surprised to see you here, sir.'

'Did you not know that both Sir Rupert and Lord Mortimer invited me to stay with them?' Now there was laughter in his eyes and she suspected that he mocked her. 'I have taken advantage of their generosity, for I thought to venture into the country for a while.'

'Have you been banished from court?' she asked, for she had heard that Lord Rochester had displeased the King by seducing a virtuous lady.

'Rochester is in disgrace,' Will said, his gaze thoughtful as it dwelled upon her face. 'Feeling it diplomatic, I took myself off, though I was not involved in the lady's down-fall.'

'I should hope not,' Angelica said, her feelings mixed as she met his serious gaze. 'It may do you good to be separated from your friends, my lord, for they are wild men.'

'As wild as the rogues and apprentices that run riot in the streets of London perhaps?' he said, a wicked smile on his lips. 'Oh, I know that you think me a terrible fellow, Mistress Angelica, but perhaps I could be reformed by the love of a good woman?'

His eyes were alight with laughter, and Angelica was not sure whether to take him seriously. She suspected that he was mocking her, and yet underlying the laughter and the teasing words was another, more deeply felt emotion. Could it be that he had followed her to her home because he cared for her?

She could not quite believe it, and yet she could think of no true reason why he should have come to this quiet part of Cambridgeshire. If he wished to rusticate for a while, he had estates of his own and did not need to visit others. He must surely have had some purpose to this journey?

'Do you truly wish to be reformed, sir?' she asked, thinking it safer to take refuge in another question. She saw that he was about to answer her and her heart quickened, but he was interrupted by the arrival of her father.

'Chesterford,' Rupert said clapping him on the back. 'I am delighted to see you here today. I hope that you have come to stay with us for a while?'

'Yes, if you will have me,' Will said and grinned at him. 'Mistress Angelica thinks I must have been banished as poor Rochester – but I have been assuring her that it is not so.'

'Rochester is in disgrace,' Rupert said, 'but for how long? I think Charles loves him too well to do without his wit for long. In time he may be recalled, and I dare say he will live to plague the King for many years – but come, my friend, I think you know only a few of us here. Let me make you known to the family and our friends.'

'I was sorry to learn of your father's illness,' Will said as he was borne away to be introduced to the other guests. 'You must say if you would rather I was gone.'

'No, indeed, Father has instructed that we continue our lives as normal. He made Elizabeth come today, for he is well cared for by our housekeeper – and I am to be married next week. You must at least give me your promise to stay for that, Will . . .'

Angelica watched as they walked away, clearly at home with one another. She suspected that her father had hopes of a match between them, and the thought made her frown. She liked Lord Chesterford despite his reputation, but she did not love him as she loved Hal. Yet perhaps Hal would never turn to her and she must marry after all. She had discovered that she would prefer Will Chesterford to any of the local gentry who had been paying her attention of late. And if she went to court, she would see her cousin more often.

Serena emerged from the bushes, having been sick again for the second morning in a row. She wiped her hand over her mouth, for the taste was vile. She wondered what had made her ill. Could she have eaten something that did not agree with her? She could not think it, because she had eaten very little for the past couple of days or so because she was feeling queasy, and the food had all been fresh.

As she walked to her caravan she was aware that Rowena was staring at her oddly, and she wondered what was in her mind. Rowena was not popular amongst the other gypsies, for though she had the true blood through her mother, she was not really one of them. However, Serena had always got on with her well enough. Perhaps for years she had tried to please her because she was Jared's mother, but from the scowl on her face, she was not happy about something.

'Is anything the matter?' she asked. 'Did you want me to do something for you?'

'It may be that you need me to do something for you,' Rowena said. 'If you are in trouble, come to me, girl. I can help you.'

Serena was puzzled as she went up the steps of her caravan. What did Rowena mean – if she was in trouble? What kind of trouble? It was only as she fetched out her basket weaving materials that it suddenly came to her. Rowena thought that she might be with child!

And yes, it was possible, for when she thought about it her courses were late. Only by a few days as yet, but she was usually regular in her flow. It was possible that she was carrying Hal's child.

Her head bent over her work, Serena pondered her likely situation. Would Hal be pleased she was carrying his child, or would he be angry with her? It was not that she desired a change in their relationship. She did not expect him to wed her in his church or take her to the big house to live, but she hoped that he might want her to stay near him so that he could see the child sometimes.

Serena did not have to go with the others when Roald returned, but if she stayed, she would need help towards the time when the birth was due. Would Hal arrange for her to have help when his child was born – would he give her money for food and clothing for the child? Perhaps a small piece of land that she might think of as her own, where she could grow food to feed herself during the winter.

She would demand nothing from him, but he had been so generous with his gifts that she was sure he would not deny her the things she needed at such a time. A little smile curved her lips. She would tell him her news when next they met, and she hoped that he would be as happy at the prospect of a child as she was.

Hal's saddlebags were stuffed with merchandise he had purchased in Norwich. He had bought Serena a silk petticoat, some gold bangles and earrings, and he would also give her a purse of money to see her through the coming winter. It would be best to make the break sooner rather than later, he had decided, since it must happen one day. He would apologize to her, give her his presents and then put her out of his mind. At the moment he felt guilty over his behaviour, for he knew that he was preparing to treat her ill, but the damage was done, had been done the first time he lay with her so carelessly. There was little he could do about it now.

His thoughts had returned to Angelica more often of late. He had been used to thinking of her as a child, but she was the same age as Claire. A frown creased his brow, for he had ordered a bale of silk sent to his cousin with a note to say that he wished her happiness on her marriage. It might not reach her before the wedding, but she would receive it later, perhaps when she returned to London from her husband's estates.

It was odd that it no longer hurt to think of Claire with a husband. It still rankled a little that she had preferred Sir Philip, but Angelica had thought her a fool to do so. He wasn't sure what had happened to ease his anger and his hurt, but he felt carefree as he rode home – or he would have, if he did not have the shadow of what he must say to Serena hanging over him.

It would be best to seek her out as soon as possible, he thought. She would be waiting for him to send word to her, and she would meet him in their special place. It would be hard to tell her, and the thought of hurting her was upsetting, because he was fond of her in his way, but he knew he must do it before he could move on with his life.

Angelica was in the gardens cutting some roses for her grandfather's room when Lord Chesterford came up to her. He smiled at her, taking one of the dark red blooms from her basket and holding it to his nose.

'We have some of these in our gardens at home,' he told her. 'They have always been my mother's favourite, for they have such a lovely perfume as well as this colour.'

'Yes, they were Lady Saunders's favourites too,' Angelica said. 'I like those big pink ones growing there. They came from France, a gift from my father to his mother when he returned. They also have a sweet smell.'

'But they are big and overblown, like a woman past her best,' Will said. 'Whereas these are small and perfectly formed buds – like a young and beautiful woman, juicy sweet and ripe for love.'

'Then you would cease to love your wife once she was no longer as fresh and perfect as this bud,' Angelica said with a little toss of her head. Her eyes sparkled at him, for she enjoyed their repartee. 'Are you as faithless as Rochester, sir?'

'Rochester is not the only faithless man at court,' Will

observed with a wicked smile about his mouth. 'His Majesty is oft unfaithful both to his wife and his mistress. I think you are harsh to me, Mistress Angelica, for I am no more faithless than most – and wed to the right woman, I might be faithful and loving all our lives.'

Angelica looked at him thoughtfully, for this was not the first time he had hinted at something like this. She believed that if she gave him leave, he would go further and ask her to be his wife. However, she had not yet made up her mind. Hal was her first choice of a husband. She had always loved him, but since Claire's wedding she had begun to think that she would like to marry – and if Hal did not love her, then she might as well take this man.

'Perhaps,' Angelica teased, her eyes bright as she looked up at him. 'I am not yet convinced, though you have a silver tongue, sir. And now, if you will excuse me, I must take these flowers in and make up a vase for Sir John's room. He takes pleasure from fresh flowers every day, and I fear there is little else to give him ease.'

'Yes . . .' Will frowned, for he was not sure whether he was making ground with her or not. 'It is a sad time for you, and I dare say you wish me to the devil?'

'No, you are welcome here as my father's friend,' Angelica said.

'And as your friend, mistress?'

'Yes, perhaps,' she said and smiled at him, giving him one of the roses on impulse. 'I like you better since you have been here, sir – but forgive me, I must go.'

Will took the rose, holding it to his nose and watching her, his eyes thoughtful as she walked back to the house. She walked proudly, like a queen and without the artifice of many women. In her simple country gowns, she was lovelier than most of the ladies he knew at court. He had grown to know her better this past week and he liked what he had discovered; there was fire and passion in her, though she kept it modestly hidden. Sometimes it flashed in her eyes, and at those times he knew that she was the woman he wanted as his wife. However, he was not sure if she would consent. He could go to her father, of course. If Rupert was pleased with the match, Angelica would probably obey her father – but that was not what he wanted.

Will had known many compliant ladies, and some of them had been eager to bed with him. He had taken less advantage of his popularity at Charles's court than he might, but he was not looking for compliance in his wife. He had discovered that he wanted Angelica to love him, and he sensed that she was still hesitant.

Well, he had time enough yet. The King would summon him to court when he noticed that he was not there, and he would go – with or without Angelica's promise. For the moment he would court her and hope to win her heart.

He looked down at the rose he held, and then slipped it inside his waistcoat. The rose was a good sign, he believed, and if he was patient, she might give him all that he desired from her.

'Your gift for Claire arrived after she had left,' Caroline told Hal when he came to her as she sat in her parlour stitching. She was working on a cloth for the church altar to replace those that had been removed during the Puritan years. The embroidery was thread of gold on a wine-red background, and it was very fine. 'It was good of you to send it, and I know she will be pleased when my letter reaches her. She was distressed by the breach between you, Hal.'

'I know,' he said and bent to kiss her cheek. 'It was wrong of me and I am sorry for it – but she hurt me. I loved her truly, and it had always been my dream that we should wed and continue here together.'

'That is true,' Caroline said and frowned. 'But it would have been a mistake, dearest. You and Claire were as brother and sister. It will be much better for you to marry someone who is not of such close kinship. Besides, I do not think you loved her as you thought – it was merely that you had planned it thus when you were a child.'

'Indeed, I have realized the truth of it,' Hal told her. 'I am sorry if I hurt either you or Claire. I hope you will forgive me?'

'Yes, of course I forgive you,' Caroline said, and then she was smiling at him. She had had some unsettling dreams of late that worried her, and she was glad to see him home safely from his travels. 'You have always been as my own son to me. Mercy begged me to take you and love you, and I have. Claire is my daughter and I love her, but I should not wish to see you wed each other.'

'Well, it is over now. I shall not be unkind to her when I see her again.'

'Good, that is all I ask.' She looked up at him as he stood near the window, sensing that he was restless about something. 'Did your business go well, Hal?'

'Yes, I believe so. Master Trethorn was pleased with our proposals, and I have brought a signed agreement back to be witnessed and given to the lawyers. He showed me the cloth produced by his handworkers, who are some of the finest in the country, and it was most impressive. I have brought some home with me.'

'Nicolas has bought some of his cloth before this and thinks it good quality. I believe Mr Trethorn uses only the finest fleeces, and we shall prosper mightily if we market our wool through him. If we are not to export our wool we must sell it here – or make the cloth ourselves.'

'I have learned a great deal of the difference between various qualities of cloth,' Hal told her. 'I think it will be of use to us as we decide our future plans.' He turned and looked at her. 'I would always wish to make you and my uncle proud of me, and do nothing that would bring you shame.'

'Of course you would not, you could not,' Caroline said. She was even surer now that something was on his mind, but she could not ask for it was clear that he was not ready to tell her.

'I must leave you now for I have something I must do,' Hal said. 'I shall see Nicolas at supper.'

Caroline stared after him as he left the room. Her latest dream had been very disturbing, and she could not shake off the fear that something terrible was going to happen.

Hal's conscience smote him as Serena turned towards him and he saw the joy in her eyes at his return. How soon that would fade when he told her that they must see each other no more. Indeed, he was not sure that he could bring himself to tell her. Yet he knew that he must. He had hidden the purse of money amongst the folds of the silk petticoat he had bought her, because he knew that if he tried to give it to her, she would refuse it.

'Hal,' she cried and ran to him, throwing herself against his chest. He put his arms about her reluctantly, holding her, dropping a kiss on the top of her head. She smelled so enticing that his restraint almost broke, but he held to his resolve. He would not lie with her again. It was not right or fitting that he should do so. He was the heir to a great title, an old name, and he must not bring shame on his family. From now on he would indulge in no more wild behaviour. 'I have missed you so much – and I have something wonderful to tell you.'

Hal steeled himself as he held her away from him, his fingers bruising the soft flesh of her upper arm. 'Hush, Serena,' he said, and he knew his tone was harsh, for it was hard to say the words. 'Let me speak first . . .' Her face clouded as she obeyed, looking up at him with such fear in her eyes that he found it almost impossible to go on, but he did. 'I must tell you that this is the last time we shall meet like this—'

'No!' she cried, shocked that he could say such a thing to her. And yet she had been afraid of it since their last meeting. 'We are promised, and such a promise is for life.'

'I know I took your virginity,' Hal said, the words tasting bitter in his mouth as he spoke them. 'It was wrong of me. I have used you ill, Serena, and I realize that I can never make up for what I have done – but if we continue, it may cause greater harm. I could never marry you, and in the end we must part. I shall marry, and—' He felt her stiffen and was torn with remorse. 'Forgive me if I deceived you. You took the ring as a promise, but it was not intended thus, merely as a gift for helping me. I never meant it to be more than a pleasant interlude . . .'

Serena drew away from him, looking at him with the eyes of a wounded fawn. Hal felt the knife twist inside him, for she had not deserved this. He had hoped that she might tire of him before he needed to tell her it was over, but the time he had spent away from her had served to show him the error of his judgement. Serena was no lightskirt to take his gifts and cheat him in the arms of a new lover. She had considered herself bound to him, and that was his fault.

'You never loved me. It was all a trick to make me lie with you . . .'

'No, not a trick. I gave you the ring for helping me when I was injured. If you thought it more that was not my intention – and yet I know that I have wronged you. I am sorry for it and I beg you to forgive me if you can.'

'You paid me like a whore,' she said bitterly and tugged at the ring on her finger, wanting to pull it free, to throw it at him. It would not budge no matter what she did, and she was close to tears as she gave up the struggle. 'You shall have it back, and all the other gifts . . .'

'No, please, Serena,' he said. 'Let me give you these things, I beg you. They are little enough recompense for the wrong I have done you – though I know nothing can give back what I have taken.'

Her eyes were wild with pain as she backed away from him, shaking her head. 'No, I want nothing . . . nothing . . .' She held out her hands as Hal offered the bundle he had brought for her. 'No, I do not want it . . .'

'I shall leave it here,' he called after her. 'Return and take it, Serena. It is owed you. Besides, I have no use for it . . .'

Serena did not turn her head to look at him. He knew that she was weeping as she ran, and he was sorry for it. He had taken her out of his selfish need, out of the hurt pride he had felt at Claire's rejection, and it was an evil deed he could not undo. He laid the bundle down where Serena might find it if she returned when she was calmer. It would ease his conscience a little, and she might have some use of it in the future.

Hal was lost in his thoughts as he walked away. He did not know that they had been watched; nor did he see the woman who came silently from the trees and picked up the bundle.

Rowena felt the weight of it, guessing that there was money wrapped inside. Serena was foolish to reject what he offered, for she might need it in the future. Life would be hard for her amongst the gypsies now. None of the men would want her because she had given herself to a man who was not one of them. Life on the road was difficult enough for a woman carrying a child if she had a man; without someone to care for her it would be hard indeed.

Rowena's case had been different. Roald had taken her as his woman even though she had born a child to Harry Mortimer, but that was because the wise woman Greta had foretold her son would bring luck to them. Even so, many of the gypsies despised her, had done so from the start. They tolerated her for her son's sake. However, as yet Jared showed no sign of doing anything to benefit the tribe, or her. She had lied to him consistently over the years, hoping that he would claim his fortune from the Mortimer family. There was little chance of his story being believed at the Manor, but perhaps they would give him money to buy his silence. Unfortunately, Jared had brooded on his ill fortune but did nothing to change it.

Opening the bundle, Rowena discovered the purse and counted the twenty gold coins inside. Her eyes gleamed with greed, because she found it hard to manage these days. Roald no longer gave her anything, and she was forced to sell her wares at the fairs they visited. She slipped the purse into the pocket concealed beneath her gown.

She would sell the other things and give some of the money to Serena if she needed it, but she would keep the purse of gold for herself . . .

Serena hurried past Jared as she met him at the edge of the clearing. He was stripped to the waist and was grooming one of the horses, his skin damp with sweat as he worked. He looked up and smiled at her, but she was too distressed to return his greeting and went on, up the steps of her caravan.

Jared frowned as he watched her go. He sensed her misery and was certain he knew the reason for it. She had been foolish to bring Hal Mortimer here, for by doing so, she had become involved with him and was doomed to be hurt. The Mortimers considered themselves too good for the likes of Serena, and Hal would tire of his sport in time. Jared hoped that she had not been foolish enough to lie with him, though he feared she might have.

His anger at the thought of Serena giving herself to his half-brother was not because he was jealous. He did not especially wish to lie with her himself – but he was fond of her, and he cared for her welfare. At one time he had considered asking for her, but then he had realized that he did not want her in that way. The woman he wanted was as unreachable as the stars in the night sky. He had seen her but a few times, spoken to her only once, but he wanted her, wanted her so much that it was like a burning ache in his guts. He had thought at first that she loved his half-brother, and it had made him angry that she should pine for a man who did not love her, but of late he had seen her walking with another man – a stranger.

Jared wondered what his half-brother would think of that. It was said that Claire Mortimer had rejected him, and it was true that she had married another man. Had that hurt Hal Mortimer? Or had his intended marriage been a matter of property only? Jared felt a spurt of unworthy satisfaction at the thought of his half-brother's disappointment. It would

154

do the spoiled heir good to taste the bitterness of losing something he wanted for once. He hoped that Hal had suffered, for his hatred of him was as strong as ever.

In his heart he had accepted that his mother had never been married to his father. If it had been true, he would have found the proof in Oxford. He was a bastard, as indeed was Hal – but *he* was the heir to a wealthy estate and the title, while Jared had nothing but what he earned for himself.

His bitterness at the injustice of it had not abated. He might have been able to forget if they had moved on after the fair as they usually did, but Roald had bid them wait here until he returned, and he had been gone some weeks. Some of the others were growing restive and arguing that they should go, because work was scarce here now that the summer was waning. Jared knew that they looked to him, and would follow him if he chose, but for some reason he lingered.

He finished grooming his horse, and then splashed a bucket filled with cold water from the stream over himself. He would wait one more week for Roald to return, and then he would go. Those who wished to follow him could do so, and the others could stay here.

It was foolish to waste his life in bitterness, and there was no chance that the woman he wanted would ever look at him. He must forget her as he must forget his mother's lies.

Nine

Angelica had been helping to decorate the church with flowers for her father's and Elizabeth's wedding. It had been a happy morning, because several of the young girls from the village had been there and they had laughed together as they worked, burnishing the silver candlesticks that had been replaced on the altar. During the years of the Lord Protector's rule they had been hidden away, but now they had been brought out with all the other treasures that made the old church beautiful.

They were fortunate that no one had damaged the stained glass windows, as had happened in other churches up and down the country. Cromwell himself had destroyed much that was beautiful in the Cathedral in Ely, which had been dedicated and commissioned by the Lady Etheldreda so many centuries before. Lord Mortimer had seen the destruction for himself and thought it sacrilege, and he had taken care to protect their own treasures.

So it was with a smile on her lips that Angelica began the long walk back to her home. She did not mind the walk, for it was a warm day and the lanes smelled fresh and leafy, the peace and solitude of her surroundings wrapping about her like a silk cloak.

She was thinking her own thoughts, which were pleasant enough, and was taken by surprise when the gypsy suddenly came out of the hedgerow to her right and stood in the middle of the narrow lane, blocking her path. He had a long knife in his hand, and a pile of dead twigs and broken branches lay to the side of the lane, as if he had been gathering firewood.

She took a deep breath, for as always he sent a shiver of apprehension down her spine.

'Good morning, sir,' she said, summoning her courage. She would not have him know that she feared him, and her eyes flashed with pride as she looked into his sullen face. 'I pray you, step aside, if you please.'

'And what if I do not please?' Jared asked. A demon was sitting at his shoulder, urging him to take what he so desperately wanted of her. Why should he not have her? She was alone, and in this secluded place there would be none to hear her cries. Why should he not take from her what he suspected Hal had taken from Serena? 'If I ask a toll of you – what will you pay me, Mistress Saunders?'

'I have no money,' Angelica said, angry now. 'Nor should I pay you if I had. You have no right to make such demands of me.'

'I have as much right as any,' Jared said, though he knew that he lied. 'I have the right of any man to take what I want – and I do not ask for money.'

'What then?' she demanded, but as she looked into his eyes and saw the fire there, she knew what he wanted of her and her stomach curled with terror. 'No – I shall not yield to you, no matter what you do, sir. Force me if you will, but they will hang you for it. You must take my life if you want me, for I shall hate you until the day you die.'

'What difference?' he asked advancing on her, his eyes cold and threatening. 'You despise me now. If I choose, I may take what I want and be damned to all of you.'

'Why do you hate me?' she asked, standing her ground, though her mind was telling her to flee while she still had the chance. Pride held her feet and saved her, for had she run, he would have followed and caught her. 'What have I done to you that you should want to hurt me?'

'You have done nothing,' Jared said. It was others who had slighted and cheated him of his rights, and as he looked into her eyes, he knew that his feelings for her were not lust alone. He wanted her, to hold her and touch her, to feel her yielding flesh close to his – but he wanted her warm and willing in his arms. It would gain him nothing to take her by force. The knowledge killed the madness that had heated his lust. 'Go your way then. I'll not harm you,' he said and stood aside.

Angelica walked past him, her heart racing wildly. Was he merely luring her on like a spider with its web waiting to catch her? She half expected that he would grab her when she passed him, but he did not, and she continued to walk steadily, her head high, shoulders straight, until she was round the bend and out of sight. And then, suddenly, her courage broke and she was running, fleeing for her life towards the meadow and her home, which lay beyond it.

It was when she was almost home that Angelica saw Will Chesterford coming towards her, and she ran to him, her chest heaving as she fought for breath. She flung herself at him and he caught her, sensing her distress and her fear.

'What is it, Angelica?' he asked. 'Something has frightened you?'

'A man . . .' She gasped, for her throat hurt and she felt close to fainting. The fear in her mind had gained on her as she ran, reliving the scene and seeing it end another way. 'He blocked my way and he threatened . . . I thought he meant to . . .' She shook her head, her cheeks flushed. 'I cannot say . . .'

'A man threatened you?' Will was angry. He knew that he and Rochester had done things that had earned them an unsavoury reputation, but he had never offered force to a young and innocent girl. 'Who was he? Tell me and I shall see that he pays for it!'

Angelica looked up at him, her foolish fear evaporating as she realized that the danger was over. She was safe, and perhaps much of it had been in her mind. It was true that the gypsy had carried a knife, and had he wished, he might have subjected her to rape or murder – but he had let her go.

'I do not know him,' she lied. She wished that she had not run to him and confessed her story. 'A stranger in these parts. It does not matter. I am safe enough now that you have come.' She smiled up at him, recovered now, her heartbeat returning to its normal steady pace. 'Shall we walk up to the house, sir?'

'Yes, of course,' Will said and smiled at her. He would take her home and then he would speak to her father. If there was a stranger in the village, he must be found and punished for daring to assault a young woman of good family.

'Angelica says that she did not know him,' Will said to Rupert half an hour later. 'She says he is a stranger here – but she was very frightened. He threatened her. She feared rape – and that cannot be allowed to go unchecked. If young girls may not walk unmolested in their own village then someone must be punished.'

Rupert frowned at him, for the charge was serious. 'Are you certain that this man threatened rape?'

'Angelica could not bring herself to say it, but I am certain that was what she meant. She was very frightened, and I think a search should be made for the stranger. Another girl may be attacked if nothing is done.'

'Yes, you are right,' Rupert said. He was reluctant to start a search at this moment, for his wedding was in two days and he had hoped that it would be a happy occasion. 'I shall instruct my people to look for a stranger and to report to me if they discover him.'

'Could you not send for someone – the shire reeve? This man is clearly a criminal and must be hunted out.'

'Do you think it necessary?'

'Angelica was terrified. You must know that she means a great deal to me, Rupert.'

'I had wondered . . .' Rupert smiled, well satisfied with his declaration. 'If you mean to ask for her, my answer will of course be yes. I should be pleased with the match – but I have promised her that she shall not be pushed into marriage, Will. You must make your case with her.'

'I would want it no other way, sir.'

'Then I wish you luck in your quest,' Rupert said. 'As for this other – well, if you wish it, I shall send my agent word that we have a dangerous stranger in the district and ask him to send us someone to deal with it.'

'Good,' Will said, pleased with Rupert's decision, and also with his permission to seek Angelica's consent to a marriage. 'I think we shall all rest easier in our beds if this fellow is caught.'

Robert Goodjohn, shire reeve of St Ives, looked at the list of women suspected of witchery that lay on his desk and frowned. It was all the fault of that damned witchfinder. There had been no peace since he had arrived the previous week and started his devil's work. Several women of the district, decent women for the most part, had been accused by their neighbours, falsely, if Robert's suspicions were right. It was all too easy to use the witchfinder's presence in their town as a way to take out their grudges against women who had upset them.

It was Robert's duty to pass this list to Matthew Hadden so that he could put the accused to the test, and yet he shrank from it. The tests were barbaric, including tossing a woman bound at the hands and feet into a river to see if she sank or swam. If the poor wretch sank she was innocent, but probably dead of drowning before they dragged her out, and if she surfaced then the judges would end by hanging her and then burning her body. And that was just one of the barbaric tortures that the witchfinder was entitled to inflict if he chose.

Robert had once witnessed a burning when he was a young boy. He had been visiting London, and had seen a woman brought out to be hanged. Still partially alive, they tossed her on to a fire. The sight of her shaven head and her white face had lingered in his dreams for months, and sometimes he could still hear her screams and taste the awful stench of burning flesh on his tongue.

He did not want his peaceful town turned upside down by

a frenzy of witch hunting, nor did he wish to see women he knew by name wantonly hanged. Besides, one of the accused was his wife's sister, and that brought the whole thing too close to home. Of course he could scratch her name out and then hand over the list, but he was sure that at least two thirds of the women were innocent. Left to himself, he would simply have dismissed the list as nonsense, but that was dangerous, for he too could be accused of flouting the Bible and might suffer at the hands of zealots.

The loud knocking at his door brought a welcome relief from his thoughts, and he smiled as his housekeeper brought him a letter some minutes later. He glanced at the seal and knew that it came from the agent who acted on behalf of Sir Rupert Saunders, a respectable landowner who had recently opened a wine business in the town.

Breaking the seal, he read the few lines enclosed. Sir Rupert had asked for help in dealing with a dangerous person in their village. He frowned, laying the letter down beside the list of suspected witches, drumming his fingers on the board in front of him, and then he smiled. It seemed that he might solve two problems with one stroke . . .

It was a lovely morning, warm but not hot and looking to be fair all day, which would be ideal for the wedding break-fast. Sir Rupert had ordered an oxen to be slaughtered and roasted whole over a spit in the grounds, also sucking pig, fowls and wood pigeon. Barrels of ale had been brought in for the feast, and the women of the house had been baking since first light.

The people of the village were bidden to the feast, for it was to be a big celebration, the like of which had not been seen in years. Even Claire Mortimer's wedding had been nothing compared to it, for Elizabeth had particularly asked that it should be a feast for the village people rather than a simple private ceremony.

'We are fortunate to live in such a peaceful place,' she had told Rupert. 'I want everyone to share in our happiness. Your mother was loved for her good works, and I would like the tradition to continue.'

Rupert was nothing loath, for his family had always been charitable, and his fortunes had restored the estate and were like to grow over the years because of the wine business he was building both in local towns and London. Despite the recent taxes the King's parliament had brought in to boost his revenues, Rupert's fortunes were flourishing. Of these measures to fill the empty treasury, the poll tax was the most unpopular, but the hearth tax was a close second, and had caused some to block up their chimneys in an effort to escape it.

Rupert had not thought to retrench, for his mind was set on the expansion of his business. He was pleased with the idea that his daughter might marry Will Chesterford, who, through his childless uncle, was heir to an earldom and a great fortune. It would set a seal on his own marriage, and assure the wealth and prosperity of both families. Will had influence at court, and that was always useful, though he had kept to his word to allow Angelica time to make up her mind. Rupert would be sorry if she resisted the match, but he would not force her. His mood was in any case one of goodwill to others, and he was looking forward to his wedding night.

They had not anticipated that event, though Rupert had been tempted more than once, but he respected Elizabeth too much to suggest it, and she had been busy with the care of his father. Fortunately, Sir John seemed a little better, and even the physician had confessed that he was hopeful of a partial recovery. Sir John had begun to sit up in a chair. He had asked to be placed by the window that morning so that he could see some of the festivities from the window of his chamber.

Elizabeth looked beautiful in a gown of cream damask over a green silk petticoat. She wore a lace cap over her hair and a hat of yellow straw trimmed with green ribbons. Around her throat she wore a necklace of topaz and pearls, and matching earrings hung from her lobes.

Rupert was dressed in blue breeches and a darker coat of brocade, Brussels lace frothing at his throat, his stockings of white silk with embroidery and ribbon bows as garters. He wore a sapphire brooch pinned to his coat, and a band of silk across it in the fashion of the court. It was an honour awarded him by the King for services past, and he wore it with pride.

Angelica thought that her father and Elizabeth made a handsome couple. Standing beside Hal as Elizabeth's attendant, she watched them take their vows and smiled to herself. Their happiness was plain for everyone to see, and she was glad that they had found each other at last. The bitterness and sorrow of the past had melted away, and it looked as if their family could now settle to a period of peace and prosperity.

She was sorry that her grandfather was not able to attend the wedding ceremony, but she knew that, against all the odds, he was much better than he had been. He might not have much time left to him, but at least he was not suffering as badly as they had feared. She glanced around the church, seeing all the people who had crammed into it, far more than had been here for Claire's wedding, which had been only for the families.

Hal was standing up with her father as his best man, and Angelica could not help thinking how handsome he looked. She had been surprised when her father had chosen Hal instead of Lord Chesterford or her uncle, but she could not know that the suggestion had come from Elizabeth.

Hal did not glance her way immediately. He seemed to be taking his duties seriously, and she thought that there was a change in him. Had Claire's rejection hurt him so badly? Or was there some other reason for his new mood?

She glanced to her left and saw that Will was sitting at the end of the second pew just behind her uncle. He saw her glance at him and grinned at her, making her heart flutter. He had been paying her more and more attention of late, and she believed that he would make her an offer soon. She

163

did not know what she ought to say to him. She liked him very well, and she thought that he might make her a good husband, and yet her heart was still Hal's. Could she marry another man when she loved Hal?

Hal turned his head to look at her as the bride and groom went up to the high altar to take their vows, and something in his expression seemed to burn her. A flush sprang up in her cheeks. Why was he looking at her so oddly? She wondered about it, dropping her gaze to her tiny, silk-covered Bible as the congregation stood to sing a hymn of praise.

Hal frowned as he saw the flush in her cheeks. He had buried himself in work for his uncle since that unpleasant scene with Serena, for it had played on his conscience, and he had stayed away from Angelica. He was not sure why he had done that, but it was something to do with wanting to be certain of his own mind. This morning, Caroline had told him that she thought there would be another wedding in the family before long. He had not understood her until she explained.

'Rupert has told me in confidence that Lord Chesterford has spoken to him concerning Angelica. Nothing is decided between them, for Rupert says that it must be her choice, but he hopes for a match. Will is the heir to an earldom, and will be very wealthy, it seems. My brother has ambitions, and it will not hurt them to be allied with such a prestigious family.'

'Chesterford is also one of Rochester's wild lot,' Hal muttered, feeling the grinding anger in his stomach. 'She would surely not wed such as he?'

'Oh, I do not think him so bad,' Caroline said. 'His reputation is perhaps worse than the truth, which is that he has been a little wild. However, he will no doubt settle when he marries.'

Hal had said no more. He could not believe that it was happening again. Angelica was going to marry a man who was not worthy of her – but perhaps Caroline had it wrong.

If it was Angelica's choice, nothing was settled, and there was time . . . time for what?

Hal pondered his thoughts, which were strange to him. Why was he angry that Angelica's name should be linked with another man? Why did he feel this pain in his chest, as if he might burst? He had been angry when Claire rejected him, but this was a slow, burning agony so that he felt he was being tortured with hot irons. He frowned at Angelica, because she had smiled at Chesterford. If she was foolish enough to throw herself away on that fool . . . but he was the fool!

Hal suddenly realized that he had been very stupid. He had allowed his childhood dreams to cloud his judgement, believing that it was Claire he wanted for his wife, when all the time the truth was there under his nose. It was Angelica he loved.

The idea was so strange to him that he almost dismissed it, but then he glanced at her once more and felt the need in his loins. He wanted her! He wanted to lie with her, but more than that, he wanted to protect and love her, to wake up with that lovely face on the pillow beside him every morning and know that she belonged to him. Except that she didn't. Angelica was very much her own person. She might show a meek manner to the world, but he knew her, knew her rebellious spirit, her courage and her loyalty. And he loved her more than he had thought possible.

He had never truly known what it was to love before. Hal realized it with a spurt of surprise. He was fond of Caroline and Nicolas, and of Claire too, but this feeling was new to him. Always, he had taken the love of others as homage due to him; he was the important one, his wishes paramount. The heir to Thornberry and adored by all his people . . . but now he saw that he was nothing unless Angelica loved him. It was a blinding revelation that seemed to sweep the floor from beneath his feet, leaving him feeling uncertain and oddly humble.

Had he left it too late to win her? Hal felt such panic that he was hard put to it not to turn to her now and scoop her up. He wanted to carry her off so that they could be alone, so that he could tell her of his love and beg her to look on him kindly. Yet why should she? He knew that he had taunted and teased her unmercifully when they were children. Why had he done that? Was it because he had sensed her power over him even then, that in his fear of loving her he had tried to drive her away?

Yes, he feared loving her. Hal understood himself as never before. To love someone was to become vulnerable, to have a weakness that might lay him low, for he could not bear to think of what he might be if she refused him. Pray God that she would look at him and smile in a moment.

Angelica looked at Hal as she followed her father and his new wife to the vestry to watch them sign their names. He ventured a smile, and she smiled back as they added their names as witnesses of the marriage. And then in a moment they were back in the church, the bells ringing out as the bride and groom walked out into the sunshine, their family and friends coming behind to shower them with rose petals and dried flower heads.

'Elizabeth looked lovely, didn't she?' Angelica said to him, feeling happy. She looked so beautiful then that Hal's stomach clenched. 'I am so glad for them, Hal. It is good to see them together after so many years.'

'You do not mind that they have loved each other for years?'

'Why should I?' Angelica asked. 'I know that my mother and father were not happy in their marriage – so why should I grudge them their happiness now? I am sad that my mother ran away from my father, and that she died tragically, but I am not sorry that Elizabeth and Father are happy. I should be selfish indeed if I begrudged them that, should I not?'

'You have a loving, forgiving nature,' Hal replied, his eyes intent on her face. 'I hope that your family appreciate you.'

'I am not as unselfish as you paint me,' Angelica said, the

lilt of laughter in her voice. 'If you could see into my mind you would know that I sometimes have bad thoughts.'

Hal looked at her and realized that she was teasing him, a wicked gleam in her eyes. He chuckled deep in his throat, for this was new. In the past Angelica had shown him her stubborn, angry side more than any other, and he had not known that she could be so delightful.

'Oh, I dare say they are very wicked,' he replied in like manner. 'Did you dare to read a book other than the Bible on Sunday – or perhaps you worked at your embroidery?'

'Oh, those times are over,' she said with a little shrug. 'Grandmama was never as strict as she ought to have been over things like that – it was staying out later than she told me or playing with boys from the village. She was very cross once when she caught me climbing trees with the black-smith's boy.'

'You did that?' Hal arched his brows, for he had not known of her adventures. He was learning so much of her that he had not suspected, and each new revelation enchanted him, snaring him deeper into her net. 'I hope she took a cane to you, for you deserved it.' He was teasing her but when he saw her eyes darken he apologized. 'No, did she? Forgive me, Angelica, I did not mean it. I would not have wished you punished like that for the world.'

'You had been unkind to me,' Angelica said looking thoughtful. 'I ran home because I was near to tears, and on the way I met Master Laughton's son. He had some sticky toffee his mother had made that day for the church fete, and he gave me a piece of it. He suggested that he climb the tree and throw me down an apple, but I went up too and we sat in the tree until my grandfather saw us and called us down. Sir John did not punish me himself, but he told me that I was a wicked girl, and Grandmother beat me for behaving like a village slut. She said that if I was not careful everyone would think I was a wanton, and I would never marry.'

'That was unkind of her,' Hal said. 'I did not know you were treated so harshly.' He frowned as a thought occurred to him. 'Is that why you refused to join in some of the games I suggested when we were children?'

'If I tore my gown I was punished,' Angelica said. 'A tear meant a beating, a stain resulted in no supper. You thought I was a silly baby, but I dare not go home with marks on my gown too often. It was easier to let you mock me than go home and face my grandmother's anger.'

'I was not aware of what you had to endure. It was cruel of me to mock you so often,' Hal said. 'I am sorry if I have hurt you, Angelica.'

'I forgave you long ago,' she said carelessly. 'Oh, look, the carriages are leaving. We must go, or we shall get left behind . . .'

Hal watched as she ran to get into the carriage taking Caroline and Nicolas back to the house. He fell behind, deciding that he would walk. It was not that far, and he needed to be alone with his thoughts for a while. He followed the crowd that was making en masse for the Saunders's home. As he walked through the lynch gate into the lane outside the churchyard, he saw a man standing to one side watching the people as they passed him.

He was a tall dark fellow with a shapeless hat pulled down over his face, his long greasy hair straggling at his collar. His face was pock-marked and scarred, and he looked an ugly brute. Hal saw one or two of the villagers glance at him as they passed, for he was clearly a stranger. However, their minds were on the feasting to be had that day, and even his sombre presence was not enough to take the smiles from their faces.

Hal decided to ignore him, for he was surely merely passing through. But he was not the only person to notice the man. Following on a little later, Will Chesterford saw the stranger and his gaze narrowed. A rough looking character – could he be the one who had assaulted Angelica? He hesitated for a moment, then went over to him.

'You, fellow,' he challenged. 'Who are you and what do you here?'

The stranger looked at him, recognizing his quality. He held back the surly retort any other would have drawn from him, and touched his head, pretending to a modesty he did not feel.

'I am Matthew Hadden, sir. I was sent here by the shire reeve Robert Goodjohn of St Ives in answer to Sir Rupert Saunders's request for help in dealing with a dangerous stranger.'

'Ah, yes,' Will said, remembering that he had urged Rupert to it. He was sorry now, for he knew the man's name and did not like him or any of his ilk. Hadden came from Puritan stock, and his trade was a foul one. 'Sir Rupert will not want to see you today. It is his wedding.'

'Aye, sir. I have been told. Fear not, I shall not trouble him until I have proof, though you may tell him that I am here. I shall do my work and present the evidence, but already I know that I am needed here. I feel it in my water. There are witches here, and it shall be my work to pull them from their hiding places and put them to the test.'

'Witches? In this peaceful place?' Will doubted it, but he was not minded to bandy words with this man. 'Well, we shall see. I bid you good day, sir.'

Matthew Hadden watched him walk away, directing a baleful stare at his retreating back. He did not like men of that kind, rich, idle, wasteful men who allowed the black arts to continue about them and did nothing to stamp out the evil. He would have liked to interrogate some of the men who had stared at him the way this one had, but he knew his limits. He chose defenceless women, women who had no powerful friends to defend them, and he proved them guilty. Sometimes they died before he could have them tried and brought to the gallows, and that was a sorry thing, for there was nothing like a good hanging.

He could smell the presence of witches in this part of the country and it excited him, making him dribble at the thought of all the pleasure to come.

*   *   *

169

Hal watched as Angelica danced with Lord Chesterford. The man had court manners, he noticed, and was an elegant figure as he led his partner through the intricate steps. Hal could not deny that they looked well together. As yet he had not asked Angelica to dance with him, and now, seeing the way she laughed up at her partner, he was reluctant to do so. Hal danced well enough, but he knew he was no match for Chesterford.

He turned aside, thinking that he had seen sufficient, but even as he walked purposefully towards the house, Elizabeth came up to him.

'You are not leaving already, Hal?'

'Not without saying goodbye to you, Elizabeth.' He gave her a wry smile.

'But without dancing at least once with Angelica?' Elizabeth arched her brows. 'Do you not think she will be hurt by your neglect? You could surely spare her a few minutes to dance with her?'

'She seems to have partners aplenty.' He could not quite keep the resentment from his tone, but did not realize that he had betrayed himself.

'Yes, she is popular – but perhaps she would wish to dance with you above most others, Hal Mortimer.'

'I cannot match Chesterford. I have not his fine court manners.'

'Faint heart never won fair lady,' Elizabeth said, a twinkle of mischief in her eyes. 'I do not think you will tread upon her toes too much. Listen, the music ends. Go to her now and secure her for the next dance. Unless you have no wish for her company?' She arched her brows at him, her look one of mischief.

Hal grimaced. Elizabeth saw too much. However, he took her advice, approaching Angelica as Chesterford led her from the floor.

'Your pardon, sir, but I would dance with Angelica if she will have me as her partner.' He bowed to her, smiling in a way that made her heart race. 'Cousin, will you dance?'

'Yes, thank you, Hal,' she said, turning to Chesterford with a smile of apology before she took his outstretched hand. 'It was pleasurable to dance with you, sir. Forgive me now.' She let Hal lead her into the throng of dancers. It was a country jig of the kind much enjoyed by the villagers, many of whom were already forming their own circles. Hal took her into a circle that was made up of people from the estate, grinning at her as the dance began.

It was a very different affair to the one she had just performed so gracefully with Chesterford. The music was fast and furious, the fiddler playing his heart out as the couples twirled and spun, joining hands with the others of their circle, changing partners as they cross-handed one to the other and came back to their own partner at last. By the time it was finished, Angelica was flushed and out of breath; she made no protest as Hal stood with his arm about her waist.

'Thank you, that was merry sport, Hal,' she said smiling at him. 'I enjoyed myself.'

'I am no dancer,' he said, his gaze narrowing, 'but I can manage a country dance, I think.'

'You dance as well as most.'

'I do not have Lord Chesterford's grace and skill – but then I have not been used to court manners.'

Something in his tone struck Angelica as odd. Was Hal jealous? She had once hoped to use Lord Chesterford to provoke him, but she had forgotten that as she came to know and like Will.

'Still, you dance as well as most. Lord Chesterford is the exception. As you say, he has learned his manners at court, both here and in France.' She gazed up at him, a challenge in her eyes. 'Will and my father knew each other in France. Will was too young to fight in the war – but he was fifteen years of age and with His Majesty when they were defeated at Worcester.'

'He must be more than ten years your senior,' Hal said frowning at her.

'Yes, that is true,' Angelica admitted. 'At first I did not

like him, but I have discovered that he is good company, and not as wicked as his reputation paints him. He is well read and shares my interest in poetry and music.'

'Then it is true – you are thinking of marrying him?'

'I might,' Angelica said looking up at him, her eyes clear and honest. 'Unless something – or someone – causes me to change my mind.' She gave him a sweet, slaying smile that robbed him of the power of speech. 'Excuse me, Hal. I believe Elizabeth needs me.'

Hal watched as she crossed the room to her stepmother's side. His eyes held a brooding expression, a smoulder of anger in their depths. What was he supposed to make of that? Was he meant to declare himself – and if he did, what might he expect from her? Would she laugh in his face, take her revenge for all the unkind words he had given her in the past, or would she melt in his arms? The thought of her melting in his arms was so powerful that he felt it like a grinding ache in his groin.

What kind of a fool was he that he had only understood his own feelings when it was perhaps already too late?

Caroline woke with a start. She was shivering, her body wet with sweat as she rose and slipped on a warm shawl, going over to the window to gaze out. It was very dark outside, for the moon had been chased from the sky but dawn had not yet come. Her dream had been vivid and she could still feel the horror of it. Something bad was going to happen, was already happening – something that could destroy their peaceful lives.

'What troubles you, my love?' Nicolas was aware that she had risen. He threw back the covers and came to her, gazing at her face anxiously. 'You are not ill?'

'No, it was merely a dream,' she told him, 'but it does trouble me. I have a feeling – a premonition that tragedy is lurking at our heels. I sense it, Nicolas. There is an evil presence nearby, and it frightens me.'

'Hush, Caroline,' Nicolas said putting his arms about her,

holding her close, feeling her tremble. 'You ate too much supper last night. It was merely a nightmare.'

'No, Nicolas.' She drew back from him, eyes wide and anxious as she gazed up at him. 'I have had the dream before, but this time it was much worse. Two men fought in the meadow, and at the end one lay bleeding . . . I fear, dying.' She shuddered, for in her dream she had seen Hal's face, and she believed that it was he who lay injured.

'It was just a bad dream, my love.'

'I think that it is something else – a premonition. But there was more, Nicolas. I feel that evil has come to our village – a man who will make trouble for us all. I saw his face in the dream and it frightened me, for there was such malice in him.'

'No one can harm us,' Nicolas told her holding her closer in his embrace. 'The bad times are gone, Caroline. King Charles is a tolerant man, and popular despite the taxes, and what some call his lack of morals. We no longer live under a dark shadow. I am lord here and there is none to challenge me. I do not fear any man, and nor should you. We have good friends, both here and at court, and there is no reason for you to have these dreams.'

'Perhaps not,' Caroline said. She allowed Nicolas to draw her back to their bed. He had never understood that her dreams were more than nightmares. Too many times she had seen things . . . things that subsequently came true. Long ago, the old gypsy woman Greta had told her that she had the gift of sight, and that it would grow with the years, and she had found that it was true. She seldom spoke of her dreams to anyone, and would not have told Nicolas if she had not felt so anxious. She was certain that terrible things were going to happen very soon, and she felt powerless to stop them. And yet she allowed her husband to kiss her and soothe her fears with his loving, for she did not want to believe what she had seen.

She had had these dreams so many times. Perhaps Nicolas was right and it was simply that she had eaten too much rich

Anne Herries

food at the wedding feast, but in her heart she did not believe it. Something had changed, a sinister presence that brooded in the shadows and would be the cause of whatever was to happen.

Caroline prayed that she was wrong, and asked for God's forgiveness. Perhaps it was a sin to look into the future, and she was being punished for her presumption, and yet she had never asked for the gift. The dreams frightened her and she would have been happier without them, but too often they had heralded something bad . . .

Ten

Rowena was sitting by her fire muttering to herself when Serena came to her. She was feeling cold despite the warmth of the day, and her bones ached. Of late she had begun to feel older, weary of her life and of the travelling that must begin again soon. She sensed a dark shadow hovering at her shoulder, and fear clutched at her belly. She had not felt like this since the villagers had hunted her down, accusing her of murdering Richard Woodville. She had escaped them then because Roald had rescued her, but it had taken her some years to forget the feeling of terror that had hung over her as she hid in the woods and waited for certain death.

'Are you ill?' Serena asked. Rowena was often sullen, but she seemed to be shivering and there was something brooding about her manner.

'Nay, not ill,' Rowena replied. She turned her gaze on Serena, narrowing it as the girl hesitated. 'I am well enough. Speak out, for I know you want something.'

'I need one of your potions,' Serena said. 'I am with child and I do not wish to give it birth.'

'You lay with the lord's son and he threw your gift away as if it were naught,' Rowena said, a note of bitterness in her voice. 'Why did you not listen to me when I told you that he was no good for you?'

'He made me a promise,' Serena said, and her face was hard, for she had wept too many tears in private and her love had turned to hatred. 'He thought that he could buy me with his gifts . . .' She looked at the ring on her finger, which she had tried to remove several times. 'This ring was his promise to me. I believed he loved me, that it was a promise in our way.'

'Promises mean nothing to such as he,' Rowena said. 'I learned that the hard way. You knew my story. You should have known that he was not to be trusted.'

'Yes, perhaps I should,' Serena said. 'But he smiled at me and I loved him – and now I hate him and would be free of his child.'

'Yes, that is the best way,' Rowena agreed. 'My mother told me to get rid of it when I was carrying Harry Mortimer's seed; I ignored her, for I thought that my child would gain me a fortune, but he brought me nothing. Without a child I might have found work and lived well in London. I was beautiful then and men desired me. Had I found a rich protector I should not be here now . . .' She shuddered, for the evil was hovering near. It hung over her like a black cloud, and she sensed that death was waiting.

'I shall make you a potion,' she said, 'but in return you must help me. I have a cure that I promised to a woman in the village, but I do not wish to go there. Take it for me and I shall give you what you want.'

'Yes, that is a fair trade,' Serena said. 'Give me your potion and tell me who it is for, and I shall take it for you.'

Rowena got to her feet. She was almost hesitant to give the vial to Serena, though she had asked for the favour. Something malevolent waited in the village. Rowena feared it. She wished that Roald would return so that they could go. Usually they only stayed a couple of weeks or so wherever they went. They had been here too long, and Rowena sensed that they might have outstayed their welcome.

'There be witches in the village,' Mistress Bacon told her daughter when she returned home from the cobbler's that morning. 'Everyone be talking of it – and they say a witchfinder has come to seek them out and put them to the test.'

'A witchfinder.' Her daughter Rose looked at her and shivered. Talk of witches and spells had been rife these past few days, and it was frightening, for many an innocent woman had been taken as a witch. 'Oh, Ma . . .' She hesitated as she recalled the love potion she had ordered from the gypsy woman a day or so earlier. 'Do you think . . .'

'What is it, Rose?' Mistress Bacon's eyes narrowed. 'What are you hiding from me, girl? Out with it! These are dangerous times.' She moved away to rescue a pot from boiling over on the fire. 'If you've brought trouble on us . . .' She was interrupted by a knock at their door. Rose started guiltily, making her suspicious. 'And who is that? No, I'll answer it!' She went to the door, wrenching it open, Rose shivering and cowering behind her. As she saw the young gypsy girl with a basket on her arm, her mouth thinned. In these times it was foolish to speak with such as gypsies. 'Be off with you! You are not wanted here.'

'But I am delivering . . .' Serena found the door slammed in her face, and turned away. Perhaps she had come to the wrong cottage, and yet Rowena had told her it was two doors from the forge. She hesitated for a moment as she wondered if she should walk a little further into the village, but then she saw that two women were staring at her in an unfriendly manner. One of them bent down and scooped up a handful of dung from the road, flinging it at her.

'Be off with you, gypsy!' the woman cried. 'And take your potions with you. Goodwife Hensby died after taking one of your cures. You and that other one be witches!'

'Be off with you if you know what is good for you,' the other woman cried. 'Witches you be and *he* will find you out if you stay.'

Serena saw the hatred and anger in their eyes and turned away. Fear was curling in her stomach, but she walked unhurriedly, refusing to show her terror to these women – one of whom had willing bought cures from them only the week before.

She did not know who Goodwife Hensby was or if she

had died after taking one of Rowena's potions, but she knew that the mood of the people had turned against them. Once she had left the village, she began to walk faster. She must speak with Rowena and the others, for if there was talk of witches it was the gypsies who would be blamed first . . .

'I have come to you, sir,' Goodwife Bacon said later that day, 'because I believe I know where be the witches you seek. There be two of them – one older that casts the spells and makes potions, and the younger, who sells them for her.'

Matthew Hadden's eyes gleamed. He had known he was right from the moment he arrived, though at first there had been none willing to raise the finger in accusation. But he had known, for he could smell the foul stink of them; it was unmistakable, and it excited him.

'Tell me everything,' he said. 'Be not afraid, woman, for those that point others out shall be blessed for their good work. Tell me where I may find these witches and you shall be rewarded.'

Mistress Bacon's eyes gleamed when she saw the silver coin in his hand. Her husband earned little enough to keep them, and they had no son, only a daughter. Rose was but thirteen as yet and foolish, but she had hopes of finding her a husband to take the girl off their hands. The knowledge that Rose had sought a love potion from the gypsy had angered her, for the lad in question was no husband for Rose. It was in her mother's mind that a certain farmer might be brought to ask for her if he was encouraged, but not if she was carrying another's brat in her belly. So she had scolded the girl until she wept and sat sullen in the corner, refusing to speak to her mother, and now she poured her tale of love potions and cures into the witchfinder's eager ears, leaving the best bit until the end.

'And it is known that she is evil, sir,' she continued, her tongue running faster than she could control. 'For Mistress Hensby recognized her as Rowena Greenslade, born of this parish and a witch's daughter – and it was proved during the war that she had murdered a good man, one Master Woodville. The villagers hunted her, but she was not to be found in the woods or the village, and how could that have been, sir, answer me that?'

'It could not – unless she was a witch and used her evil powers to hide herself,' he said. His eyes gleamed and his tongue slid over his lips as he thought of the pleasure to come. There would be none to speak up for these women, for gypsies were universally despised and often hated. It would be easy to have his sway here. 'Now, tell me where I may find these witches?'

'We should leave,' Serena told Rowena. 'They flung dung at me from the road and cursed me, accused us of being witches – and they said that Goodwife Hensby had died from taking one of your potions.'

'No, that is a lie,' Rowena said but the fear was in her eyes. 'What I gave her was harmless, something to ease her pain. She had a lump in her stomach, and I have seen such things before; the victim of such an illness always dies.'

'Then you should not have sold her anything,' Serena said. 'They are blaming you – both of us – for bringing death to them, and there is more.' She hesitated trying to put her feelings into words. 'I sensed something in the manner of the people. There is evil and hatred there . . .'

'Yes, I have felt it,' Rowena agreed, and the colour drained from her face. She looked grey as she went into her caravan and brought back a small vial. 'This is for you as I promised. It is not your fault that you could not deliver the potion. I should not have sent you. I knew that something was wrong.'

'Thank you.' Serena took the potion from her. 'Will you speak to Jared? We linger here waiting for Roald and he may never return. It should be for Jared to lead us now.'

'Yes, you are right,' Rowena said. 'I shall speak to him in a moment.'

She turned back into her own caravan. She was trembling from head to toe, and she needed some ale to steady her nerves before she approached Jared. The fear that had been building in her mind these past days was stronger now, and she sensed that death hovered nearby. She had defeated death once before, but Roald had helped her then. He no longer cared for her, and Jared was not like him. Her poisoned words had done their work too well, for her son was eaten up with bitterness and cared for no one. She wished that her former lover was with them, but she had felt for some days that he would not return. Perhaps he had met with an accident. It was unlike him not to send them word.

She sat on a little stool, clutching the jug of strong ale to her breast and muttering to herself. She was afraid of what was waiting for her, but she did not know what to do. This evil thing that hovered near her might follow wherever she went.

Serena took the potion to her own caravan. She sat on the steps and contemplated it for a moment. Rowena had claimed that her potion had not harmed the village woman, but had she lied? Would she die if she swallowed this stuff? She pulled the stopper and sniffed, drawing her head back in disgust. It smelled awful and would taste worse – and yet did it matter if she died? It might be the best thing for her. She had no chance of making a good life here amongst her people, for she had seen them look at her, and she knew that once she began to show her condition they would despise her.

She lifted the vial to her lips, but even as she did so she heard a shout and stayed her hand as Jared came striding towards her. Something made her wait as he came up to her, and then, as he knocked the vial from her hand it was too late. The dark liquid was spilling on to the earth and disappearing.

'Why did you do that?' she asked.

'Because I know what it was for,' Jared said. 'You got it from my mother, didn't you?'

'She did not tell you?'

'No, but I have seen her make these things before, and I

saw you with her earlier. It was a vile potion to make you lose the child. Have you no sense at all, girl? It is bad enough that you carry the child, but you make your sin worse by taking a life – and it might have taken yours as well.'

'Rowena said it would not harm me.'

'My mother would not tell you that it might kill you,' he said angrily. 'She dabbles with these things, but she does not truly understand them. Her mother was a wise woman and she showed Rowena some of her potions, but she has experimented with others, and they are dangerous. I believe that they may as like kill as cure.'

Serena turned white. 'Then it is true what they say in the village . . . a woman died after taking one of her cures . . .'

'What are you saying?' Jared gave her a hard look. 'You had best tell me, Serena. Where did you hear this?'

'In the village . . .' Serena explained about taking the love potion to a house in the village. 'She slammed the door in my face and then a woman threw dung at me in the street. She said that we were witches and told me to leave this place.'

'It is dangerous to stay now that these whispers have started,' Jared said. 'I have heard that a witchfinder has come to the village, and that means you could be taken and put to the test.'

Serena shivered, feeling cold and frightened. 'What should we do?' she asked. 'Roald told us to wait for him . . .'

'Roald has been gone too long,' Jared said. 'We shall leave today, as soon as everyone is ready. You must spread the word, Serena. You, Rowena and I shall leave this place. Those who wish to come with us may, and those who prefer to wait for Roald must do so.'

'Where are you going?' Serena asked as he turned and started to stride away. 'We need you to lead us, Jared.'

He turned to look at her, his face a mask she was unable to read. 'I shall return and I shall care for you, Serena. Your child shall be mine, and any that dare to look ill at you will answer to me. Do as I tell you now and all will be well.'

'But where are you going?'

'There is some business I must finish, business that should have been settled before this.'

Jared walked away from her, his expression one of grim determination. He had a score to settle with his half-brother, and then he would shake the dust of this place from his feet for good.

Hal mounted his horse, leaving Hillgrove and turning towards the village. He had been told that Angelica had gone visiting the sick with Elizabeth, and he hoped to meet them on their return. He had thought long and hard about his feelings for her, and reached a decision. He would ask her if she would marry him and take the consequences. If she would not have him . . . He reined in his horse as the man stepped out into the lane before him, staring down at him angrily.

'Stand aside, man. You are impeding my way.'

'That was my intention, brother,' Jared said, his dark eyes glinting with anger. 'We have a score to settle, you and I.'

'Have I not told you that your claims are nonsense?'

'This has nothing to do with our father or the estate,' Jared said. 'You seduced Serena and now she carries your child. She wanted to rid herself of it, and would have had I not stopped her. She might have taken her own life too, and I think she would not have cared. You have broken her heart, Hal Mortimer, and you must answer for it.'

Hal stared down at him, angry at this accusation, which he could not deny. He might excuse it in his own mind, but he knew his guilt, and he would not lie, especially to this man.

'What was she to you? Not your woman,' he said as he dismounted, tethering his horse to a branch where the lane widened and it would come to no harm.

'She is one of my people, and as a sister to me,' Jared replied. 'You owe me for what you have done to her.'

'Come take your dues then,' Hal invited, for he had always known that this fight must happen one day. 'But do not think you will trick me as you did before. I have learned a few things since the last time.'

'We cannot fight here,' Jared said, looking about him. 'Come into the meadow.'

He climbed over the stile, and Hal followed. The grass had begun to grow long again, and there were sheep grazing at the far end. It was such a peaceful scene that it seemed foolish to fight, and yet as he looked at his half-brother, he saw that the hatred was strong and would not be denied.

They began to circle one another warily. There was no ringmaster to call their fight, and it would not be a matter of rules and falls, but a grudge match that would end with one or the other unable to continue. Grunting, Jared leapt at him and brought him to the ground. For some minutes they were locked together as they rolled over and over, testing their strength and using whatever means they could to subdue the other. Punches, kicking, even biting were not barred and it was a vicious struggle. Finally, Jared brought a knee up sharply into Hal's groin, and for a moment it paralysed him.

Jared got to his feet, backing off to eye him warily, for he had received a few bruises to his face and neck where Hal's hands had seemed to squeeze the very breath from him. Then they were at it again, tussling, arms locked about each other in a more natural wrestling hold, which Hal managed to break at the last, catching Jared by his hair and forcing his head back until he yelled out. Then they joined again, each throwing the other several times, their breath becoming harsh and difficult as the struggle went on and on. Both were young, strong men and equally determined to win, Jared because he wished to teach his half-brother a lesson, and Hal because he wished an end to this feud.

In the end, it was Hal who had his revenge for his defeat at the fair. As they were locked in a seeming stalemate, he got his leg round to the back of Jared's and brought it up sharply, taking him off balance and causing him to stumble. In an instant, Hal had him over on his back and flung himself on top of him. Jared lay beneath him, winded and stunned,

183

for he had hit his head against a large stone hidden in the grass. Seeing that his half-brother could not rise, Hal got to his feet and stood over him, wiping his mouth where it had been cut earlier in their struggle.

'You are beaten, brother,' he said. 'Come, take my hand, rise and let us forget this quarrel. I will admit that I wronged the girl. I gave her money, but if you think it was not enough, I shall give you more.'

Jared pushed his hand away. He knew that his half-brother had defeated him with the same trick he had used on him at the fair, and had it been anyone else he would have taken his hand and laughed, for they had both forgotten the rules. It had been a good fight, but he could not forget that Hal was the heir and he a despised gypsy, nor that his brother had ruined an innocent girl.

He struggled to his feet, staring at him angrily. 'You have beaten me this time. I give you best – but it does not end here.'

'Do not be a fool,' Hal said. 'I will make recompense to the girl – and to you, too. If Lord Mortimer believes your story, I shall ask that you be given some land here.'

'Keep your land and your promises,' Jared snarled. 'I curse you and yours, for you bring nothing but sorrow to those you touch.'

He turned and walked away, leaving Hal to stand staring after him. He was feeling chilled, the sense of his victory as bitter ashes in his mouth. It was true that he had wronged Serena, and nothing he could do would change that.

He found his horse and mounted it, turning it homeward. He must wait for another day to speak to Angelica.

'It was good of you to come, my lady,' Widow Hayes said to Elizabeth as she looked up to her from her mattress of straw where she had lain for some many days now, unable to move for the crippling ague that plagued her. 'I do not know what I should have done without you these past weeks – but be careful what you do or say. Fear stalks our village, and *he* will have his dues in flesh, one way or the other.'

'What do you mean, mistress?' Angelica asked for she could see that the widow was anxious. 'Do you speak of God's justice?'

'Nay, lass.' The widow smiled at her, for she was a pretty girl and as kind as her stepmother. 'It is that man – the witchfinder. Matthew Hadden, he calls himself. He is evil, a man who takes pleasure in torture.'

'A witchfinder?' Elizabeth looked at her in alarm. 'Yes, I think I have heard that name before. There was a trial when I lived in London . . .'

'And a hanging,' Angelica said, remembering that awful moment. 'I heard it spoken of at court – I am sure it was the same man. I think His Majesty did not approve of such things, but the woman was proved to be a witch who had taken a man's life, and it was the church courts that ordered her death.' The Act of Free and General Pardon had deliberately left open the question of witches and their punishment. To use witchcraft was to desert the teachings of the Bible, and though some believed that there was no truth in talk of witches, it was thought prudent to leave scope for their trial and execution.

'Aye, Hadden has been the scourge of many a poor woman,' Widow Hayes said. 'I am thankful that I am tied to my bed, for if he lighted eyes upon me I should be taken. It is always the old and helpless that he preys on, those who have none to protect them, but they say it is the gypsies who have brought ill luck to the village and they speak of arresting them.'

'Arresting who?' Angelica asked for she was puzzled. 'What have they done that has brought ill luck to any here?'

'All manner of things,' the widow said. 'Goodwife Hensby died after she drank a potion one of them sold her – and Mistress Bacon says that the young one put a spell on her daughter. She says she drove her from the door, but the girl sits in a trance and will do nothing for her keep. And then there is Master Brook's cow that took sick and died . . .'

'Can any of this be true?' Angelica said, looking at

185

Elizabeth. 'Surely it is all tales? Goodwife Hensby died of the wasting sickness. She had been ill a long time.'

'This is what happens when a witchfinder comes,' Elizabeth said and crossed herself. 'Widow Hayes is right, my love. We must be careful. Even we might be accused of witchcraft, though what we bring is mostly gifts of food and drink – but I have given simple cures to some villagers, and I think I shall not come again for a while.'

'You'd best get home as soon as you can,' the widow told her. 'You are a stranger to the village, though wed to Sir Rupert, and now that folk have started to see witches everywhere you could be named.'

'Elizabeth!' Angelica looked at her fearfully. 'We must go home and tell Father what is happening here. He will do something to stop this wickedness before it goes too far.'

'Yes, you are right,' Elizabeth said and looked at the widow. 'Take care of yourself, my friend. If I were you, I should keep to my bed until this is over.'

'Aye, I will that,' the widow said and gave her a toothless smile. 'Take care, my lady. I shall do well enough now. Come not here until the evil shadow has moved on.'

Elizabeth nodded her head, for she knew that no woman was truly safe from the witchfinder. It was unlikely she would be accused, for she had good friends and her husband was a powerful man – but it was best to be careful. Superstition and malice together were a powerful force, and had caused much ill feeling before this. She would not come to the village again for a while.

'You must do something, Rupert,' Elizabeth told him when he came in later that day. 'The villagers are shadowed by fear, and the talk of witches is everywhere. We even had some look at us askance when we left Widow Hayes' cottage.'

'If that wretch dares to look at you, I shall make him sorry he ever came here,' Rupert said with a frown. 'Do not fear, Elizabeth. Hadden will not dare to point the finger at you

186

or my daughter. Men like him are cowards at heart, and he knows that I am too powerful.'

'But he will do untold harm to others,' Elizabeth said, still uneasy. 'Why should he have come here? Did someone send for him?'

Rupert frowned and did not answer her at once. He had gone to meet the man after Will told him that he was in the village, and he did not like him. Knowing that he had come in answer to his request for help to the shire reeve weighed on his conscience, for he knew that such men brought only trouble and sorrow.

'I asked the shire reeve for help and he sent Hadden,' Rupert admitted at last. 'I thought he would send one of his men to make inquiries for a stranger who had caused some violence – but he sent the witchfinder. I think he wanted to move him on, and it is difficult to get rid of that kind. He has the backing of the church, more's the pity, and some would say his work is needed to root out evil.'

'I think him the evil one,' Elizabeth said. 'Most women taken as witches are innocent, Rupert. They are good women who make simple things to help others, and it is wrong that they can be falsely accused and have no redress.'

'I agree with you,' Rupert said, 'but we all have to be careful when dealing with such men. It is unusual for a man to be taken for witchcraft, but it can happen. They will say he has been bewitched and that the witch has taken over his soul. If the church believes that he is guilty, he may be arrested and tortured to drive out the devil – while the witch is hanged. Yet to speak out against it is to deny the Bible, and few dare that, I think.'

'But he would not dare to point his finger at you.'

'No, perhaps not,' Rupert agreed. 'We must hope that he moves on soon, and that no witches are marked out by him.'

'Yes . . .' Elizabeth frowned, for she had expected more from him. She could not know that he had heard whispers about her and was thinking only of protecting her. 'Can you not do anything to rid us of him, Rupert?'

'I shall try to persuade him that he is needed more else-where,' Rupert said. 'But perhaps he will tire of his search here, which must be fruitless, for we have been too peaceful to be harbouring witches in our midst.'

'We were peaceful,' Elizabeth said, 'but I think the peace has gone, and I fear that evil will happen here if he is not stopped.'

'You and Angelica must not go far alone,' Rupert said. 'I think he dare not point at any of us, but we shall not tempt him.'

Elizabeth had to be satisfied, though she could not help wishing that she had more power. A woman must accept her husband's bidding, and if Rupert did not wish to move against Matthew Hadden, there was little more she could say or do – but she would speak to Caroline when she saw her, and ask her if Nicolas could do something.

Serena sat staring into the fire. Jared had promised to return soon and the others were growing restless. Rowena had been drinking throughout the day and sullenly refused to speak or make preparation to move on. It was as if she had fallen into some kind of a stupor and could not be brought to realize the danger they were in.

'Leave me alone,' she said when Serena tried to rouse her to pack her belongings. 'I shall wait for Roald. He will protect us . . . that worthless son of mine does nothing but scowl and fight.'

When Jared did not return by morning, the others muttered amongst themselves, casting sullen looks in Serena's direc-tion. One of them, stronger than most, came to her at last and demanded to know why Jared had not kept his word to return.

'I do not know,' she said. 'I am sorry, Miguel. He told me he would return soon and to make ready, but I do not know where he is now.'

'We are of one mind,' Miguel said. 'There is an autumn fair in Huntingdon, and if we go now we shall be there in time. We are for leaving – do you come with us?'

'I must wait for Jared,' Serena told him. She had never liked him or the way he looked at her. He was a large man, fat and ugly, his hair greasy as it straggled about his neck. His last woman had died after giving birth to their sixth child, and she knew he was looking for someone to take her place. Most of the women were afraid of him, for he was violent, especially when in drink. She shuddered inwardly as she saw a gleam in his eyes, and knew that he was considering her as a replacement to care for his brood. 'He told me he would come and I must wait.'

'Please yourself,' Miguel said with a shrug of his shoulders. 'You know where we go if you wish to follow.'

Serena sat on the steps of her caravan and watched as the gypsies began to leave, each caravan following the other without so much as a backward look. She felt that they had abandoned her and Rowena, and while she understood why they wished to go, it made her feel unwanted and unloved. She knew in her heart that it would always be this way in the future, for the man she had taken to herself was not of the tribe, and they despised her.

Where was Jared and why had he not come back as he'd promised? She looked across to where Rowena sat, lost in a drunken stupor, rocking herself and muttering words that she could not hear.

The horses were restless. They had been disturbed by the departure of the others, and, Serena realized now, they had not been watered since the previous morning.

She went to fetch the bucket Jared normally used, setting off through the wood to the stream. It was unfair that the horses should suffer, and if Jared did not return, there would be only her to care for them. It was clear that Rowena was not capable of doing anything for herself.

It seemed quiet and eerie in the woods without the voices of her people, and she felt the loneliness settle about her. She did not know what she would do if Jared had abandoned her – but surely he would not? He had promised to care for her . . . but he had promised to return soon and he had been gone for hours. And she knew how faithless men could be . . .

When she reached the stream, Serena saw that some of the women from the village had come to do their washing. They looked at her, and then gathered their things, walking past her without a word. The accusation in their eyes told her that she was an outcast, a witch who had been marked out.

Shivering with fear, Serena bent to fill her pail with water, and as she did so, someone came up behind her and gave her a big push so that she fell into the water. She gave a little scream, for the bank was steep here and she was out of her depth. Always she had kept to the shallows when she bathed, for she was not a strong swimmer.

'Help me,' she cried as she saw a man and two women on the bank looking at her. 'Please help me . . . I cannot swim . . .'

'You shouldn't have pushed her, Mavis,' one of the women said. 'You don't know she is a witch after all . . .' She moved towards the water's edge as though she would offer her hand, but the man pulled her back.

'Leave the witch to sink or swim,' he muttered, 'and good riddance to her either way. Gypsy or witch, she is naught but trouble.'

Serena screamed, splashing about in the water as she tried to save herself, and then, just as she felt herself starting to sink, a man jumped into the water and grabbed her, hauling her out and dragging her to the bank. She was gulping for air, her senses all but gone as he turned her over and pummelled her chest until the water gushed out and she lay gasping, her eyes shut.

'Poor wench,' Will Chesterford said glaring at the man and the women who had watched from the safety of the bank. 'You should be ashamed of yourselves!'

'She be a witch, sir,' the man said, though he looked shamed. 'She be done for when Master Hadden gets her for sure. Better she go like that than strangle on the scaffold.'

'She shall not be hanged or drowned,' Will said angrily. 'Be off about your business and leave me to mine.'

He lifted Serena's limp form in his arms, carrying her to his horse and draping her over his saddle. Then he mounted behind her and set off for Hillgrove, determined to do what he could to protect the girl, who was pretty and young and deserved better than a watery grave.

Angelica saw him coming from the landing window. She ran down the stairs as she saw him dismount, and was in time to see him lift the girl in his arms. Serena was beginning to recover her senses and moaned a little, clearly in fear.

'What happened?' Angelica asked, for she could see that he was as wet as the girl he carried. 'Where did you find her?'

'She had been pushed into the stream where it is deepest, and she could not swim,' he said. 'They were jeering at her and would not help her for they thought she was a witch. I went in after her and brought her here. With that madman in the village, I think she would not be safe even with her own people.'

'I thought the gypsies had gone,' Angelica said. 'I saw some of their caravans leaving an hour or so ago – but bring her in, sir. The servants will take her to one of our spare chambers and I shall see that she is well cared for.'

'That is kind of you,' Will said smiling at her. 'Any man who won you for his wife would be fortunate indeed.'

Angelica returned his smile shyly. He had done a brave thing today and she thought the better of him for it. She was almost sure now that if he asked her to be his wife she would accept him. Hal had not been near her since the wedding, and she had almost given up hope of him. It might be better if she allowed Will to speak to her. She knew that he would have done so before this if she had not stopped him.

Serena coughed and spluttered, taking Angelica's attention. She hurried to her as Will lay her gently on a settle, and then went off to dry himself. Servants had come to see what was wrong, and Angelica instructed them in the matter of a chamber for the girl. She saw doubt in their faces and shook her head at them.

'For shame,' she said. 'Would you have left her to die? I know that she is a gypsy, but she has been near drowned and needs our help. Come, carry her up and see her to bed. I shall come and look after her myself.'

'It is whispered that she is a witch,' one of the servants offered hesitantly.

'It is a false whisper,' Angelica said. 'She is hardly older than I am – do you think me a witch because I sometimes try to help others?'

'Oh no, mistress,' the man said and looked ashamed of himself. 'Bless you, 'tis true she is not much more than a child. I'll carry her up and see that she is comfortable. Do you come up when you are ready.'

Angelica left him to do his part and hurried to find Elizabeth, who was in her still room. She told Elizabeth what had happened, asking what might help the girl most.

Elizabeth smiled at her. 'I dare say a drop of your father's brandywine would be as good as anything,' she told her. 'Go up to her, Angelica, and see if she is recovering, and I shall bring it to you.'

Angelica did as Elizabeth bid her, running up the stairs. The gypsy girl had been taken to a room that was kept for the use of unexpected visitors, and was furnished richly with silken drapes about the bed and fresh sheets.

She had been stripped of her wet clothes and lay wrapped in clean linen, the covers pulled over her decently. One of the maids was tidying the girl's clothes, and she looked at Angelica.

'It was me that undressed her, Mistress Angelica. I shall take these things and wash them for her, but I dare say I have a gown she could wear until they are ready.'

'She will not be leaving us just yet,' Angelica said. 'Thank you, Tilda. I shall ring if I need anything more.' She walked to the bed and looked down at the girl lying there. Her eyelashes were flickering, and as Angelica bent over her she jerked away and looked frightened. 'Do not worry. You are safe now. Lord Chesterford pulled you from the water and brought you here. We shall take care of you.'

'You . . . I think you are Mistress Saunders, the daughter of Sir Rupert,' Serena said, her throat rasping, for it felt sore where she had gulped the water. 'You are very kind . . . but you should not try to help me. They say I am a witch . . .'

'And that is but foolish nonsense,' Angelica said. 'I know that you are innocent. How could you ever have harmed anyone?'

'It is not me they blame, but I have helped her and so they think me like her,' Serena said and her eyes widened in fear. 'She is alone now, for Jared has not returned as he promised and the others have gone. I fear what they will do to her if they take her . . .' She moaned and rubbed at her chest for it hurt where the man had pummelled her, though she scarce remembered it.

Angelica saw the ruby flash on her finger and thought it a fine ring for a girl such as this to wear. She caught Serena's hand, looking at it, for she suspected that she might have seen it before.

'That is a beautiful ring,' she said. 'Was it a gift from your husband?'

'I have no man,' Serena said. 'It was given to me by a man, but he was false to me – and I would take it off if it would come, but it cuts into my flesh and reminds me of his faithlessness.'

'I see.' Angelica stared at the ring uneasily. She could not be sure that it was the one Lady Saunders had left to Hal, for she had seen it but once. Her grandmother had not cared for it as much as others, and claimed that it hurt her finger. Besides, Hal would surely not give away something as precious as that, and there must be others similar.

'Have you tried soaping your finger?' she asked and frowned as the girl nodded. 'Then I think you must have it cut off by a goldsmith, for there is no other way.'

'I have no money for goldsmiths,' Serena said. 'But one day, perhaps . . .' She was prevented from saying more by Elizabeth's arrival with the brandy, which she drank obediently. It warmed her inside and she stopped shivering. 'Thank you . . .' Her eyelids were heavy and she lay back, falling asleep as they watched.

'Come away, my love,' Elizabeth said. 'She will sleep now, and I wish to talk to you. It may be best if we do not mention this to your father when he returns, Angelica. I think he fears that the witchfinder might point his finger at me if we become involved in this business, and he would not thank us for bringing that girl to the house.'

'But Lord Chesterford brought her here so that she would be safe,' Angelica said. 'We cannot abandon her. My father would not expect it.'

'No, perhaps not, but it may be best if we do not tell him immediately.'

Angelica nodded her agreement. She would do as Elizabeth bid her, though she thought that her father would be even more displeased if he discovered the deception before he was told.

Eleven

Serena awoke just as it was getting light. For a moment she did not know where she was and she was frightened, but then she realized that she was lying in a soft bed and that the linen smelled of fresh herbs and lavender. The memory of what had happened to her the previous day returned, sending a shiver through her. She knew that she had been pushed into the river, and that people had jeered at her from the bank as she struggled to keep afloat in the cold water. She would probably have died if that man had not pulled her out.

She could vaguely recall his voice, angry at first as he berated the villagers, and then kind and gentle as he spoke to her, telling her that he would take care of her. Serena knew that she owed him her life, for the village folk had turned against her . . . and Rowena.

Remembering that Rowena was now alone, Serena knew that she must get up and go to her, for she was in no fit state to care for herself. She threw back the covers and swung her legs over the side of the bed. Her head swam a little, but in a moment it had cleared, and she regained her sense of balance. She lit a candle with the tinder that had been left on a trestle near the window, looking about her with interest. She had been too ill the previous day to take much notice of her surroundings, but now she saw that the room was furnished with solid oak furniture, the drapes soft and pretty. She experienced a moment of reluctance, for she would have liked to stay here a little longer, but she owed her loyalty to Rowena, who had been good to her in her way.

She saw that a gown had been left lying on a wooden chest, and thought it must have been put there for her to wear. It was grey and old, but she thought it would fit her, though she would rather have had her own clothes. She wondered where they had gone, but decided that in their absence she must wear the gown she had, for she did not wish to raise the household. They might be angry with her, though thus far she knew they had been kind – but they might stop her leaving, and she had to go.

Dressing swiftly, she carefully put out her candle with the snuffer left beside it, for to leave it burning might cause a fire. Then she opened the door of the chamber and peeped out into the hallway. At the moment all was quiet, and she thought that perhaps the servants had not yet risen. With good fortune, she might be able to escape without being seen.

Creeping down the hall on bare feet, for no shoes had been provided and she had lost her own in the stream, she reached the hall at the bottom of the stairs. Avoiding the main door, she went down the hall at the back until she found a small side entrance that was probably used by the servants. It had just one large black iron bolt to secure it and was easily drawn back, for it had been recently greased.

Once outside, she began to run across the smooth lawns as fast as she could, not wanting to be seen from the house. She felt guilty at leaving without thanking those who had cared for her, but felt that it was necessary, and wondered what she would find at their camp. Had Jared returned while she was gone – and what of Rowena?

Rowena awoke with a sore head and an empty belly. As she struggled down the steps of her caravan, she saw that most of the others had left the clearing. When had that happened? The previous day had been a blur to her and she remembered nothing. She looked about her for signs of activity but could see none. No one had yet lit a fire that morning, which was a pity, for Serena would have given her something to eat and drink, but there was no sign of her or Rowena's worthless son.

The horses were making a fearful row. She looked at them, but it did not occur to her that they were thirsty. Despite feeling so poorly, Rowena knew that she must gather wood before she could build a fire. She wandered as far as Serena's caravan and called to her, but, receiving no answer, she trundled off in search of twigs and broken branches that she could use to make a cooking fire.

Apparently, she had been deserted, though at least Serena and her son intended to return for their possessions. It was just like that good-for-nothing Jared to go off and leave them all in the lurch, she thought angrily as she walked slowly from the clearing. Her bones ached and her head was spinning so much that all she truly wanted was to lie down and sleep. Something was wrong with her, and she suspected it was more than just a headache caused by too much drink. She was ill, but there was no one to care for her, and so she must fend for herself. She walked heavily, one foot in front of the other, picking up a small twig now and then, but making no real efforts to collect what she needed.

All she could think of was the day she had first met Harry Mortimer and he had smiled at her. She had been beautiful then, with her black eyes and curling hair that fell down over her shoulders in a shining mass. Harry Mortimer had not been the only man who wanted her.

Lost in her dreams of the past, Rowena stumbled on through the woods and when she came out of them, she continued walking down the lane that led to the village . . .

Jared entered the clearing perhaps five minutes after his mother had left it. He had already been to the clearing once that morning, and having discovered that the other gypsies had left and the remaining horses had not been given water, he collected a bucket and set out for the stream. He had seen that one of the buckets was missing and thought that Serena must have taken it to fetch water for the horses – and that was his fault.

He had spent the previous day and two nights wandering, agonizing over his thoughts. His defeat at his half-brother's hands had left him even more bitter than before, and he had walked as far as the next village before stopping to drink a tankard of ale. It was there that he had seen a poster advertising the big horse fair at Huntingdon, and he had met Roald.

'Where have you been?' he demanded of the older man. 'We had all but given you up. Rowena said she thought you must be dead, for she has never known you to stay away so long.'

'I have been looking for work to tide us over the winter,' Roald said. 'I think that we should go down south, for there is little here after the Huntingdon fair. The winters are milder there and the spring comes early. Besides, I had to walk miles out of my way to avoid the plague; there have been several outbreaks of it in the country and I have seen men lying dead of it on the road. Has it visited you here?'

'I have heard nothing of it,' Jared said. 'In your absence I told the others to make ready to leave. I knew there was a fair somewhere, and I walked here to see the poster that I had heard about. It seems there will be wrestling, and I may enter the contest. I have thought that it would be a good life for me if I followed the fairs.'

'Then you will not come to the south with us?'

'Not unless there is a fair,' Jared said. 'I shall ask when I am at Huntingdon, where I may find another wrestling contest.'

'Yes, perhaps it is time you found a different life,' Roald told him. 'You were not truly one of us. Rowena has the true blood through her mother, once diluted, and you are a lord's son – though born on the wrong side of the blanket. You might do well to join up with the travelling fairs, either to wrestle or find some other work.'

'Yes, that was in my mind,' Jared said. 'If I could get

enough money together, which is why I need to win it at the fairs, I might set up some kind of business of my own.'

Roald stared at him, and then nodded. 'Yes, that might be your way. It is not ours. I have business in the morning, some horses I may wish to buy. Come with me, Jared. You may find some profit it in for yourself.'

Jared had agreed, though the walk to the farm that Roald knew of had been long and he knew that Serena would grow anxious – but she would wait for him. If the others moved on without him it would not matter. He was ready for a new life, and once he left Thornberry he would never return.

Jared came out of his reverie when he reached the stream. He saw the bucket lying abandoned on the bank and knew that it was his own. Someone must have left it lying there – but why?

'Serena?' He called her name, looking about for any sign of her, but there was none. Something must have disturbed her, for she would not have left a bucket there without good reason. Bending to fill both buckets he saw a dark object caught in the reed bed and recognized it as a shoe – Serena's shoe! So she had slipped as she tried to fill the bucket. He frowned as he stood up, his anxious eyes moving up and down the banks. Had she fallen into the water? He knew that she usually kept to the shallows when she bathed. He was concerned for her safety, but knew that the horses were near maddened for lack of water. He must return to them and then come back to look for her, though he called her name again several times. 'Serena . . . Serena . . . where are you?'

There was no reply. Leaving the stream, he walked swiftly back to the clearing, a bucket filled to the brim in both hands, for it would not last long between three horses, and his next task must be to look for Serena. However, just as he began to water them, he saw her come hurriedly into the clearing and run up the steps to Rowena's caravan. In another moment she was down them, and seeing what he was doing came towards him.

'You were gone a long time,' she said, accusation in her voice. 'The others were restless and would not wait.'

'I met Roald and he asked me to help him buy some horses. I could not refuse, for I have told him that I intend to go my own way after the fair at Huntingdon, and he has been good to me in his way.'

'I asked them to wait but they would not,' Serena said, 'and your mother spent the day drinking herself into a stupor. I am glad you have seen to the horses, poor things. I intended to, but . . .' She broke off as she recalled her ordeal in the stream. 'Have you seen Rowena? I came back as soon as I could because I thought she might be in danger.'

'Where have you been – and what happened to you? You left the bucket by the stream and I saw a shoe caught in the reeds. Did you fall in?'

'I was pushed,' Serena said. 'They stood on the bank laughing at my struggles – two women and a man. They said I was a witch.' She hesitated then, 'A gentleman plunged into the water and pulled me out. I had lost my senses, and the next thing I knew I was in a bed up at Hillgrove. The daughter of the house tended me and was kind to me.'

'Gentry!' He scowled at her. 'Damn them! Damn them all to hell!' Jared's face was dark with anger. 'Forgive me, Serena. It was my job to water the horses, and you would have been safe here with the others if I had returned when I promised.'

'Why did you really stay away?' she asked. 'I know you met Roald, but . . .' she faltered as she saw the bleak expression in his eyes. 'Forgive me, it is not my business.'

'No,' he said. 'It is not and I shall not tell you.' He frowned at her. 'Do you know where my mother might have gone?'

'She was in some kind of a stupor when I saw her last,' Serena said, and faltered as she saw the flash of anger in his eyes. 'As soon as I woke this morning I slipped out of the house and came here to see if she was all right.'

'She must have thought she had been abandoned,' Jared said. 'Will you finish watering the horses while I go and look for her? Pack her things and your own for as soon as I return we shall leave.'

'Yes, if you wish it,' Serena replied. 'I do not know which way she went.'

'I entered the clearing that way, and I went that way to fetch water,' Jared said. 'I saw no sign of her. Therefore, she must have gone in that direction . . .'

'But that way lies the village,' Serena said, her face white. 'If she goes near the village, she will be seen . . .'

'Then we must hope that I am in time to stop her,' Jared said grimly. 'Wait here for me, Serena. If anyone comes here you must hide, but if I do not return within a few hours you should go – follow the others to Huntingdon.'

'Take care,' Serena whispered for she felt cold with fear. 'Bring her back if you can, Jared . . .'

He strode away from her without answering. Serena watched him go, but her heart was heavy. Would he be in time, or would the witchfinder have laid his eyes on Rowena? Once he marked her out, she was finished . . .

'She must have gone first thing this morning, Mistress Angelica,' the young maid said as she explained that the gypsy girl's bed was cold and empty. 'She had taken the dress I left for her, and slipped out by the side door.'

Angelica frowned. 'That was foolish of her. My father says that the witchfinder has been whipping the people into frenzy. If he sees her . . .'

'Yes, mistress. I am sorry I could not stop her.'

'It was not your fault, Tilda. Speak to no one else about this, but tell my groom that I would ride and that he and one other is to accompany me. I must go and look for her, but I dare not go alone.'

'Yes, mistress . . .' Tilda hesitated. 'Are you sure you should go alone, mistress?'

'Elizabeth is too busy to be bothered,' Angelica said. 'And

my father would forbid me, but I cannot allow that girl to be murdered – can I?'

Tilda hesitated. Had it been up to her, she would have abandoned the girl to her fate, but she knew her mistress was stubborn and would not listen to her.

'Not if you say so, mistress,' she said and went off to do Angelica's bidding, though she had a good mind to go to Lady Saunders when she got back.

Angelica changed into a riding gown and followed the servant a few minutes later. She slipped out by the side door as Serena had done earlier that day, and just managed to avoid bumping into Elizabeth who had gone upstairs to look for her.

Alerted to Angelica's intentions, Elizabeth had meant to stop her. She knew that her husband and Lord Mortimer had taken a party of men to the woods. It was their plan to move the gypsies on and, hopefully, end this nonsense before anything terrible happened. She frowned as she saw that the girl's room was empty. It was foolish of Angelica to go on such a wild mission, even though she was taking two of the grooms with her – but it was too late to stop her now.

Hal had joined the party of men that Lord Mortimer had raised to put a stop to this talk of witches. He did not think that the gypsies would cause any trouble, for if they were told to move on for their own safety they would surely do so. It was in case they met a mob from the village that they needed their own men to be armed and ready.

'That man has been raising them to fever pitch,' Rupert had told them earlier that morning. 'I had hoped to reason with him, but he is like a madman and will not listen to anyone. We must band together in this, Nicolas. First the gypsies must leave, and then we shall deal with Hadden.'

'Yes, we shall deal with him,' Nicolas said looking stern. 'I shall not have this kind of madness in my parish. Let him take himself off to London. They say the plague has been running riot between here and there. God send that he may take it and visit us no more.'

It was mid-morning by the time the large party of men reached the clearing. They saw at once that only three caravans remained, and there was no sign of anyone.

'Damn this for a sorry sight,' Rupert exclaimed. The empty caravans had an eerie feel about them and a shudder went through him. 'Think you we are too late, Nicolas?'

Hal had noticed the small fire burning outside Serena's caravan and he dismounted, walking towards it. He had a gut feeling she was hiding inside, and as he approached, she came to the door and stared at him, her dark eyes angry.

'Why have you come here?'

'My uncle has brought a party of men to warn you to leave,' Hal said. 'Where are the others?'

'Most are on their way to Huntingdon,' she said. 'Jared has gone to look for Rowena. We do not know where she has disappeared to, but we think she may have wandered down to the village. She was . . . unwell yesterday.'

'I heard what happened to you, Serena,' Hal said. 'I am sorry for it.'

'I do not need fine words from you!'

'Do you need anything – money?'

'Nothing! I hope never to see you again. When Jared finds his mother we shall leave.'

'The child . . .'

'There is no child,' she lied. She faced him angrily. 'If Jared told you that, he is wrong . . .'

Hal stared at her for a moment, and then turned away. He knew that he had deserved Serena's hostility, and he was sorry that he had lain with her so carelessly. Had he not allowed Claire's rejection to twist his mind, he would have known that his true love lay elsewhere.

'Where have the others gone?' Rupert asked as he returned to them. 'What does the girl say?'

'Most of the gypsies have gone on to Huntingdon,' Hal said. 'Jared is looking for his mother, who may have wandered as far as the village. Apparently, she is unwell.'

'Then we must go on to the village,' Nicolas said. 'If the witchfinder sees her, the mood of the people may turn nasty. I will have none of his evil practices in my parish.'

Hal remounted his horse, swinging away from the gypsy camp. He did not look back. Remorse would do no good now, and he would not think of Serena again.

'There she be!' Mistress Bacon called out shrilly. 'There be the witch! She have put a spell on my Rose and she is known for her foul ways. There be Mistress Greenslade, born of evil and steeped in it. 'Tis she who has brought this wickedness upon us.'

The small group of villagers murmured amongst themselves, looking at each other uneasily. Few of them cared for Mistress Bacon, for she had a shrill tongue and grumbled constantly. However, they could not deny that Rose had not been seen in the street since the witch visited her house, and it was true that a healthy cow had died suddenly. The death of Mistress Hensby had been expected by those who knew her, but there was talk of the plague coming this way, and Matthew Hadden had told them that it was witches who spread that dread disease through their familiars, often in the form of animals.

Rowena stumbled onward. She was feeling very ill, her head spinning and her breath catching in her throat. She had experienced faint pangs of pain in her chest before, but never like this, and she believed that she was dying. Her sight was misty, and though she saw the small group of villagers staring and pointing her way, it did not seem of any significance.

Suddenly, a hush fell as a man pushed his way through the crowd towards them. His eyes glittered with a fearful radiance that frightened them, his ugly face eager, and his mouth dribbling at the corner. Most of the villagers were normally decent folk, and the sight of him made them wonder at what had come to their village. He called the witches evil, but looking at him made several men cross themselves.

'Point out the witch to me,' Matthew Hadden said, his hands

clenching at his sides in excitement. 'I smell her . . . she is near . . .' His gaze fell on Rowena and he smiled horribly. 'I see her. Her wickedness is writ clear upon her forehead to me. We need not bother to put her to the test, for you all know she is guilty of murder and all manner of evil . . .' He raised his arm, pointing at her deliberately. 'Take the witch. Take her now and she shall be tried before you all and brought to the rope . . .'

Rowena stopped. All at once she had become aware of the silent menace of the crowd and the man who pointed at her. She felt his evil, felt the strength of it and knew that he would be the cause of her death.

'Take the witch!'

'But she has not been proven,' one of the men cried out. He was the blacksmith and had taken over the forge, which had once belonged to Rowena's father. He had claimed it through a distant relationship, and found that he felt pity for the poor woman who hardly seemed to know what was happening. 'She must be shown to be a witch . . .'

'I need no more proof than my poor Rose,' Mistress Bacon said, though she knew her daughter's sullen fit was nothing more than the sulks because she did not wish to wed the man her mother had chosen for her. She bent down to pick up a loose stone from the road and flung it at Rowena with all her might. 'Stone her! Show her what we think of trash in this village.'

Three other women picked up stones and threw them at Rowena. They struck her arms and her body, but she hardly flinched. It was as if she were turned to salt like Lot's wife when she looked back in disobedience to God's word, unable to speak or defend herself.

'No!' Hadden's voice rang out, for he did not wish to be cheated of his pleasure. 'Take the witch alive . . .'

Some of the men looked at each other nervously and then began to move forward, but even as they did so, three horses galloped into the street and rode between them and the witch.

'Stop it!' Angelica cried. 'This woman is no witch, just a

poor gypsy who has tried to help you with the cures she makes from berries and herbs. Mistress Hensby died of the wasting sickness, as you all know . . .'

'Be quiet, wench,' Matthew Hadden moved forward, reaching within a foot of her horse before one of the grooms edged his own between her and the witchfinder. 'Out of my way! Who is this woman? Mayhap we have another witch here . . .' His eyes gleamed with excitement, for he would enjoy putting this one to the test. Her flesh was firm and sweet, and he liked it best if the witches were young and comely.

'Stand away from her,' the groom nearest him said. 'My mistress is the daughter of Sir Rupert and niece to Lord Mortimer. Harm her and you will answer to them.'

'Kill the real witch!' Mistress Bacon screamed and picked up another large cobble, aiming it at Rowena. This time her stone found its mark, and Rowena stumbled as it hit her in the eye. She turned away, falling to her knees as the blood poured down her cheek.

'You wicked woman,' Angelica said looking at Mistress Bacon. 'You may be held accountable to my uncle if you have caused that poor woman serious harm.'

'She deserved it,' Mistress Bacon cried, but she did not look so certain now. Amongst the crowd some agreed with her, but others murmured that it was a bad day for them. 'She is a witch . . . you all know she killed Master Woodville . . .'

Some of the villagers moved away from her, as if they wished to disassociate themselves from her. Angelica slipped from her horse and went to Rowena as she lay on the ground, kneeling beside her in the dirt and taking a clean kerchief from her sleeve to hold against the wound. Rowena did not stir. She had thankfully slipped into an unconscious state.

'Oh, you poor thing . . .' Angelica said, stroking her brow and wondering what to do next. Matthew Hadden was shouting something, but all of a sudden he fell silent. Looking up, Angelica saw Jared approaching. He was carrying a thick wooden staff and the expression on his face was grim. He looked to neither right nor left as he came up to them. Angelica rose to her feet and met his stony gaze. 'I am sorry for what they have done,' she said. 'You must take her home, and I shall follow—'

'No!' His gaze was angry as he looked at her, and then his face softened as he sensed her sympathy and her kindness. 'I thank you for the offer and for what you have tried to do,' he said. 'But we need no help, and it would not be fitting that you should tend her. You and she are from different worlds. Let it be. It is enough that you cared.'

'Oh, I am sorry,' she said on a choking sob for she saw the ravages of grief in his face and knew that he had not been given a fair deal from life. 'I am so very, very sorry . . .'

Jared nodded but said nothing more as he bent to pick his mother up in his arms. Her head lolled back, and Angelica thought that she was dying or already dead. Why had she come to the village? Why had she not gone away with the other gypsies? It was a mystery, and one that she would never solve. She watched as Jared walked away. The witchfinder was muttering, but his baleful eyes were on her now. She shivered as she saw their malevolence, but lifted her head proudly as one of her grooms came to help her back into the saddle.

'There still be witches here,' Matthew Hadden cried, determined not to be done out of his dues. 'Mark my words, there be witches here. I can smell them.'

Angelica turned her head to look at him. The look she gave him would have silenced any other, but Hadden was not to be put in his place by any woman, and she would not be so proud if put to the test. He had seen the strongest of them break and weep as they begged for their lives.

'Be careful, witch,' he told her. 'I am a powerful man, and if I mark you out, you shall be taken and . . .' His voice was drowned out by the sound of horses' hooves as Sir Rupert, Nicolas, Hal and the others galloped into the street.

'Angelica!'

'Daughter!'

Hal jumped from his horse and came to hers, gazing up at her. 'Are you all right?' He saw the blood on her gown and on her hands where she had tried to staunch Rowena's blood. 'What has happened here?'

'I think they have killed Rowena,' she said. 'I tried to help her, but Mistress Bacon felled her with a stone that hit her in the eye. I believe that she was already ill and the stone hath killed her . . .'

'But you . . . ?' he said, anxious for her sake. 'The blood . . . ?'

'Is Rowena's,' Angelica said, and smiled at him. The expression of fear for her had warmed her, and she knew that he truly cared for her safety. 'I am well, Hal – except that Master Hadden has named me as a witch.'

'What is this?' Nicolas had heard the last part of the conversation. 'He dared to point his foul finger at you?' Whirling round, he confronted the witchfinder, who turned pale and stepped back as he saw the fury in the lord's face. The crowd had melted away now, hurrying back to their homes, except for Mistress Bacon, who stood her ground defiantly.

'She tried to help the witch,' she cried. 'She is a fool, if nothing more . . .'

'Be quiet, woman,' Nicolas commanded, and it was said afterwards that no one in the village had ever seen him look at a woman as he did then. 'Go to your home. You will be brought before me at sessions, and we shall see whether you are guilty of murderous intent or not. Be thankful that I do not have you cast into the prison at St Ives at once, but be warned that I may do so if you dare to utter another word.'

Mistress Bacon stared at him, the colour draining from her cheeks. Her hand crept to her throat and she backed away from him, slinking back to her cottage like a whipped puppy.

'As for you, sir,' Nicolas said, directing his fury at Matthew Hadden, 'you are no longer welcome here. Take yourself off to Norwich or some such place where they may have need of your services. I hear they have the plague there, and that is surely a curse brought by witches.'

'The plague is a curse,' Matthew Hadden replied. He felt his knees buckling as he looked into Lord Mortimer's cold eyes. It was unfair that he should be sent away when he had been bent on God's work, for such the purging of witches surely was? 'But you still have need of me here.'

'No,' Rupert said. 'We have no need of your services, Master Hadden.' He threw the man a purse of gold. 'Take this and go. You have been paid and we want no more of you. Cause more trouble here and you will be paid in a different coin.' His hand went to his sword, his look as hard and menacing as Nicolas's own.

Hadden weighed the gold in his hand, and the situation in his mind. He had been sent for a purpose, and if it were true that the witch was dead, his work was done. He looked at Angelica, relinquishing the pleasure of putting her to the test as he realized she was too well protected. He had the authority of the church courts and he might make trouble for these people, but they were rich, powerful, and possibly ruthless in protecting their own. He knew that one day he would probably meet a violent end, but for the moment he preferred to take the safest way out.

'I have been paid,' he acknowledged reluctantly. 'And the witch is dead. I think there is urgent work for me elsewhere. I shall leave on the morrow.'

'You will leave this instant,' Nicolas told him, his voice harsh. He was used to command and, though a lenient master, once roused to anger, a man to be feared. 'Four of my men will remain here to guide you on your way, sir. Do not return, for your reward might not be as rich as that you have today.'

Hadden's eyes dropped. He made no further protest, though he smarted beneath the insulting looks he was getting from Lord Mortimer's party. Instead, he turned away, hearing the steady clop of hooves behind him. It seemed that he was to be shadowed to make sure that he could not slip back into the village.

'You must get Angelica home,' Nicolas said to Rupert.

'You go with them, Hal. I shall follow later when I have made sure that things are as they should be here.'

'Come, Angelica,' Rupert said. 'We must do as Nicolas says.'

They turned and rode back towards Hillgrove in silence. It was not until they had dismounted and gone into the house, that Rupert looked at his daughter.

'You were brave but thoughtless, Angelica. What made you do such a foolish thing?'

'Forgive me,' she said, for the incident had chastened her. 'I did not think he would dare to point the finger at me. I thought only to save the gypsy girl from harm. And then they started to stone that poor woman, and I did what I thought right without thinking.'

'If Nicolas had not acted so swiftly you might have suffered the same fate as Rowena Greenslade. I cannot believe that you would so flagrantly disobey my orders when I told you that you were not to leave the house until this affair was over.'

'I am sorry, Father . . .'

'That is not good enough . . .'

'Do not scold her.' Hal intervened and received a glaring look for his pains. 'I beg you, sir. Angelica has suffered enough for her mistake. She will not be so foolish again. Please do not be harsh to her. She has been punished too often in the past.'

Rupert's gaze narrowed, intent on her face. 'Is this true? Was your grandmother harsh to you?'

'Sometimes,' Angelica said. 'But she begged my pardon before she died and I forgave her, Father. I know that when she beat me it was because she feared I would be like my mother.'

'Damnation!' Rupert's curse made her draw back, and Hal put his arm about her as if to protect her. 'No, no, do not fear me, Angelica. I had no idea that you had been treated thus. You must forgive me. When I left you to the care of my mother I did not think . . .' Rupert acknowledged silently that he had not thought of his daughter at all. He was silent as he realized that she might have been many things, resentful and sullen being just two. In fact she was a good dutiful girl, and if she had disobeyed him in this instance, it had been for the sake of others. She was very different from her mother. 'I am sorry, Angelica. I have been harsh, and what you did was a brave, selfless thing – though foolish.'

'Angelica has always been brave and true,' Hal said. 'I wish she had not been quite as brave today, for if she had died I do not think I could have borne it – but I beg you not to scold her further.'

Rupert's gaze narrowed as he looked at Hal. 'What are you saying to me, Hal Mortimer? You speak fair words, but I have heard none from you before this?'

'I did not know my own mind, sir. But if I have been slow to understand how much I love her, I have realized it now.' He turned to Angelica. 'If we were alone I would go down on my knees to you, but I beg you will spare me that – and say that you will make me the happiest of men by consenting to be my wife.'

'Oh, Hal, do you truly mean it?' Angelica's face lit with happiness. 'Yes, yes, of course I will marry you. I have always loved you . . .'

She gazed at him as he moved to take her into his arms and kiss her lightly on the lips. None of the three who stood there in the hallway were aware that Lord Chesterford had just come to the top of the stairs in time to witness the declaration and Angelica's answer, nor did they see him frown and walk quietly away.

'Well, Angelica, I had thought your future lay in a different direction,' Rupert said thoughtfully. 'But it seems that once again I was mistaken . . .' He nodded his head, for it would do well enough. The families were close, but there was no real blood tie between them; they were cousins only by marriage. 'If it is what you truly want, Angelica, I see no reason to deny you. I give you leave to talk to her alone, Hal – unless your recent unpleasant experience has made you wish to go to your room, daughter?'

'No, Father.' She smiled at him and then at Hal. 'Will you walk with me in the garden, sir?'

'Yes, of course.' He took the hand she offered and led her outside. Rupert watched them go and frowned. He must see Chesterford and break the news to him, for the man had played fair with them. He called for a servant to attend him, and then went into his library. He would ask Will to visit him and tell him that Angelica had chosen to marry Hal . . .

'Are you certain that you do not wish to rest?' Hal asked as they went out into the garden. The sun was shining, though it was not as warm as it had been earlier in the day. 'That was a wretched thing to happen, and I think you were very brave.'

Angelica looked at him, her eyes searching his face for the truth. 'Did you mean what you said just now – do I truly mean that much to you, Hal? Have you forgotten *her* now?'

'If you mean Claire, the answer is that I have come to my senses,' he said, his expression serious. 'It was a young lad's dream, Angelica. I made up my mind that I would wed her when I was too young to understand what marriage truly meant, and I never let myself wonder if I loved her as a man should love his wife.' He smiled ruefully. 'Sometimes when I looked at you I was aware of feelings I ought not to have for you. I did not have them for Claire, but I imagined that would happen when we married. I was angry when she chose Philip Rathbone over me, but it was merely hurt pride. I know I behaved badly, but it is over now and I shall be all that you would want me to be in the future.'

'I have never wanted you to be anything other than your-self,' Angelica said, and his heart caught, for sincerity was in her eyes. 'I loved you even when you were unkind to me. All I ever desired was that you would smile at me some-times . . .'

'Oh, Angelica, you shame me,' Hal said and caught her hand, pressing it to his lips. 'When I think that I might never have understood until it was too late. If Claire had not had the good sense to reject me . . .'

Angelica laughed as she saw the expression in his eyes. At that moment she could not doubt his love for her. 'You would probably have told yourself that everything was as it should be, and mayhap you would have believed it.'

'Perhaps,' he agreed. 'But supposing one day I had woken up to all that I was missing. You would have been married to someone else, and I would never have understood what true love really was.'

'And do you now?' she teased, a naughty smile on her lips. 'Be sure that you are certain of your heart, Hal Mortimer – for if you betray me I shall cut it out with my knife.' She showed him the little knife she wore on a chain at her waist, together with all manner of trifles that she might need for her housewifery duties. 'Oh, Hal, do not look like that. I am only teasing you – as you have teased me so many times.' She tipped her head to one side, looking up at him mischievously.

'You do right to remind me,' Hal told her. 'I have not always treated you as I ought. I do beg your pardon, Angelica. I beg you to forgive me.'

'Hush,' she said and placed a finger to his lips. 'I shall hear no more of this, Hal. I do not wish you to be humble. You are my love and I would not change you for the world. Be as you have been, but love me well and do not break my heart.'

'I swear that I shall be faithful to you,' he said and swept her into his arms. Pictures of the gypsy girl crowded into his mind, but he forced them out. He would not think of Serena or the possibility that she was carrying his child. The gypsies were leaving. He would never have to see her again. 'I love you, Angelica. I feared that you had it in mind to wed Lord Chesterford, and I was jealous. I shall always be jealous of any man you look on kindly.'

'You have no need to be,' she said. She looked down at her gown and her hands, which were still stained with

Rowena's blood, a little shiver running through her. 'I am glad that my uncle rid us of that evil man. It is a pity that it was too late for that poor woman.'

'Yes,' Hal said, 'and that you were there to see it.'

'I must go and wash away her blood,' Angelica said. 'If it is true and her son is your half-brother, do you not think you should speak to Lord Mortimer? Surely he ought to be compensated in some way for the wrong that has been done him – and I do not mean only the brutal attack on his mother . . .'

Hal was silent for a moment. Something of the kind had been running through his mind, and he knew that she was right.

'I should have done it long ago,' he admitted. 'When he first came here claiming to be my father's son. I think there must be some truth in it, for we are much alike in looks. I do not believe that my father married his mother, but still he is entitled to something. I shall speak to Nicolas when I get home.'

'Then go, my love,' she said, 'and return to us this evening. I am sure that my father and Elizabeth will be glad to have you sup with us. I must go and change my gown, and then I shall speak to Lord Chesterford. He meant to ask me to marry him, and I might have said yes if you had not spoken.'

'Do you care for him?' Hal's eyes flashed with anger.

'I like him,' Angelica said. 'But my heart is yours and always has been. Go now, Hal. It is best that this is finished now.'

'Yes. I shall see you this evening . . .'

Angelica watched him call to the groom, and then turned and went into the house. She was smiling to herself, for it seemed that she had her heart's content at last. She must go up and change, and then make her apologies to Lord Chesterford, for she had perhaps allowed him to believe that he might win her in the end . . .

She had thought to settle for second best, as perhaps her mother had before her, but she was fortunate. Fate had decreed otherwise, and she was to have all that she had ever wanted. She must be the most fortunate girl alive.

She was smiling as she ran up to her room, to change her gown and freshen herself. It would be hard to tell Will Chesterford that she was to marry another man, because she believed that he truly cared for her, though he had not spoken out. At least she had made him no promises, and she was glad of it. She was free to love where she would, and to marry the man she had loved for as long as she could remember.

Nothing now could spoil their happiness.

Twelve

Serena watched as Jared prepared his mother's caravan for the burning ceremony. She had kept a vigil by Rowena throughout the night, but now it was time. It was their custom to destroy everything the dead person had left behind. Once Jared had prepared the inside of the caravan he would drive it to an open piece of wasteland, unhitch the horse and set fire to it with his mother inside. The horse would be set free to roam where it would, and gain a living for itself on the common. To keep anything that had belonged to the dead would be bad luck.

'May I help you?' she asked as she saw him come down the steps of the caravan. He was carrying a small casket, and she frowned as he sat on a fallen tree trunk and opened it. 'What are you doing? That belongs to Rowena.'

'It belonged to her, but she is dead. Now it belongs to me. There might be money or papers in here that I need.'

'But it is the custom to burn everything . . .'

'That is a foolish custom, and one that I shall not follow to the letter. Most things may burn with her for they are of no use to me, but I shall not throw this away.' He showed her a purse of gold coins. 'And I shall keep the horse. I can trade it at the fair in Huntingdon.'

'You will bring bad luck on yourself,' Serena said with a little shiver. 'And her spirit will not rest if things are not done as they ought to be.'

'Rubbish,' Jared said, and scowled at her. 'She is dead. You know that as well as I do. If there is anything you want, you may help yourself to it. Better that you should have it than that it should be burned.'

'No! I want nothing,' Serena said and walked away from him. She went into her own caravan, and when she came out she was carrying a bundle. She walked past him without looking at him.

'Where are you going?'

'I must return this gown to Hillgrove,' Serena said. 'It was loaned to me by one of the servants, but it is not mine.'

'Why bother? We shall not come here again. I intend to join up with the fair and travel on with them. I can earn a good living from wrestling, and then I shall find a place of my own – perhaps an inn where I can be the landlord and you my wife. I shall marry you, Serena, but not in the gypsy way. A priest shall marry us, to give that brat of yours a name. No child deserves to be a bastard all its life.'

'No, I do not wish to wed you,' Serena said. 'Once I loved you, Jared, but now I do not like you. You are like your half-brother. You both think only of yourselves.'

Jared shrugged as he tossed the empty casket into the flames of the fire he had built earlier. 'Please yourself. I shall return here once I have done what I must, and if you are here I shall take you with me. If not, I shall go on alone.'

Serena did not answer him. She did not know what she wanted of life. Now and then she had thought of taking her own life, for the alternatives were bleak. She did not want to return to the gypsies, but it would be a hard life on the road alone, and with a child quickening in her belly.

She supposed that she would follow the others to Huntingdon, because though the women might despise her, they would help her when the child came. But she would not marry Jared. She did not wish to be his wife. She hoped that he might be gone when she returned to the clearing, for she did not wish to travel with him. He had changed, become harder.

'Forgive me, sir,' Angelica said as she saw Lord Chesterford come down the stairs that morning. 'My father said that you

Anne Herries

were to leave us today – and I believe he has spoken to you
of my marriage to Hal Mortimer.'

'Yes, he has told me.' Will's eyes went over her. She looked
for anger, but saw none, merely regret. 'I wish you joy,
Mistress Angelica. I had hoped that you might look on me
with love, but I do not blame you. I was never worthy of
you, for I have lived too long in the company of rogues and
seducers.'

'No, do not say that,' she said moving towards him, her
hand stretched out. 'I no longer think ill of you, sir. You are
my friend, and I do like you . . .'

'But you love him?' Will saw the answer in her face and
nodded. 'That is fair enough. I wish it were otherwise, but
I shall take my disappointment as a gentleman ought, mistress.
I bid you farewell – and a long and happy life, Angelica.'

'I thank you, sir. Do you return to court?'

'Not for the moment. I have it in mind to visit my estates.
Who knows, I may discover contentment there.'

Will walked past her and out of the house. He was not
sure how long he could continue to give her fair words. He
was hurting deep inside himself, because she was the woman
he would have married for love. Any other he might take in
the future would be for the sake of his estate and the heir
his uncle had long demanded of him.

His carriage was ready and waiting for him. He climbed
inside and gave the order to move off, leaning back against
the squabs with his eyes closed. To hell with all women! He
had had enough of them all, and . . . the carriage had not
gone far down the road when it slowed, and he glanced
out of the window to see that a girl was walking in the middle
of the narrow road. He was about to tell the coachman to
shout at her to move, when he realized it was the gypsy girl
he had saved from a watery grave. She had disappeared the
next morning before he had had time to speak with her. He
tapped the roof of the carriage, instructing the man to halt,
and when it had, got down and ran after the girl, touching
her arm.

218

'Stay a moment, mistress, if you please.'

Serena turned to look at him. For a moment she was frightened, and then as he spoke, she knew him. 'You are the gentleman that saved me,' she said. 'I was at the house a moment ago and I asked them to thank you, but they said that you had left.'

'No doubt they thought I had, but I was kept talking for longer than I expected.' His eyes went over her. 'Are you well, mistress? I do not know your name?'

'It is Serena, sir. I am glad to have seen you, for had you not come to my aid I might have drowned that day. I wished to thank you for your help.'

He smiled down at her. Now that she did not look like a drowned rat, she was comely. 'You are very pretty. I was glad to help you, Serena. Your name is attractive also. Do you have another?'

'None that I know of, sir. My people do not bother much with names.'

'You are a gypsy. They told me so – but you carry yourself with pride.'

'I am of the true blood, sir. I am proud of my heritage. Why should I not be?'

'I see no reason, none at all,' Will said, finding himself intrigued. 'Where are you going? I had heard that your people had moved on.'

'Yes, most have gone. I suppose I shall follow them to the fair at Huntingdon. I have my own caravan, and I know the ways of the roads, for I have been travelling them since I was a child . . .' She sighed; she was not looking forward to joining the others at Huntingdon, but did not see what else she could do.

'You do not seem as if it is what you truly wish?'

'Things have changed.' Serena lifted her head and looked proudly into his eyes. 'I am with child, and the father was not one of my people. They will let me stay with them, but I shall be an outcast . . . they despise me.'

Will's eyes narrowed as she told her tale, and then he

smiled as an idea came to him, an idea so outrageous and amusing that it banished his megrims. 'What if I were to offer you a different life? A life in which you would wear beautiful silk dresses and jewels . . .'

'You want me to be your whore,' Serena said, and would have walked on had he not taken hold of her arm. 'I gave myself to a man I loved. I shall give myself to no other, unless I love him.'

'No, no, you mistake me,' Will said and there was a gleam of wickedness in his eyes, for it was a grand jest that he would play, and it would help him to shake off this mood of despair. 'You need never share my bed unless you wish it – but you must learn to act and behave like a lady. I shall teach you, and you will do everything I tell you. I give you my sacred oath that I shall not play you false. Once my purpose is done, you may go your way and none the wiser. Or if you choose live in luxury for the rest of your life.'

'Learn to live like a lady?' Serena stared at him. 'How could I do that – and for what purpose?'

'I shall teach you everything,' Will said. 'You already have a regal bearing, and you seem intelligent. I think you will learn easily.'

'For what purpose would you make me a lady?' she repeated.

'I wish to play a jest on someone,' Will said. 'He recently worsted me in a wager and I want my revenge. I mean to tell him you are my cousin, a widow and a wealthy heiress, and you must let him think it and lead him on a little. You must play with him until he falls in love with you and begs you to wed him, and then we shall tell him the truth. But you will have enough money to go where you choose and bring up your child in comfort.'

'And that is all?' Serena asked, looking at him in suspicion. 'You will not force me to lie with you – or this other?'

'I give you my word as a gentleman, and that I have never broken yet,' Will said, smiling at her beguilingly. It would be a fine jest, and he was sure that they could pull it off. In the meantime, he would find it amusing to make a lady of this gypsy girl. God knew she was lovely enough to drive most men mad with wanting, and dressed in clothes that befitted her face, she would be a sensation in London. Besides, he would not have to go back with his tail between his legs, and if his friends saw him with a woman like this they would think her his mistress if they did not believe her his cousin. And if she was like most women, he would charm her into his bed yet. 'What do you say, Serena – will you come?'

Serena hesitated. She had little hope of finding happiness with her own people, and this man had saved her life. Some of her people would say that to save a life was to own it – so she already belonged to him.

'I have a horse and caravan in the woods,' she said. 'I must go back and collect my things.'

'Is there none to care for the horse?'

'Jared may be there . . .'

'I shall send a groom to see that the horse is taken care of,' he said. 'Get into the carriage, Serena. You need nothing that was yours before. I shall provide you with all you want.'

Serena gave him her hand, allowing him to take her back to his carriage. She was not sure that she believed his fine words, and he would probably demand that she become his mistress, but better this lord who had saved her life and spoken to her kindly than Miguel. Miguel would get drunk and beat her. He would force her to lie with him, and in truth it would not be so very hard to lie with this man, though she would keep him to his word as long as she could.

She settled back against the squabs, trying to imagine what it would be like to live as the gentry did, and then she smiled. Winter was coming, and she would rather be warm than wet, cold and hungry. No doubt this man would feed her, and she would see that he gave her the money he had promised. This time she knew exactly what a man's promise was worth.

He joined her in the carriage a moment or two later. 'I

have sent my groom to look for your caravan. He will bring the things inside to you at my estate, and see that the horse is cared for. Will that content you?'

'Yes, my lord,' Serena said, unconsciously raising her head in the manner which she had observed in the gentry, expertly mimicking a woman who had once sent her packing from her door. 'I am well content – if you keep all your promises.'

Will threw back his head and laughed, for she was a clever mimic, though she knew it not. He would make a lady of her in no time, and then the fun could begin . . .

'He claims to be my half-brother,' Hal said, looking at Nicolas and Caroline. He had asked to speak to them on a serious matter, and they were gathered in the small, comfortable chamber that Caroline liked best. 'We have argued over it, for he said that his mother was married to my father and I called him a liar – but, in truth, I think he may be my half-brother, for he looks very like me.'

'I know,' Nicolas said surprising him. 'I saw him leaving as we arrived in the village yesterday, and I noticed the likeness. I asked questions about him, and I was told he was Rowena Greenslade's son. No one wanted to tell me more, but I gathered that he had boasted about being the true heir to Thornberry once when drinking at the inn.'

'Oh, Hal,' Caroline said. 'Why did you not tell us this before? Nicolas searched for Rowena's son many years ago. I knew then that she had had a child, and when, once, I saw him in St Ives, I believed that he was Harry's son. I have always been concerned that he must have had a dreadful life, and I would have helped him if we could.'

'I think we should give him a piece of land,' Hal said. 'He is bitter and may not accept the offer, but I believe it should be made.'

'Yes, I agree,' Nicolas said. 'Do you know where we may find him?'

'I know where the gypsies were camped,' Hal said. 'If we go at once we may be in time to see him before he leaves.'

'Then we shall go immediately,' Nicolas said. 'I feel that I ought to have made more effort to find him. He is my brother's son after all, and though his mother was a whore and a liar, that does not mean that we can ignore his existence.'

'I shall get the horses ready,' Hal said. 'I am sorry now that I did not tell you sooner. Forgive me.'

'You could not have known,' Nicolas said. 'Had your father survived the war, I believe he would have married Mercy. Your position as the heir is not changed by this, but it will not harm us to give Jared a share of the estate.'

'Then I am glad that I have spoken to you,' Hal said and went out, leaving Caroline and Nicolas together.

'I am worried,' Caroline said. 'Jared must be angry over his mother's death, and he probably resents us . . . I pray that you can make your peace with him, for I fear the consequences if you cannot.'

'That dream . . .'Nicolas frowned at her. 'It bothers you greatly, does it not?'

'I have had it many times before, but it grows stronger.'

Nicolas nodded. 'I must go. Pray God that we may see an end to this injustice, for I would not have had bad blood between us . . .'

He left his wife and went outside. Hal had the horses waiting and within minutes they were riding towards the woods. Seeing the plume of smoke on the common land, Nicolas drew rein and pointed it out to his adopted son. They puzzled over it for a moment and then decided to investigate before seeking out the gypsy encampment. The summer had been dry and a fire could do untold damage if it spread to the woods or the village.

'I would like to send a message to Widow Hayes,' Elizabeth said to Angelica later that morning. 'Rupert assures me that it is perfectly safe for you to go; the villagers are much chastened and cannot do enough to make up for what happened. They sent a deputation to your father and begged his pardon, but I would prefer it if you took a maid and one of the grooms with you, just in case.'

'That would surely look as if we did not trust them?' Angelica said. 'I shall take Tilda with me, but I do not need a groom. The gypsies have gone and so has that wicked man, and we are as we always were. I have played in these lanes and walked to the village all my life, and I do not intend to be thwarted by Master Hadden.'

'Well done, my love,' Elizabeth said, for she had wondered if Angelica would feel nervous of walking alone as she once had. 'But to please your father, take the groom as well, even if he walks behind you and waits at the edge of the village for you.'

'If it will please you,' Angelica said and kissed her. 'But Father must not worry for me. The villagers were shocked that the witchfinder pointed his finger at me, and I do not believe they would have harmed me, even had he and my uncle not arrived when they did.'

Angelica set out some fifteen minutes later. Both she and Tilda were carrying baskets containing foods and gifts for the widow. The groom had been told to walk some distance behind them. He would be near enough to come to their aid if they should need him, but far away enough so that he could not intrude, and he had been given strict instructions that he was not to enter the village.

The girls talked and laughed together as they walked. It was a cloudy morning, a little chillier than of late, but they were wearing their cloaks and it did not bother them. Tilda was promised to a young man from the estate, and she talked happily of her plans to wed him.

'I shall miss working for you, mistress,' she told Angelica, 'but I do love him so. And you will be going to the Manor soon.' Her eyes sparkled with mischief. 'We shall both of us be wedded ladies then, mistress.'

'Yes, we shall,' Angelica agreed. She saw a plume of smoke rising from beyond the woods. 'What do you think that is, Tilda?'

'It be common land over that way,' Tilda said and frowned. 'Mayhap someone has lit a bonfire.'

'Yes, perhaps,' Angelica said. They had almost reached the village. She stopped, beckoning to her groom, and telling him to come no further. 'We shall not be long. You are to wait here for us, do you understand? Come only if you hear screams or cries for help – or if Tilda comes running for help.'

'If you say so, mistress.' He looked at her doubtfully for his master had told him otherwise, but there was something about her that would not be denied. 'But do you be careful . . .'

'I shall be perfectly safe,' Angelica said and her smile bewitched him. 'I do not think that Master Hadden dare return for fear of his life, and no one else would harm me. My family has always been good to the village people and most remember that.'

'Yes, mistress.' The groom smiled at her. He would wander down in a few minutes and see that all was safe and then come back to meet her here.

Jared waited until the fire he had lit to burn his mother's caravan, and most of her possessions, had dwindled sufficiently. It should be safe now, for the wind was in the wrong direction to blow sparks towards the woods. Then he turned and took the reins of the horse he had used earlier, mounting it. He sat for a moment, surveying the land about him, looking towards the village and then to the woods. He had had dreams of making this land his own, but it was useless to pursue a hopeless course. He would go back to Serena. He had been harsh with her earlier, but now he would make it up to her. Somehow he would find a new life for them.

Jared was filled with a kind of hopeless despair as he rode into the woods. He knew in his heart that his mother had lied to him. She had never been married to Harry Mortimer; and therefore he had no right to this land. Unlike Hal he had not been adopted by Nicolas. It was more likely that Harry had used her for his pleasure and then discarded her – as Hal Mortimer had Serena. He was still angry over the way he had fallen for the trick that Hal had used on him during their wrestling bout. Few men had beaten him in a wrestling match, and the defeat had done nothing to ease the bitterness inside him. And yet he knew that he should move on; he should forget this place and its people, for only more harm could come if he stayed.

He was suddenly impatient to reach his caravan. Because the woods were thicker in places, he had to dismount and lead his horse until he came to the clearing. It was then that he saw that the cooking fire he had lit earlier had gone out, and there was no sign of Serena. However, as he secured his horse, he saw a man coming down the steps of her caravan carrying a bundle of her things.

'Hold!' he shouted. 'What do you there? Would you steal from us? We have little of value, sir.'

The man stared at him hard before he spoke. 'The gypsy girl has gone with my master, and I was instructed to bring her clothes and personal possessions. If you are the man called Jared, she asks that you take her horse and make what use you will of her other possessions.'

'What are you talking about?' Jared said, a red mist forming before his eyes. 'Has she gone with Mortimer? Damn it, man! Tell me the truth or I shall cut your heart out. Where is Serena?'

'She went with my master in his carriage. I think they have gone to London,' the man said, lying recklessly, for it would go hard with him either way. The gypsy would attack him if he did not tell him something, and his master would have him flogged if he told the truth.

'Is your master Hal Mortimer?' Jared's eyes sparked with fury, his hand at the knife he wore strapped to his belt.

'No, sir. His name is Chesterford – Lord Chesterford.'

'You lie . . .' Jared felt the anger rising inside him. 'Do you say that she is a whore to go with any man who chooses her?'

226

'I do not know how that may be, sir. My master saved her life when she had fallen into the stream, and she seemed pleased to go with him. I know that she went of her own free will, and that is all.'

'You swear that she was not abducted?'

'I swear it on my mother's life, sir,' the man replied. His poor sainted mother had been dead many a year, but the gypsy was not to know it. 'Mayhap she went to be a servant in his house, I do not know. I do as I am told.'

'Aye, I dare say you do.' Jared jerked his head at him. 'Get out of here. If I see you here again you will be sorry.'

He was not sure if the man was a thief or merely doing the work of his master, but Serena should have been back by now. She had gone to Hillgrove to return a gown, and would surely have returned before this if she had intended to. His first reaction was anger, followed swiftly by despair.

She was a whore and a slut! First she had lain with Hal Mortimer, and now she had gone off with some lord or other. Jared snarled in disgust. Be damned to her and the man she had run off with! She would find that his promises were as useless as Mortimer's – but it was Hal who had corrupted her, destroying her innocence. His half-brother, who was younger by some months, but would inherit the estate.

He went into his caravan, found the jug of strong ale his mother had brewed and shook it. There was very little left and he needed drink in his belly, something to ease the grinding ache inside him. He lifted the jar, swallowing the contents and wiping his mouth. It had been his intention to leave Thornberry at once, but now he was undecided. Without Serena and her unborn child to care for, his life seemed worthless, empty. He was not even sure that he wanted to wrestle at the fairs. Why should he work for his living when a share of all this should be his?

He needed something to drink! He turned and walked from the clearing, ignoring the horses as he quickened his pace. He would go to the inn and drink a few tankards of ale. If

Serena had not returned when he got back, he would go without her, whether that rogue had lied to him or not.

Angelica had completed her task, pleased that her friend seemed on the mend. As she left the widow's house, she was met by a small group of villagers. They looked at her uncertainly, as though they were afraid to speak, and then one of them came to meet her.

'We wanted to tell you, Mistress Saunders . . . we are sorry for what happened here. Mistress Bacon has a surly tongue and she will be punished for it. She has been sentenced to a day in the stocks, and her husband has taken a stick to her. We hope that you will not hold it against us that we harboured that man in our midst?'

'I have already forgotten it,' Angelica assured them with a smile. 'Master Hadden cast an evil shadow over this village, but he has gone now. I shall not seek vengeance and neither should you. Do not punish Mistress Bacon for my sake.'

'You are a fine lady,' one of the men called. 'God bless you and keep you – and Master Hal. We shall dance at your wedding, mistress.'

There was a murmur of agreement, and Angelica smiled as she walked on. How did they know that she was to marry Hal already? It had not yet been called in church.

'Somebody be talking out of turn,' Tilda said as they looked at each other, merriment in their eyes. 'Nobody knows you be going to marry yet.'

'It seems that they do,' Angelica said, and laughed softly. She was feeling very pleased with life, for it seemed that everything was right again and she had her wedding to look forward to.

It was as they left the village that they saw the man walking towards them. He was nearer to them than the groom, who, having discovered the mood of the village was contrite, had wandered off again. Angelica's heart pounded, for she had not forgotten the last time she had met the gypsy. She took a deep breath as they came up to him.

'Good morrow, sir.'

Jared stared at her, and the anger swept through him like a forest fire. His world was in ruins and he could taste the bitter gall in his mouth, for she had helped his mother when no other would, and it had brought home to him his feelings for her. She was beautiful and he desired her, wanted her with a grinding ache that ate away at him night and day. Feelings that he knew she could never return for the son of a gypsy woman, even if his father had been Harry Mortimer.

'I see nothing good about it,' he muttered. 'I suppose you know that *she* has run off with that lord you've been harbouring up at the house? It was Hal Mortimer that ruined her. She is carrying his bastard, and now she has gone off with another.' His eyes glittered. 'Be damned to all of you, Mortimers and those that love them. They are cursed to a man . . .'

'Who are you talking about?' she stared at him, but then she knew. The ring that Serena had been wearing. Only a wealthy man could have given it to her – and she had instinctively known it as the one that Hal had inherited from Lady Saunders. 'You speak of Serena?'

'Aye, I speak of her – an innocent child corrupted by my half-brother. She is an outcast from her people. I would have cared for her, but she has no pride left. He destroyed that when he abandoned her and her child . . .' he said and brushed by her before the anger in him erupted and he did something he might regret.

Angelica turned to stare after him. He was angry and bitter, and with his careless words he had destroyed her happiness. She did not expect Hal to have lived like a monk all his life, but to take a young girl's innocence and then abandon her . . . it made her feel sick to her stomach.

'Oh, mistress,' Tilda said looking at her white face. 'Take no notice of him. He is but a rough gypsy and has a wicked tongue.'

'No . . . no, of course not,' Angelica said. 'We must go home, for if we are too long, Elizabeth will worry.'

She lifted her head, controlling the urge to weep or shout as the pain ate its way into her heart. How could Hal have done such a thing? It was only a few weeks since Claire had decided to marry . . . but he had been so angry. Had he taken his anger out on the gypsy girl? Used her to ease the sting of Claire's rejection and then abandoned her?

Angelica was weeping inside. It hurt so much! She could hardly believe Hal so base, so callous. It called into question all that she had believed of him these many years and . . . her love. Could she truly love a man who had behaved so ill?

The groom came up to her, looking past her at the gypsy who was striding towards the village. 'Did he abuse you, mistress? Shall I go after him?'

'No, there is no need,' Angelica said, lifting her head proudly. 'It was only some foolishness. But there is something you can do for me if you will?'

'Yes, mistress. Whatever is your pleasure.'

'I wish you to go to the Manor. Inquire for Hal Mortimer and give him a message. Tell him that I would see him as soon as it is convenient.'

'Yes, mistress. I'll go now,' he said, and grinned because everyone knew that she was to wed Lord Mortimer's heir.

Tilda looked at her after the groom had set off at a run. 'It was just lies, mistress,' she said. 'Bitter lies. That one has been spreading lies for weeks now – about Lord Mortimer and him being the true lord of the manor.'

'Yes, of course. I know,' Angelica said. 'Do not worry, Tilda. I am not upset.' She was lying, of course, for her heart felt as if it were breaking, and inside she was weeping tears of blood.

Hal and Nicolas had just returned to the Manor when Angelica's messenger arrived. He thanked the man, telling him that he would visit shortly, and sent him off again.

'What will you do now?' he asked as Nicolas dismounted. They had found the burned-out caravan on the common, and seen the two empty caravans and three horses in the woods, but there had been no sign of the gypsies. 'Jared would not have left the horses to die of neglect. I am certain he will return for them sooner or later.'

'I have men looking for him,' Nicolas said. 'They have been told to bring him here. I would have preferred to meet him on his own ground, but he must be found, Hal. This feud cannot be allowed to go on unchecked.'

'It was my fault,' Hal said looking thoughtful. 'I should have told you when he first made his claims . . .'

'It would have been better,' Nicolas agreed, 'but there is no going back, Hal. That is a lesson we must all learn in life. But if you learn by your mistakes, you will do better in future.'

'I shall try to be less hasty of temper,' Hal said. 'I have learned a lesson, sir. I believe I took too much for granted . . .'

'And that may have been our fault, because we all spoiled you and let you charm us into giving you your way,' Nicolas said, and smiled at him. 'Well, go to Angelica, see what she wants so urgently. She is your future, and I must tell you that I am pleased with your choice. I wondered if she might be like her mother. Sarah led Rupert a merry dance and all but broke his heart – but Angelica is a good girl. You are lucky that she has given you her love. See that you deserve it.'

'Yes, sir.' Hal smiled as he turned and began to walk away. He did not summon the groom for he had been in the saddle all morning and a walk would stretch his legs. He wondered why Angelica wanted to see him.

Angelica saw Hal coming from the window at the back of the house which looked out towards the meadow and beyond that Thornberry Woods. She hurried downstairs and went out to meet him, because she did not wish to be overheard. What she had to say was private, and must be said when they were alone.

Hal saw her coming and his heart lifted. She was so beautiful, and he had learned to love her so very much. He did not understand how he could have been blind to his own feelings for so many years, but now that she was his, his promised wife, he intended to make up for lost time. He would make her happy and never give her cause to distrust him.

'Angelica, my love,' he said and went towards her with a smile on his lips and his hands outstretched. 'I was coming to see you as soon as I returned from the business that I had with Nicolas . . .'

They were in the meadow. Angelica stopped a few paces short, her eyes dark with a mixture of pain and accusation as she looked at him. 'No, do not touch me, Hal. There are things I must say to you . . . things that I must ask . . .'

Now that she was here, she was reluctant to accuse him. Her heart felt as if it were being torn in two, and she wished that she had never met the gypsy, never heard his bitter words. But she had, and she knew that she would never rest unless she unburdened herself of this grief. And yet she longed for Hal to tell her that it was all a lie, and that he had never lain with the gypsy girl.

'Angelica . . .' Hal was puzzled by the look in her eyes, a cold chill spreading down his spine. Only yesterday she had declared her love for him and they had pledged themselves for life. Now she was looking at him as if he were someone she had never seen before in her life. 'What is wrong? Please tell me why you look at me that way.'

'Yes, I shall tell you.' She lifted her head and now there was only pride in her eyes, a cold, slaying pride that cut him to the heart. 'As I came from the village this morning I met your half-brother, Hal. He was angry and he told me something . . . something that shocked and distressed me. It concerned you and the gypsy girl Serena . . .' She looked into his eyes, praying that she would see denial, righteous anger that Jared had lied, but she saw shock and guilt and she knew that her instincts had been right. 'I hoped that he lied, but I see he did not. How could you do that, Hal? How could you destroy her innocence? How could you abandon her when she carries your child?'

'I did not . . .' Hal felt choked as he protested. His own guilt was bad enough to bear, but that Angelica should know . . . It shamed him, and his gaze fell before hers. What could he say that would take away the look of hurt and shock in her lovely eyes? 'I gave her money and gifts. It was not quite as you have been told. I do not deny that I lay with her, but I did not think her virgin until it was too late.'

'But it is only a few weeks since . . .' Angelica's eyes were bright with accusation. 'Did you use her to ease the sting of Claire's rejection? For your pride's sake?'

'Yes.' Hal saw the withdrawal in her, felt her sense of disgust. 'I cannot excuse myself, Angelica. It happened when she took me to the gypsy camp and nursed me after the fall. She was kind and generous, and I was feeling angry – but I did like her. She made me feel better about myself, and I did not know that she expected me to love her . . .'

'And then you abandoned her . . . left her destitute when she was carrying your child. Your child, Hal! Have you not experienced what can happen when a man deserts the mother of his bastard? The hatred your half-brother feels for you—'

'She swore to me that there was no child,' Hal said. 'I admit that I used her, but I would not have abandoned her. Had she told me of the child I would have supported her. I would have paid for the child's welfare . . .' He looked at her appealingly. 'You must believe that I would have done at least that much, Angelica?'

'Yes . . .' she said slowly. The pain was still balled inside her, but some of the feeling of revulsion had eased. 'Yes, I shall believe that if you say it, Hal – but how could you . . . when you say that you love me?'

'I do love you. You are the first woman I have truly loved, and shall be the only one,' he said, his voice throbbing with passion. 'Please believe me, Angelica. Please do not turn from me. I love you so much. Without you, I should not wish to live.'

'Oh, Hal,' she said, her voice catching with tears. 'I love you . . . but I do not know if I can marry you. I am not sure that I could trust you again.'

'Please, please do not say that,' Hal begged. He moved towards her as if he would take her into his arms, but she held up her hands to ward him off. 'Do not cast me off, Angelica. I beg you to forgive me.'

'I shall try,' she said in a choked voice. 'But do not come to me for a few days, Hal. I need a little time to think about this . . .'

She turned away and began to walk towards the stile.

'Angelica . . .' The anguish was in his voice and his face as he called to her, but she did not turn back. 'Forgive me . . .'

Thirteen

Angelica walked with her head high until she was almost home, and then she stopped, leaning her back against a tree as the tears began to fall. Anger had driven her thus far, but love was making her weak. Her feet would take her no further. She could not walk away from the love that bound her to Hal. No matter what he had done, she could not stop loving him. As the realization that she still loved him as much as ever dawned on her, she turned back towards the meadow. It was as she reached the stile that she saw Hal was no longer alone. Jared was there. He had a jug in his hand, and it was obvious from the belligerence of his manner that he had been drinking deeply.

A chill of fear ran down her spine as she climbed the stile, for even at this distance it was clear that they were arguing fiercely, and she could hear them shouting at each other.

'Damn you!' Hal cried. 'You are a lying bastard. You did it out of revenge because you think you have been cheated of your rights, but if you had been where you should have been and not drinking in some stinking ale house, you might have learned something to your advantage this day . . .'

'I care not for your charity,' Jared muttered. His voice was harsh, slightly slurred from the drink. 'I curse you and all your kind . . .' He gave a roar of anger and threw the jug at Hal. He ducked and it missed him, but in the next moment Jared had drawn the knife at his belt. Angelica saw the blade as his arm came up; it flashed through the air, stabbing the unsuspecting Hal even as she screamed a warning.

'No!' she cried as she began to run towards them, but she

could see that Hal had slumped to the ground and that blood was staining his white linen shirt. She screamed out at Jared, 'Murderer! Murderer! You have killed him. You have killed him . . .'

She raced to Hal's side and threw herself down on her knees beside him, uncaring of the gypsy who stood there with blood dripping from the wicked blade in his hand. Falling across Hal's body, she cupped his face in her hands, looking down as the colour drained away.

'Oh, my love, my love,' she wept. 'Do not leave me. I beg you not to leave me. What is my life to me if you are dead? I love you . . .'

'He is not worthy of your tears . . .' The words came from Jared's mouth though he hardly knew he spoke them. 'You are far above him . . . both of us. Neither he nor I were worthy to kiss your feet . . .'

Angelica glanced up. What she saw in the gypsy's face shocked her. There was anguish, grief, hatred and love . . . yes, love for her. She saw it, understood it and rejected it in an instant.

'Go away,' she hissed at him. 'Stay, and they will hang you for what you have done this day. You have murdered your brother, Jared Mortimer, and you have broken my heart. Get away, or I shall dance as they hang you and laugh as the crows peck out your eyes.'

Jared looked into her face, seeing the anger and the despair and knew that he had broken her heart, as others had broken his. He had destroyed her – the one person he had ever loved. She was right. He was a murderer and a vile thief to have stolen what she valued most.

'Forgive me,' he said. 'I care not if they hang me. I have nothing left to live for, but I am sorry for what I have done. For your sake I wish it had never happened.'

Angelica hardly heard him. She was bending over Hal. She thought that his eyelids had flickered, and prayed that perhaps there was a chance that he still lived. As Jared walked away from her, she was tearing strips from her petticoat, stuffing them inside Hal's shirt and trying to bandage the wound. His eyelids flickered again, and for a moment he looked at her.

'It is going to be all right,' she told him, her eyes stinging with the tears she must not shed. To be weak now would lose all. She must be strong for his sake. 'I love you, my darling. I am going to staunch the bleeding, and then I shall fetch help. You will recover. I promise that you will get better. And when you are well enough, I shall marry you. I love you more than my life itself, Hal. It does not matter that you . . . nothing matters. I shall always love you. Always!'

'Forgive me . . .' Hal's lips formed the words though no sound issued, just a bubble of blood. 'I love you . . .'

Angelica pressed hard on the wadding she had formed with her petticoat, and then bound him with the sash she wore about her waist. It was but a crude dressing, but it would serve for now. She had blood on her hands and her face, her gown stained with it, for it was everywhere. She must fetch help immediately. She had stopped the bleeding for a moment, but he needed a physician's care, and that meant that she must leave him, which was very hard. Yet even as she got to her feet, she saw that people were coming towards her: Caroline in the lead, her feet flying, Nicolas hard behind, and several servants in the rear, all running as if they knew what had happened here.

'Thank God,' Angelica said. 'Oh, thank God you have come. He is badly hurt – but how did you know?'

'I felt the knife,' Caroline said, her face white. 'I have dreaded this for months – dreamed of this day for years – and when it happened, I felt the knife as if it had entered my flesh. It was Jared, his brother, who did this, was it not?'

Angelica nodded, wondering at the gift that had made Caroline sense what was happening, and feel her beloved son's pain, for Hal was her son in all ways but one.

'Yes, it was Jared. I saw them when I came from the stile, and heard them quarrel. Hal was trying to tell him something to his advantage, but he would not listen.'

'He shall hang for this,' Nicolas said as he looked down at Hal, seeing the blood and his pale face. 'The murder of a brother is a heinous crime.'

Caroline was on her knees beside Hal, feeling for his pulse. 'I think he still lives,' she said and looked at Angelica who nodded her agreement. 'We must get him home and see that he is tended.'

'Take him to Hillgrove,' Angelica said. 'Elizabeth has nursed my grandfather and he lives against the odds, for the doctor was sure that he would die. She will help Hal, and I shall sit with him and take care of him . . .' A little sob rose in her throat. 'Please, do not deny me this, for I love him so.'

'Hillgrove is closer,' Nicolas said. He gestured to the servants. 'Bring that gate – the one that hangs on its hinges over yonder. I had been meaning to have it mended, but it is as well it slipped my mind. We must carry him to Hillgrove.' He looked at Caroline, for he knew that she was in agony. 'You can stay there, my love. The three of you will share his nursing, and if God be kind, we shall save him . . .'

'Oh, Hal . . .' Caroline said. 'Forgive me. I knew that this would happen if we did not make reparation to Jared . . . forgive me . . .'

'The fault lies not in you,' Nicolas said and his expression was hard, unforgiving. 'Harry was selfish and careless. Had he not gambled away his inheritance and treated Rowena better, the boy would have been brought up as another son. It was my brother who brought this upon us . . . the seed of his sin that has brought us to this evil day.'

Angelica sat by the side of Hal's bed. It was late and the candle had burned low, but there was still enough light from the fire for her to see Hal's face. He was sweating again, and she knew that this was the fever they had been expecting. The physician had visited and done what he could to treat the wound, cauterizing it with a hot iron. Angelica had been banished from the room while it was done, but the sound of Hal's screams still echoed in her ears.

For two days they had been changing the bandages, and she knew that the blood was no longer draining his life. With the help of Elizabeth's balm, the wound looked as if it might heal, but now the fever was on him.

'We must watch for signs of festering in the wound,' Elizabeth had told her, 'but so far it appears to be clean. Also there is the possibility of fever. If he takes the fever we may lose him, but we shall pray, and we shall do all we can to save him, my love. He shall not die if love and our nursing can prevent it.'

Angelica had been comforted by Elizabeth's kindness, but now, seeing the sweat upon his brow, she was seized with apprehension. If he should die, she did not know how she would bear it. To lose him now would be like losing a part of her very self.

She fetched a bowl of cool water and a cloth, bending over him as she smoothed it over his heated brow and down his throat and arms. She smiled as she stroked his head, his hair darkened by sweat, his cheek unshaven, and then she bent to kiss his lips.

'Please live for me, Hal,' she whispered. 'Please do not die, my dearest. I love you so very much. I have forgiven you for all that has gone before. Live for me and we shall begin again.'

'Angelica . . .' The words were on Hal's lips, though she knew that he did not know what he said in his fever. He had called for her many times, throwing out his hand as if in entreaty. 'Do not leave me . . .'

'I shall never leave you,' she vowed as she lay her hand against his cheek. 'I swear that I shall never desert you, my love.'

She tended him, for he was hot with fever, but then, later in the night, he was cold and shivering, and she lay beside him on the bed, gathering his body close so that he was warmed again. The fever came once more, then waned, and then she felt the change in him as it was eased and his breathing became less laboured. She stayed beside him all that night, refusing to go when Elizabeth begged her to sleep. Something in her told her that she must not leave this night, for if she did, he might slip away.

Towards the dawn he stirred and she went to him, stroking his forehead as his eyes opened and he stared at her. He was cooler now but his skin was dry, and she believed the worst of the fever was gone.

'Angelica,' he said. 'Are you truly here or do I dream?'

'I am here, Hal. You have been ill and I have been helping to nurse you. I feared for you when the fever was at its height, but I think that you have come through it now. Elizabeth says that if you survive the fever all will be well.'

She rose from the chair beside his bed and went to fetch cool water from a pitcher on a side table. Returning to the bed, she supported him with her arm, holding the cup to his lips so that he could swallow a few sips.

As she laid him gently back against the pillows, his hand moved on the covers and she took it, kissing it and then holding it to her cheek. He looked at her uncertainly and sighed.

'I hurt you,' he said. 'What I did was wrong. I know it, and would turn back the clock if I could. I want only you, Angelica . . . have you truly forgiven me? In my dream I seemed to hear you say that you loved me . . .'

'I have forgiven you,' she said. 'When I saw you lying there on the grass, your heart's blood ebbing away, I knew that my life would be nothing without you, Hal. The past is over; we shall forget it and live for the future.'

'If I live, I swear that you shall have no more grief of me,' Hal told her. 'You are my life, Angelica. I regret that I harmed the gypsy girl with my selfishness, and I have asked her pardon. I would have helped her had she let me, and if you know where she may be found I will give her money.'

'I believe she went with Lord Chesterford,' Angelica said. 'Jared told me it was so. He was angry and bitter, and hurting too, I think . . . but what he did was wicked. He was your brother, and to try and take your life was a terrible sin. I do not think I can ever forgive him that.'

'He was as much sinned against,' Hal said. 'Our father used my mother ill, for she was young and innocent, and he deserted her. It seems that he promised marriage to Jared's mother and then abandoned her too – and it is because of his sins that we have come to this sorry day.'

'Yes, perhaps,' Angelica said, 'but Rowena had nurtured her lies in him, teaching him to be bitter, and his life must have been hard with the gypsies, for he was never truly one of them, even if his mother had the true Romany blood.'

'If I had listened to you that day, if I had spoken with Nicolas then . . .' Hal closed his eyes and lay back, feeling exhausted. 'Forgive me, I must sleep. We shall talk later . . .'

Angelica watched over him, but he was peaceful now, and when Elizabeth came to her again, she smiled and agreed to take some rest. She believed that the fever had gone at last, and with care and love, Hal would recover.

'Have you found him?' Caroline asked as Nicolas came in looking weary one evening a week later. He had been out constantly with his men every day that week searching for Jared, often from dawn until dusk. 'I think he will have gone far away by now.'

'The caravans are still in the woods, and I have ordered a constant watch on them,' Nicolas told her. He sat down in a chair and stretched out his legs. Caroline knelt before him to remove his riding boots, for she could see that he was exhausted. 'You should not . . .' he protested, but she smiled and shook her head. 'I am blessed in my wife . . .'

'You take too much upon yourself,' Caroline said. 'Let others search for Jared. I doubt that he will return to Thornberry. He must know that he would be arrested and tried for his crimes.'

'Two horses were gone,' Nicolas said. 'The other was left to wander as it would. I have ordered that it be cared for, poor beast . . .' He sighed heavily. 'If I had done as you asked years ago, this might never have happened.'

Caroline gave him a forgiving look. 'You made a search for him then. It is my belief that Rowena did not wish to be found. She feared that she might be tried for the murder of Richard Woodville, though we wanted only to help her and your brother's son.' Caroline laid her cheek against his, and he turned his head to kiss her so that they looked into each other's eyes. 'You must not blame yourself, Nicolas. Had Hal told us of his meetings with Jared we might have healed the rift – but after his mother's death it was too late.'

'I think there may have been more,' Nicolas said, but shook his head when she raised her brows. 'I have heard whispers, but I shall hold my tongue. Whatever cause Jared had to hate us, he had no right to try and take his brother's life. If I find him I shall see that he is brought to account for it.'

'I pray that he will not return,' Caroline said, 'and in my heart I believe that he is punished enough. He is an outcast, and he has his brother's blood on his hands, for he cannot know that Hal is recovering. He will never be free of what he has done, and may spend his whole life looking over his shoulder.'

'Yes, I dare say,' Nicolas said and reached out to touch her face as she still knelt beside his chair, gazing up at him. 'God has been kind and Hal may live to be happy – and in truth, it would be hard to send my brother's eldest son to the gallows. What he did was wicked, but the fact remains that he is of Harry's blood, and therefore mine.'

'Then leave his capture to others,' Caroline said getting to her feet. 'I shall have wine and food brought to you, my love. Hal was well enough to smile when I saw him today. I shall visit again tomorrow, but he has Elizabeth and Angelica to care for him, and I think he will mend.'

'We must pray that he will,' Nicolas said. 'Had the blade gone deeper, we might have been burying him instead of dancing at his wedding.'

'Yes. Indeed, I feared it would be so,' Caroline said, for

the shadow of that terrible day had hung over her for too many years. 'I shall order your supper now, husband. Sit there and rest and it will not be long in coming.'

Nicolas sat staring into the fire as she went away. His mind travelled back to when he was young and in awe of his elder brother. It had been accepted that Harry would marry Caroline, and that Nicolas must make his own way in the world. Well, he had done that, for he had repaired the ravages of his brother's extravagance, restoring and improving the estate so that Hal would inherit far more than he had after his father's death. He could only hope that Hal had sown his wild oats, for it would need a steady hand if the prosperity he had built were to be maintained.

Had Harry been other than he was, Nicolas might never have known the happiness of being wed to Caroline. Harry had thrown away her good opinion as he had gambled his father's money, carelessly and without a thought for the morrow. His seed had been nurtured in waste land, and it was from that seed that tragedy had sprung, but now, at last, perhaps they could put the past behind them.

He pictured his brother's face as he had seen it last, when they quarrelled: handsome, selfish, and careless, his brother had ridden away to war, leaving others to heal the harm he had done. His actions on the field of battle had been brave, for he had saved Rupert's life before dying. Yet the truth of the matter was that he had lived only for his own pleasure, leaving nothing behind but tragic consequences.

'Harry, my brother,' Nicolas murmured. 'You were our father's firstborn son and he loved you, but did you ever care for any of us?'

Hearing the servants at the door, Nicolas put his mood of retrospection behind him. To look back in regret was useless. Caroline was right in what she claimed. Jared would spend the rest of his life looking over his shoulder. He would not dare to return to the scene of his crime, and it would be better if that was an end to it. Had he managed to take him, he would have done his duty as he saw it, but it would have been hard to send Harry's son to his death at the hangman's noose.

He smiled as he saw Caroline return after the servants had brought in the food. She was as lovely in his eyes now as the day he had first kissed her in the meadow, claiming her for his own. Fate was strange, he mused, for when it took, it also gave.

For some days Jared had moved on constantly, selling both his horses to buy a better mount that would carry him faster. He believed that Nicolas Mortimer would hunt him down if he lingered, and he feared that he would end at the gallows if he were taken.

It was no doubt what he deserved. Jared had felt remorse as well as fear when he looked down at the body of his brother. As Hal's blood seeped into the earth, he had felt the bitterness and hatred drain away from him. And in its place had come regret – regret that he had never truly known his brother.

He was alone in the world, and he would constantly need to move on to avoid the punishment that awaited him if he was taken. The gypsies would reject him if he went to them, for with a price on his head, he could bring them nothing but ill fortune. So much for the old prophecy that he would bring them luck. It had been false, as had so much that had been told to him by his mother and the gypsies.

His plans to follow the fairs and earn his living wrestling were at an end, for if he were successful, his reputation would grow, and in the end it might come to the ears of someone who knew that he was wanted for murder. He did not know what to do with his life – had in the darkest hours considered ending it – but some instinct for survival held his hand.

And then, after some days of wandering, never stopping for more than a few moments to buy food, he had discovered that his fear had faded. He no longer felt that he was being hunted. Now there was only remorse, and a restless urge to do something with his life.

If he were to continue living, it must be for some purpose. Had he been a Christian, he might have entered a monastery and devoted his life to God, but he had never been inside a church in his life, and the ways of the clergy were alien to him. So he travelled on, day after day. Finding himself in Portsmouth after more than three weeks of riding back and forth across the country, he stopped at last. Walking to an isolated spot on the shore, he stood staring at the ocean, breathing in the crisp, slightly salty air.

A storm was on its way across the sea, and he watched the dark clouds gather overhead, the waves rolling in as the wind whipped them to a frenzy to crash against the shore. It occurred to him then that he was like a piece of flotsam caught by the tide and carried with it, dictated to by forces outside itself. Rowena had filled his head with lies, passing on her hatred to him, urging him to take back what was his, when all the time she had known that it was a lie.

She was dead now, and the bitterness had gone. The fear of pursuit had gone too, though the regret lingered. Now he must find a new life for himself, and the restless water fascinated him, held him as it raged with such force and energy as the storm took hold. To battle against such elements might give a man a purpose in life, to dare all and live or die – and death was not so terrible if it came on a wild night like this.

There were many ships in the harbour sheltering from the wild weather, but in the morning when it abated, they would leave for wider shores. The prospect of adventure, of new lands, and perhaps fortune made by his own hands, beckoned him. He knew that life at sea could be hard, and it might be years before he rose from being a mere seaman, but suddenly he was filled with hope and energy. This was his opportunity, his chance for a life without hatred or resentment.

In the inns that clustered about these shores there were men looking for crew. Often they took them by force, plying the unwary with drink or simply abducting those who came their way, but he would sign on willingly, and thus earn himself a place on board a decent ship. He was smiling as he turned towards an inn he had noticed earlier. It was clearly a tavern frequented by seamen, and he would find what he needed there.

He would take another name for himself – Harry Blackthorn. He was amused at the idea of calling himself by his father's name. It was a new name, and a new life, and he would make the best of it he could, forgetting the past and the woman he knew could never have been his.

It was cold out, for the prelude to winter had come in the past week and ice hung at the windows of the houses and cottages in the village. Angelica had been down earlier to deliver food and fuel, for Elizabeth was continuing the traditions begun by her late mother-in-law. She hurried to the fire when she entered the parlour at the back of the house, holding her hands to the flames to warm them.

'You should have left it to the servants,' Hal said as he came into the room behind her. His voice was tender, filled with concern for her. 'You will catch a chill if you go out in weather like this, my love.'

She turned to him, her eyes lighting with love as she saw him. 'Are you well enough to be visiting?' she asked, because it was taking much longer for his wound to heal than they had anticipated. It had puckered and taken harm, and he had been forced to rest these past few weeks, though he had returned to his home three weeks since. She had been to visit him every day, but this was the first time that he had been further than the gardens of the Manor to her knowledge.

'I am well enough now,' Hal told her. 'I wanted to see you, but when I got here Elizabeth said that you had gone in the carriage to take food and fuel to the villagers, so I sat with your grandfather for a while. He is very weak, but seems to bear up well?'

'Elizabeth takes great care of him, as she does of all our people. Some of them might starve if we did not take them

The Seeds of Sin

food and fuel in this harsh weather,' Angelica said. 'It is our duty to look after them, Hal. You would not have me neglect my Christian duty?'

'No, of course not,' he said and came to her, drawing her into his arms as he looked down at her face. 'You know that I would not – but have a care for yourself as well. It will not be long now before we are wed, and I cannot bear to think of you ill.'

'You are the one who has been ill,' she said and looked at him anxiously, for his face was still thin. These last few weeks had changed him. She thought that he had lost the boyish arrogance that he had once had, and was more thoughtful, even serious now – very like his adoptive father. He still had his father's fair good looks, but he was Nicolas's son in all other ways. What part of him that had been Harry's had been put away. 'How do you think I would feel if you were ill again?'

'I shall be well enough for our wedding, I promise you.'

'Oh, Hal . . .' She went to his arms, looking up at him with concern. Her body flooded with love as she laid her head against his chest. It was still hard for her to believe that she was to be granted her dearest wish, and at the back of her mind a small fear lingered. 'I cannot wait for that day.'

'Nor I,' he said and bent his head to kiss her. 'But my strength does not return as fast as I would have it, and I want to be well when we become husband and wife, Angelica. By Christmastide I shall be as strong as ever.'

'Yes, of course, and I shall wait,' she said, lifting her face for his kiss, which was sweet and gentle. 'But I am impatient . . .'

'No more than I,' he told her, and looked rueful. 'I have never been truly ill before and it irks me, but it will pass . . . as everything passes.'

She saw an odd, wistful expression in his eyes. 'Do you think of him, Hal? Do you hate him for what he did to you?'

'Hate is too strong a word,' Hal said. 'I think regret or

247

pity would be better ones. We were both of us strong-willed and angry. It may be that what happened was our destiny, for Caroline had feared it for many years. Had I told her and Nicolas at the time, Jared might have learned to forgive, but now . . .' He shrugged. 'I neither know nor care where he is or what he does. The past is over, finished. It cannot be changed. If he came here, he would be taken and tried, most likely hung. For my part, I hope he has the sense to go as far away from Thornberry as he can.'

'Then you are not bitter?'

'Why should I be bitter?' Hal smiled at her. 'I am alive, and I grow stronger with the days. And I have you . . . I need nothing more.'

Hal and Angelica came out of the church to the sound of bells pealing joyfully. They smiled at their friends, who had gathered for the wedding, laughing and running towards their carriage as a deluge of dried rose petals was thrown over them. Once inside, Hal sat looking at her for a moment, and then drew her close, his lips tender and soft as he kissed her. Then, in a moment, the kiss deepened becoming hungry, demanding as he pressed her to him.

'Oh, Hal,' she said, reaching out to touch his face with her fingertips. 'You are truly well again, aren't you?'

'Yes. As well and strong as ever, which was what I wanted to be for this day – and this night.' A wicked gleam sprang up in his eyes. 'I would not have you lie with an invalid this night, my love, but a strong man who has waited too long for his lover.'

'You need not have waited,' she said softly. 'I would have come to you had you asked . . .'

'But I did not want it that way,' Hal said. 'It was my father's way, and I have done with all that. You are my love, my life, and I swear that I shall never break your heart as Harry Mortimer broke my mother's.'

'I love you,' Angelica said, trembling with delight as she gave herself up to another kiss. If the feelings he was arousing in her now were a prelude to the pleasure to come that night, then she must be the happiest of women 'Oh, Hal, I love you so much . . .'

Angelica rose from her marriage bed and walked over to the window to gaze out at the night. Snow had fallen during the hours of darkness, and they would have a white Christmas. This year it would be celebrated in the old way, with all the customs restored to what they had been before the Civil War that had torn the lives of so many people apart.

They had been to mass the previous night in their own chapel. Afterwards they had celebrated with friends until it was time to retire to their own apartment – and their marriage bed.

Turning to gaze at the bed where her husband lay sleeping, Angelica smiled. Everything she had ever dreamed of had been hers that night. Hal had loved her tenderly, passionately, sweeping her on to a crest of delight that made her scream out his name and clutch his shoulder. He had shown his love so many ways, taking her virginity with such care that she hardly felt the pain, giving her more pleasure than she had dreamed could be hers.

'I shall never look at another woman,' Hal had vowed to her, as they lay entwined afterwards. 'I swear that none hath ever given me such joy, Angelica. I know my heart now and I shall not betray it or you.'

'I want only you,' she told him, her face buried in his shoulder. 'It is all I have ever wanted, Hal.'

As she watched, he stirred, moved his hand to find her and then opened his eyes looking for her, such alarm in his face that she laughed. He saw her and held out his hand to her.

'I thought you had gone, that last night was but a dream . . .'

'No, dream, my love,' she said and went to sit beside him on the edge of the bed, 'but a prelude to the life that awaits us for now and the future.'

His eyes searched her face. 'And are you happy?'

Angelica nodded, and then bent down to touch her lips to his. 'Happier than I have ever been . . .' she said, and shrieked with laughter as he drew her down on top of him, before rolling her beneath his body. 'So very, very happy, my dearest Hal . . .'

① 11/09